THE ONE WOMAN

THE ONE WOMAN

LAURA MAY

ISBN: paperback 978-1-956183-80-1
Ebook 978-1-956183-69-6
Library of Congress Control Number:
2022939021

Any references to historical events, real people or real places are used fictiously. Names, characters, and places are products of the author's imagination.

Cover Design by Diana TC, triumphcovers.com

First Printing Edition 2022
Published by Creative James Media
Pasadena, MD 21122

To all the books that came before.

Chapter 1

"*D*id you pack your passport?" Mark asked.

I had never once forgotten it, but he always inquired.

"And the money? Charger?"

"Yes, all packed," I replied.

"I'm going to miss you." Mark wrapped his hand around me and kissed my forehead, then my lips. My fingertips brushed his light brown hair for a fleeting moment, but I let go. It was a quick kiss since we were at the airport, and it was not a place to make a scene. Not that we made them anymore.

"I'll be back soon."

I looked in his green eyes and I already missed him. But it was only for three days.

It was my first solo trip without him I'd be taking since our three-year relationship started, we always traveled together.

I grabbed my blue suitcase and hauled it to the security check. The airport was crowded today; families with kids and grandparents were hurrying to their charter flights.

Moms' and dads' faces were red from excitement, already getting ready for a week in Egypt or Turkey with a swish of vodka or whiskey from a Duty-Free store. And the constant announcements of the departures and changing gates tried to be heard among the clamor.

The air inside was suffocating, pressing on my chest. A mighty ventilation system doing a poor job on refreshing the air. The skin on my cheeks burned, and a warm hoodie I wore made me feel like I was slowly cooking from the inside.

I loved flying and airports in general. The thing I hated was getting ready at home, always having a feeling that I forgot something important. But when I was at the airport and realized I had miraculously packed everything I needed, I relaxed. Here among so many foreigners, I felt that I was already abroad.

This conference I was flying to was about the latest trends in software development and design. I got the ticket when my colleague Diane canceled her trip because her son got ill and she had to stay home with him.

The web design department in the company I worked for, Benzon Technologies, was quite small, at least in the Ukraine, so I was the next in line for this trip.

I still had an hour before my flight from Kyiv to Tel Aviv, so I bought a cup of takeout coffee and found a quiet place to sit near the empty gate. It was cooler here, and much quieter. Instead of scrolling Instagram, I took out a print-out of the conference program and scanned underlined workshops I needed to attend. There'd be lots of people from Benzon at this conference. One of the top speakers was a software architect from there, a big star as I was told.

I'd been to Tel Aviv twice, so I knew what to expect from the city. And one of the main things I looked forward to was the sun. It was December, and in Kyiv, it was not snowing but felt almost like it. I was so excited to feel the warmth on my skin, even if it was only for three days. Thank God my company booked a seafront hotel for its employees. And since there wouldn't be anyone I knew, I'd spend my free time with the one thing I knew and loved: the Mediterranean Sea.

On the flight, I watched my favorite romantic movie from the 90's on my tablet. This, along with the shining sun from the illuminator window, created a warm fluttering feeling inside me as we landed.

During the taxi ride, I was glued to the window. People were not wrapped up in scarfs, puffy coats, and mittens; some were actually wearing t-shirts. I looked down at my white woven hat laying on my lap and smiled.

My room was bright, but it didn't have a sea view, the windows showing the flat roofs of neatly stacked houses. The cream-colored walls held the paintings of faraway cities. Crisp white linen of a bed crunched under my fingertips, its smell coating the room.

Even though it was four in the afternoon, I still had about forty minutes to enjoy the sunset. I changed into much lighter clothes—no more hoodies—which included a white t-shirt with a swooshing logo and jeans and ran outside. The evening was warm, just a bit sticky to my skin. And when I saw the water, it took my breath away. I stopped to watch the sun going down, the water playing with red, orange, and violet colors, reminding the canvas of an advanced artist, who poured the soul into every brush stroke.

As I strolled down the Promenade, my eyes fixed on the horizon, a few runners swished by my side, and one newbie rollerblader bumped into my back, muttering an apology. All these people saw this beauty every day, but they stopped to watch the miracle of the sunset with me, their eyes reflecting the hues of a dancing light. I turned around, finding huge glass skyscrapers around me were glistening like popsicles in a candy shop. I didn't know why, but sunsets always brought me peace, and the sound of waves soothed me much better than any guided meditation on YouTube. I took a deep breath and felt my chest expanding with a seasalt air, a tender smile playing on my lips.

When I entered the hotel lobby, I turned to the bar. It was dimly lit; bare concrete walls were decorated with intricately carved dark wood panels. Black lamps hung from the ceiling reminding of dark icicles. A slow ambient music muffled the murmur, and a flowy scent of jasmine mixed with citrus tickled my nose. I assumed the bar was crowded with Benzon employees, but since I didn't know anyone, I figured maybe it was a good place to find an ally for the conference. I ordered gin and tonic and perched on the dark green barstool. I started with a relaxing technique: scrolling through social media pages and sending Mark photos from the seashore.

All my networking knowledge was based on the business book I never finished and a newsletter from a career website that I opened only once in a while.

"Don't know anyone in here?"

So, it appeared that my nonchalant technique was working.

I shut the screen and looked up at the speaker. It was a woman in her thirties with ocean-blue eyes and dark, chin-length curly hair. She had pale skin, which was highlighted by the clothes she wore: black jeans and a charcoal t-shirt. She had strong, sculpted arms, and slenderly cut cheekbones.

"Yes," I admitted. "The idea was to get a friend for a

conference, but I decided to start with a gin and tonic and Instagram," I smiled. "I'm Julie."

"Ann." She also ordered a gin and tonic and sat on the stool near me. "Is it your first conference?"

"Abroad, yes. I wasn't even supposed to be here in the first place. My colleague couldn't come, and I got her place. I'm not sure I'll find lots of useful information since I'm a graphic designer. Did you see the timetable? Lots of stuff for software developers and business growth. And there will be a speech from a Benzon celebrity, which I will probably need to see."

I was babbling, and I didn't even know her. It was time to hold my tongue. Ann just looked at me and sipped her drink from a Copa glass.

"Where are you from?" she questioned.

"I am from Kyiv, Ukraine. We have a small office. You know, it's so chilly and grey there now, so one of the primary reasons I was happy to come to the Mediterranean was to see the sun and the sea. Say hi to warmth even for a couple days."

Her quiet gaze made me talk non-stop. Maybe it was not a marvelous idea to tell a stranger that I didn't really care about the conference, and I just wanted to get away from the gloomy winter.

I cleared my throat. "Where are you from? What do you do?"

She glanced at me, and her ocean-blue eyes were so familiar. Her gaze lingered, but she shook her head and took one more sip. It seemed she had forgotten what to say.

"I live in LA, work in HQ. I'm in software development."

And that was all. I got the idea that she was thinking about something else; maybe she didn't want to talk to me. For sure she didn't blabber as much as I did.

"How do you like Tel Aviv?" I asked.

Easy topic: the last resort would be asking about the weather.

"Oh, Israel is like my second home. My grandmother lives in Tel Aviv now. When I was a kid, my parents sent me here to spend the summer. My granny, Mary, used to live in Jerusalem till I was thirteen, and then she moved here. I flew in two days ago to spend time with her. She is getting old, but this city of young people gets her moving. She takes so many art classes and does yoga and dancing. I'm beginning to wonder if she has any free time."

Ann laughed, and the sound was so warm it lit something inside me. Her eyes shone brightly when she talked about Mary, and kindness wrapped around every word.

"She sounds," I paused for a moment before continuing, "awesome. I don't see my grandparents often, as they live in another city, and I only visit on holidays. But we never really got close. My parents moved with me and my brother to Kyiv when I was little. I think you need to have grandparents living close by to form a connection. I am trying now, but it seems the time is lost. My mother is my pillar of strength. What about your parents? Are you close?"

Something shifted in Ann's posture, and her face fell a little, but she hid it fast and eyed her watch.

"Oh, gosh, it's late," she remarked. "I need to be getting ready."

I scared her with my personal questions, but I enjoyed talking to her. Even if I did most of the talking, her eyes never left mine, and she was really listening, trying to see something inside of me, and I was comfortable in her presence. Usually, I didn't come out of my shell so easily.

Ann noticed that I got upset and gave me a small, warm smile.

"I'm sorry, but I really need to get ready for tomorrow," she said, running a hand through her black hair. "I enjoyed your company and would love to know more about Kyiv and your family tomorrow." She winked. "What do you think?"

My face lit after these words. What was wrong with me? Ann looked at me as though she was trying to understand something, with so much intensity. But I was an open book, and it was always so easy for everyone to read me.

"Sounds perfect," I replied with a nod. "Good night."

She nodded and grabbed her keys and phone and went to the stairs, not an elevator. I watched her go, feeling so strange. I realized that I wanted to know more about her.

I was awful at making new friends. I had a couple of girlfriends from university time, but lately, they were deep in their personal lives: babies, husbands, and let's face it: We weren't that close anymore. I had no idea how to make new friends when daily life changed so fast. We had less and less common topics, and we spent our time so differently that there was no chance to relate to each other even to ask for advice. And the more I tried to explain, the more judgment I seemed to receive.

I was all right by myself, but I thought that soon some kind of Tinder for finding friends would come in handy.

I could feel that Ann could be my person. Finishing off my gin and tonic, I wondered how I could judge that within less than an hour of talking. I didn't know, but I felt it. And I usually trusted my feelings.

Going back to my room I thought that at least I wouldn't be so lonely for the next two days.

Chapter 2

JULIE

$\mathcal{T}$he next day, I woke up early. The sun crept in through my window, sending honey-colored hues over the room. I put my running shoes on and flew towards a Promenade. This was only my second morning here, and I needed to savor the view as much as possible. I ran for twenty minutes, but then slowed and came down to the water edge, scanning the waves.

Water always had a pull on me; from my childhood, my mom had to force me to get out of the lakes, rivers, and seas. Now it was chilly to go in, but still, I needed a connection.

With my shoes off, I breathed in the sea salt and took a few pictures to send to Mark. He was probably on his way to the office right about now.

At ten in the morning, a shuttle bus from my hotel took Benzon employees to the huge exhibition center right outside the city. The modern-looking building with a triangular overhang reminded me of an open sail, full of wind. The side walls were covered with partner logos, and famous names like Google and IBM were listed. The entrance was framed with a huge monitor, a promo video playing. This event was a big deal in the software world.

The smartly dressed hostess met us at the bus and gave us maps of the place. Lots of eco, green, recycling points. Nowadays it seemed that everyone in the IT industry needed to save the planet. It was an important trend, but it felt like lots of showing off to me.

At 11:30 there'd be a welcoming speech with a program overview.

It was so crowded that it would be almost impossible to find Ann. And as she didn't take the bus I was in, so she probably left on the previous one. I stood on tip toes trying to spot her, but there was no chance with so many people swarming around, talking to each other, standing in groups. Why didn't I ask for her phone number?

I grabbed a coffee and some snacks as I headed inside; free food was the norm for these events because of course hungry IT people should be fed.

The central hall was huge, but you could see the stage even when you were standing far away at the back, which was my case.

The introduction rolled in, sponsors were thanked, and organizers gave a short description of events on the main stage. The timeline consisted of a wide range of speeches, available to everyone. Secondary stages were more tech and development focused. I would need to attend a few UX workshops. Also, there would be a masterclass from a guru designer I was excited to hear, along with a Benzon star at 3 p.m.

By lunchtime, I had lost all hope in finding Ann and became one of the lost IT souls in the crowd. Thank God I wasn't here to network. But I started to truly enjoy the program. For sure, the conference creators had gathered the top experts who knew how to explain and present. My bag was filled with flyers and my mind with ideas.

It was almost three when I returned to the main stage after a class on user experience, and it was time to find a place in the already crowded central hall. It seemed not only Benzon employees came to listen to the speaker. So many people were here that I got crammed into the wall. I caught bits of conversations around: "She's so empowering," "She truly loves what she does and shares the love," "She is an expert, but also she is a women protector in the IT-sphere."

Hm, *she*? I was sure Benzon's representative was a man. Maybe I should have paid more attention to the program.

My heart started beating erratically after the host presented the name of a Benzon speaker: Ann Weis. Lots of phones shot into the air just as my jaw dropped to the ground. Ann was standing on the stage. She was calm, and she was fierce. And she began.

Ann told the story of how she came to Benzon six years ago. She was a nobody and got an assistant position, but she wanted more; she needed knowledge but didn't know where to start. It happened that her boss saw the intelligence in her eyes and believed in her. Believed enough to become Ann's mentor. The next two years were spent in books and education, and with the steady support of her mentor, she gained a new profession. She got transferred from an assistant position to the software development department.

What amazed her was that of the thirty people in the department, only two were women. During her next few years in software development, she found out that for some reason women were avoiding going deep into tech. Because of this, she initiated a mentorship program for women in IT in Benzon. They already had the first round and found out that a lot of brilliant women had fears of not being recognized and that the IT niche was only said to be diverse when in reality it was a male-dominated area. Still, women were not truly welcome, and their knowledge wasn't trusted.

Ann showed a few examples of how when adding women to tech teams, they skyrocketed new projects and brought new ideas with them.

Her eyes were shining, her voice was steady, but the audience held their breath. Some guys lowered their gazes; it was true that women usually went to management, HR, and design jobs. But Ann was convincing these men to give a chance to women, and they just needed a little encouragement.

The second part of the speech was about the latest updates, new technologies, and trends in software architecture. Here, I didn't understand half of what she was talking about. But as time passed, men around were enchanted by the magical language she spoke. Now they saw her as an equal, and it made sense that after suggesting a mentorship program for women she needed to prove that women could be trusted. In the end, she said that Benzon now helped with setting programs for diversity, and anyone interested in being a mentor could apply at the link shown on the screen. Much to my surprise, lots of people around started typing the short link and scanning the QR code.

In the end, she managed to convince them. I did hope they would act on her suggestion because women were needed here. It could even be seen at this conference that only 25-30 percent of those attending were female. And they mostly went to HR and design workshops. If you peeped at the Node React lecture, you'd see only five women in a male audience.

The hall boomed with applause at the end. Those

lucky ones who managed to find a seat stood up, clapping, nodding. Shouts of approval and encouragement tried to outcry the roar. Ann smiled and thanked the audience, bowing her head lightly. She said that she'd be happy to discuss any questions in fifteen minutes in another room and that everyone was welcome.

When I went to the room to say I appreciated the work she was doing, there were so many people and absolutely no chance to get a word in edgewise. She was a star, an advocate for women, and I was merely one of many in the crowd. There was no way for us to be friends, and it sounded crazy that only yesterday I was drinking with her at the bar. All I wanted to say was that she did a great job on the stage and that I admired her passion for sharing knowledge and bringing more trust in women. But it seemed every person approaching her said the same, and more.

As I was turning to leave, Ann glanced back, and our eyes met. She froze for a second. I was trying to say everything with my eyes, but how could one talk with their eyes? I had no idea, so I showed a thumbs up and beamed. She smiled and nodded, placing a hand on her chest. And then she shifted her gaze to the excited woman who was speaking to her, and I left.

One more workshop on UX and I could go back to the hotel, change, and go on a date with the evening sea.

The bus delivered us to the hotel, and I dropped my bag of flyers, ads, notepads, magnets, pens, and even a couple of mugs at my room, changed, and strolled to the beach.

It was dark already and there were almost no people left around. The cool breeze grazed my skin, and it was a welcome feeling after the day in the crowd. It was time to call Mark. I didn't have any time to think about him through the day, but now as I stood here alone, I missed him. He picked up the phone after the third beep.

"Hey," he said, his voice so soft.

"Hey, how was your day?"

"The usual. Work, home. It's so quiet here without you."

"It's quiet here too, besides the waves and the wind. It's quite lovely, and they are keeping me company," I replied with a smile.

He chuckled.

"Of course. Where would you be in your free minutes except on the beach." He knew I was a water addict. "How was the conference?"

"You know what? It was interesting and empowering. I thought it would be too techy for me, but I attended classes and workshops on design, and the speakers were magnificent. They did a great job on the program. And guess what?"

"What?" There was a hint of amusement in his voice.

"Yesterday, I went to the hotel bar where Benzon put all its employees. I hoped to find a buddy for today. One woman spoke to me named Ann. I thought she would keep me company today browsing the lectures, but I couldn't find her on the bus and nowhere in the conference. But then I found out she's one of Benzon's top speakers. Other speakers on the main stage were from Google, Facebook, and IBM, so I suppose I had a conversation with a celebrity yesterday."

"Sorry you had to spend the whole day alone, but it sounds that it wasn't awful after all. Was this Ann good on the stage?"

"Actually, she was exceptional. She talked about getting more women into IT."

"But you already are a woman in IT," Mark pointed out.

He was proud of me, but I was not an IT person. I drew cute pictures that were used in website designs and created app visuals. But what Ann did was real tech magic, and I had no idea how it all worked.

"No, Mark," I laughed. "I am a painter who works at an IT company. The only difference is that instead of paper, I use a tablet."

Mark worked as an attorney; the intricate world of law fascinated him. He enjoyed working with people and with his work he tried to balance justice in favor of the company he worked for.

"But what Ann was talking about is that more women should get inside real tech stuff like software development and that companies should provide guidance and individuals can become mentors. I think lots of people will at least try after her speech. Now she helps companies develop diversity programs. Then she switched to a language I have no knowledge of, explaining the trends and new technologies, but guys around seemed to understand and took notes. I think in the end she won them over and proved that women can be experts. It was interesting to witness," I said.

"A noble thing she did there." Mark chewed something. "I am going to have my *ME* evening now. It's time to refresh my memory on Lord of the Rings."

Oh, he liked his *ME* evenings. They usually included watching his favorite old movies.

"What time does your plane land tomorrow?" he asked.

"Around 10:30, I guess. I need to check, though. I will send you a message when I find out for sure."

"I'll be there, but right now, Saruman awaits. Miss you and see you soon."

"See you tomorrow. Enjoy your time. Bye."

I shut the phone and breathed in the salty air. Oh, how I missed this smell when I was at home. Kyiv was a great city, but it would be greater if the sea was there. I spent an hour walking the Promenade before going back to the hotel. In the hotel lobby, I turned to a bar again. The chances were not high, but maybe this time I'd find a buddy for tomorrow.

"Gin and tonic, please," I told the barman.

"Same." Ann appeared silently by my side.

Chapter 3

ANN

Since I met Julie yesterday at the bar, I couldn't stop thinking about her. She was so out of place, sitting alone, when everyone was huddled in groups. What was she even doing here? She should be curled in her bed in a hotel room with a book.

From the moment I saw her, I sensed the pull. It was like there was a cord between us, but as far as I knew, only I felt it. It was as though I knew her from another time or life, but I never remembered till now. I had no clue what to do with this feeling.

Yesterday was the worst time possible to get such a distraction. I should have been preparing for the speech. It was the first time I was talking to such a huge audience.

When I left her at the bar, she had appeared distraught. Maybe she remembered too? I would have spent more time with her, but I had to do so much stuff before the speech: polish the presentation and rehearse, rehearse, rehearse. Of course, I didn't see her in the morning, as I had left early. During the speech, she was there; I didn't see her, as the hall was filled to the brim, but I could feel her.

What was she thinking about my ideas? Would she support them? But instead of being distracted, knowing that she was there gave me power. It was like I was talking to her when trying to explain. Afterwards, when I went to Q&A, I glimpsed her staying back. When our eyes met, time froze for a second. It was the strangest feeling. I needed to know what she was thinking. She smiled and gave me a thumbs up.

That smile shifted something inside me, a part that wasn't used for a long time and was forgotten. All my stress on preparation, all the time I spent, it was all worth getting the smile from this girl I almost knew nothing about. Her light brown hair went to her shoulders and highlighted the freckles on her nose. I had made an effort to look away from her to the woman by my side.

One thing I knew for sure: I needed to know more about her, and if she would have me, I'd want to have her in my life.

I practically ran to the hotel bar when I came back. She wasn't there. Where was she? My heart hammering, I ordered water and sat at the table to see the entrance.

"May I?" a dark-haired guy asked; he pointed to the chair at my table across from me. He saw that I was hesitating and continued, "I wanted to say how much I loved your ideas today. I have a friend who is brilliant in Java. She is much more talented than the guys I work with at the office; the girl would have boosted the performance of our team, and I managed to organize an interview for her with my team leader. And guess what? After the interview, he says that yes, she is smart and has the knowledge needed for the job, but she's not for us. One of the reasons is how we can't have a girl in a team of guys. Also, I had a feeling that he was afraid that she was smarter than him."

His nostrils were flaring, and he breathed noisily as he was telling this story.

I finally said, "Okay, please sit."

The world needed more people like this man. He actually allowed the idea that a girl can be smarter.

"Now she is working as a freelancer on projects like flower shops and hair salon sites while she could revolutionize the technology we all are using. She is a great professional but unseen in the world of men, and it undermines her self-worth. So, when I heard you speaking, I thought that was it. I already applied to the program, and I want to help women get into tech, so there won't be such situations like what happened with my friend, and we don't lose the professionals we could get."

I'd heard so many stories like this one already, and how I admired these men who were ready to fight. It was listening to them that got this program launched.

"Thank you," I said. "Thank you for taking our side."

He smiled and went on talking.

Julie did something with my time perception because when she entered the bar, I saw her moving in slow motion. Everything around got blurred, and the guy talking to me was muted. Her hair was disheveled, and there was pink on her cheeks from the wind outside and sand on her white sneakers. She had gone to the beach. I wanted to run to her, to embrace her. What was happening? I shook my head, trying to ground myself.

"I'm sorry, but I need to go," I told the guy, who continued talking non-stop, oblivious to the fact that all my attention shifted.

Julie reached the bar and sat on the same stool from yesterday as she ordered a drink. "Gin and tonic."

"Same," I said to the bartender sitting beside her.

Chapter 4

JULIE

*A*nn smiled at me and searched my face for something. I was glad she was here.

"So, you are a famous person here," I remarked. "I loved your speech. Please tell me more about the program."

The bartender placed our drinks on leather coasters and hurried away. Ann moved her finger on the iced glass drawing lines.

"For some time, I worked side by side with an HR department, and I saw the people they were interviewing. Once, they needed to hire a big addition to the software department. Twenty people, I think," she explained. "They were interviewing day and night. What stunned me was that 95 percent of candidates were men. Was it a male-dominated job? A couple of women did get an interview, but they were never approved. They lacked confidence going in, as it was three guys who performed the interviews. Watching all this, I realized women needed to have support in the industry. That's how it all started."

Ann had seen the problem, and she had decided to do

something about it. Now her ideas were picked up by different tech companies.

"That's a great thing you're doing," I said, and I believed it.

She glanced at me, a small smile playing on her lips.

"Thanks. How was your day? And I never caught what you're doing in Benzon."

I shrugged. "I am a graphic designer. Basically, I draw what I'm told. It's primarily home pages and forms, so it's not as creative as it may seem. I am given strict rules to follow, and my task is to visualize what project managers are thinking.

"I thought I would meet you at the conference today," I continued. "Well, I met you, but my initial idea was that we would browse happily from one workshop to another. I needed a buddy," I laughed and cleared my throat, looking down at my glass. "That's why I came to the bar yesterday. I am not a skillful networker, but I did speak to the speaker, so I am not a lost cause after all."

Ann shifted just slightly, leaning in. Her eyes never left my face, and I felt my cheeks warming. Why did I talk so much? It seemed so easy with Ann. Where was my usual reserve I had with strangers? It was melting like ice cubes in my gin and tonic.

"But I managed just fine today. I quite enjoyed the lectures I attended. They were explaining new features and ways of implementing them," I said and tucked a strand of hair behind my ear. "The one negative thing with all the activity is that I almost don't have a free minute. I'd like to spend more time by the water and roam through the city, but my plane is leaving tomorrow at seven in the evening."

"What about tomorrow morning? You still have that," she pointed out.

"Yes, and I am planning to use it fully."

She nodded. "Sunrise?"

"Maybe. It depends on how things go tonight. Maybe I'll get drunk with you." I winked and blushed. What was the matter with me? Why would I say that? I tried to hide my embarrassment by taking a sip of my drink. She should be running from this fanatic woman, me. But Ann laughed and gave me a mischievous look.

"That's a great idea. I don't remember the last time I got drunk in Tel Aviv. I know a few bars. Do you want to leave here?"

Girls' night out in the middle of the business trip. Why not?

"Sure." I stood up and pulled on my jacket. "It's not a good idea to get tipsy in front of colleagues, though."

"I know one place that is by the beach. You can hear waves crashing while sitting outside."

We left the hotel and walked for ten minutes on the Promenade. Ann told stories from her summers here and how she and her grandmother went to the sea all the way from Jerusalem once a week. How it was so hot here in summers, but they went anyway. How she got dangerously tanned in just a couple of days.

She took a deep breath. "It's so different here compared to LA. This country has a history, and every time I visited, I was taught about culture and traditions. I think I could give tours now in Jaffa," Ann said, her eyes focused on the dark horizon of the sea. Her features softened as we walked, her posture became more relaxed.

We entered the bar. Strings of warm light ran along the walls with vintage art in fraying frames. Small wooden chairs were covered with pillows of different shape, color and ornament. The white ceiling was adorned with a golden net, which hung low. And a faint smell of wine and ginger contrasted with the sea smell outside.

People were drinking cocktails from oddly shaped glasses, and each one was different. The bar was called "The Glass," and it seemed their specialty was to serve drinks in every shaped glass one could imagine. A soft murmur mixed with a chill music, and people were here lounging, not drinking wildly. It was like a favorite coffee shop in the morning, but for the evening.

I ordered an Aperol Spritz, a safe choice for every place. Ann went for a custom-made cocktail with rum mixed with juices and a drop of chocolate liquor. We found ourselves a table near the door, sheltered from the chilly evening breeze, but still, we could hear the waves.

"This place feels relaxing," I said, looking around. "Especially the lights. I usually don't go to bars and am not a big drinker. Maybe once a month, Mark has his friends over, and he mixes up these crazy cocktails."

"Mark is your …?"

"Mark is my boyfriend," I explained, and I could have sworn something in Ann's face shifted; her eyes darkened just a notch.

"How long have you been together?" she asked, her eyes never leaving my face.

"We met four years ago at the summer festival. Three years ago, we decided to move in together."

Her chin dipped down. "You said once a month he has his friends over. What about your friends?"

"I don't really have friends," I admitted, burying my embarrassment in the glass. I rarely told this to people, as they might think there was something crucially wrong with me. What kind of person didn't have friends? This time, I was trying to explain myself. It seemed important for me to prove to Ann that I was not a crazy sociopath.

"Well, I *do* have friends," I continued, "but we are not close. I had a girlfriend back in university, but she pursued her career to Dublin. We video chat, but it doesn't work as well as when you can feel the person sitting next to you. When she visits, we spend a great deal of time together, but I wish she'd be there more often for me. We try to rekindle our friendship, but it slowly fades," I sighed.

Ann studied me. Bar lights were reflecting in her blue eyes, and her features were warmed as she lightly inclined towards me. Usually, she was a warrior, a fierce one, but here she took off her armor. All her attention was pinned to me, like what I was saying was interesting to her. And her eyes, they never left my face, and I would be uncomfortable if it was anyone else, but in her gaze, I swam like in the balmy sea waves. She didn't say much, but she listened, and I had a feeling that she understood. I wanted to show her what kind of person I was.

"You said you have a brother. How's your relationship with him?" Ann questioned after a while.

I chuckled. "Alex. He is four years older than me. He's great, and he's always there for me. And his wife, Christina, is the kindest human being. Always doing something. She works in a fashion marketing company helping companies build brand images. She's four months pregnant. And now that you know my people, what about you? Any siblings?" I asked.

Ann sipped her hideous cocktail and leaned back, rubbing her wrist. "No, it's only me, I was a big project for my parents. They wanted to raise a scientist. They partially succeeded. I think they would be happy with my career at least."

She spoke about them in the past tense, but I didn't press with questions.

"What about other aspects of your life? It sounds like they had big expectations."

Ann chortled. "They had big expectations all right. But

I failed them spectacularly. They wanted me to be a big scientist, have a family, and take part in the community. I partially covered the scientist part, getting an online degree in computer science. Again, it was later than they expected me to do it. It was after I started working in Benzon when I decided to proceed to software development. The part with building a family and integrating into the community just won't work," she said, gazing outside to the distant sea. "They just don't accept me now. It's difficult to explain." Ann ran a hand through her hair.

I didn't want to push her, but there was something wrong with her family. "What about friends?" I asked.

Chapter 5

ANN

*H*ow could I explain that I was a loner? But Julie didn't have friends either, so that gave me hope she might understand.

"Some time ago I decided to dedicate all my time to work," I said, my chest tightening. "I do have friends, and I am close to my neighbors. I moved to the house I live in now three years ago, but they are more like family now. Also, I enjoy surfing and there is a big community in LA." I tried to come up with something, hiding the fact that after my parents stopped talking to me, I got disappointed in people and couldn't keep anyone close. It hurt too much when the people you love shut you out of their life.

Julie noticed my discomfort and said, "It's okay. Maybe we are similar in some ways."

These words echoed in a long forgotten chamber inside me. Her gaze studied my face, and I caught her eyes, light chocolate brown. She was so at ease, her body inclined in my direction, listening closely. She smiled, and for a fleeting moment I wanted to touch those lips.

"Do you like surfing?" I asked instead.

"I never actually tried it. I paddle boarded a couple of times, but not surfing. Once in Portugal, I saw a group of surfers. They were just sitting on their boards waiting for a wave. It was a calm day, and they were looking in one direction, so peaceful. This I could do," she laughed. "I was planning to go to see the sunrise tomorrow. Do you want to come with me?"

Of course, I wanted to come. Julie had some kind of power over me, and she had no idea that I would go anywhere with her, just to stay close, to know more of her. How could it be when I met a person just yesterday and it felt like there was a cord between us. It confused me. And she lived in a city I've never been to, a country I knew almost nothing about. On another continent too, for God's sake. And she had a long-term boyfriend.

How could I be a part of her life? Could I be a friend?

"Sure," I agreed. "I usually hate waking up early, but sunrises are worth it."

I would only have time with her in the morning. I needed to come up with an idea on how to see her again, and I had a night to think.

She looked at my empty glass and asked, "More?"

I grinned, and we ordered the same drinks.

Julie had style; she wore a white jacket with jeans, a white shirt, and a massive necklace with an amethyst stone and golden chain laid on her collarbone, highlighting her delicate neck. She touched her hair a lot; it was like a shield she liked to play with.

We talked about traveling. She appeared to be an avid traveler, and together with Mark, they'd been everywhere. Benzon policy encouraged employees to take vacations, and it seemed her manager shared the idea of traveling, so every two weeks Julie packed a bag and went to Europe for a weekend. Ukraine was so close to Europe, so it was easy: two-to-three-hour flight and you were in Paris, Berlin, or Amsterdam. Every three months, she and her boyfriend disconnected from the world and flew to Asia or South America.

"Sometimes I get so tired of constant exploring, and we rent a house in the middle of nowhere and just do nothing. *Week of nature* I call it, and afterwards, crowds of people and city buzz isn't so pressing," Julie explained.

I imagined what she and Mark were doing during those weeks out, my mind painting vivid pictures. I tried to push the thought away, as alcohol was already playing tricks on my imagination. My eyes fell to her cleavage just for a second before I looked away, but my cheeks were burning hot already. I decided to talk because my mind was running in the wrong direction.

I told her that when I was a kid, I traveled with my parents all over the US. Camping was our family thing. Now I enjoyed being close to water. I could usually find nature retreats in California, and it was a complete change of scenery. But what I truly loved was exploring giant cities. It all started with New York. It was so different from LA where I grew up. Then I loved seeing Tokyo and London. And my second travel love was history travel.

"I am like one of those old Chinese tourists with headphones who trot after a guide with an umbrella. I like group tours," I laughed. "I know, it's embarrassing."

Julie snorted in her cocktail. "I can't imagine you in such a group, mixed among elderly tourists who always take these tours."

"I am usually the youngest there, but you won't believe stories you hear from those people, how they met their spouses, what they did in life. Compared to their stories, my life pales to boringness. And guides usually load so many facts in the programs. Anyway, it works for me."

Julie stared at me with amazement. She was a bit drunk by now. Her replies became slurry at the edges. I enjoyed her company, and the strange part was that she seemed to have fun as well.

I told her that it took me five trips to Rome to visit all the museums and sights I wanted to explore. Now I was in the process of exploring Barcelona.

"There's going to be a massive Benzon party next month in Barcelona," Julie told me.

I knew about that one. One of the essential Benzon offices was in Barcelona, and company management decided to save money and not organize it in LA but move the party to Europe. Barcelona was a safe choice, having lots of sightseeing and places to eat.

I nodded. "Yes, I know."

"Are you going?" she asked.

"Yes."

"Of course you are. You're a valuable asset," Julie said with a wink.

I blushed. Really? All it took was a small compliment and I felt my cheeks burning.

"We should be going," I said, clearing my throat. "It's an early wake-up tomorrow if we want to see the sunrise."

Julie tried to hide her surprise in the last sip of the drink, and we stepped outside. It was much colder, as temperatures dropped in Tel Aviv at night. Julie hugged herself and pulled the jacket up to cover her neck, goosebumps visible on her skin. She stopped, facing the sea and inhaled deeply, closing her eyes.

"I love the sea smell," she murmured.

Light wind caught her hair as she stood there, not moving, listening to the waves. A smile tugged at her lips.

I couldn't take my eyes off her, her white jacket practically glowing in the night, her face so serene. Julie opened her eyes and looked at the black vastness of the night sea. I peered at my watch so she couldn't see me staring at her.

Chapter 6

JULIE

*S*he wanted to escape me. Did I bore her? She sat across from me and after I praised her, she just shut down. But before that, she was genuinely interested in our conversation. Ann was the most unusual person I had ever met. So independent, doing what she liked and actually changing the world in small ways. A way that got her to the conference stage. It took courage and time. I didn't think she gave herself enough credit for it.

I caught her checking the time and said, "Let's go."

She looked away and exhaled nervously. And I did one thing that I was sure I would not do if not for the alcohol blurring my world: I took Ann's hand in mine.

"Are you still coming with me in the morning?" I asked.

Her skin was so soft, a tiny bracelet wrapped her wrist, a simple chain with a small silver house on it. Her nails were short and painted black.

Ann looked down at my hand holding her, and I couldn't read her expression.

Why did I even touch her? Those few cocktails were

enough for me to slur the edges of familiarity and
appropriateness. I only knew her for two days and I
already grabbed her hand begging her to come with me in
the morning. Those drinks were strong.

"Sorry." I let go of her hand. Ann watched me with her
blue eyes, tucked her hair with that hand, and smiled
shakily.

"It's okay. Sure, I'll go with you in the morning," she
said.

Thank God. I must stop scaring her. The moment she
relaxed in my company, I said or did something to scare
her. But we likely wouldn't see each other ever again after
tomorrow, and it tugged in my chest.

Ann walked silently by my side. She wore a black
leather jacket, black boots, black jeans, and only her shirt
was white. Her pale skin was highlighted by the dark waves
of her hair. She scanned the horizon with her huge eyes,
the darkness of the sea. Only ship lights were scattered in
the middle of nothing.

"I enjoyed the evening," I told her. I needed to make
sure we were alright after that awkward hand grab.

She turned her head to me, and she beamed. So,
everything was fine. And I smiled back.

"I did too," she said.

We soon entered the hotel lobby.

"Let's meet here at six?" Ann suggested.

I nodded. "Sounds perfect."

"I am going to take the stairs. My room is on the
second floor. Good night," she said, but then she paused,
opening her mouth to say more. She stopped herself and
turned around.

"Good night!" I said to the closing door to the stairwell.

I took the elevator to the fourteenth floor. In my room,
I took a shower and buried myself under the covers.

What an unusual evening. One moment, we were engulfed in conversation, and the next, she shut me out. It was such a strange feeling. It would be great to keep in touch with her after tomorrow, but I knew perfectly well that remote friendships didn't work.

I closed my eyes and was lulled by the faraway noise of the waves.

Chapter 7

ANN

I ran up the stairs. What the hell happened? When Julie touched my hand, I honestly felt the spark and then a current of her energy warming my hand. I was surely going crazy. And my stupefied reaction had offended her. I opened my room door and sat on the bed.

There was a connection between us, I knew it. Did she feel it too? I wanted to be close to her, I needed it, but the next day she was going back to her life, to her boyfriend. One morning was all we had together. And the day after tomorrow, I'd be on the plane back to LA.

I slowly peeled off my clothes and shuffled to the bathroom. The shower was my favorite place to think and generate ideas, but this time I didn't know what to do with my thoughts as hot water trickled over my skin.

I dove under the crispy hotel sheets, set an alarm for 5:30 a.m., and stared at the ceiling. As minutes went by, I closed my eyes and finally fell asleep.

∾

An alarm screamed at 5:30, it was still dark outside. Oh, I was not a fan of early wakeups. I dragged myself out of bed, mournfully wishing I could just stay there and close my eyes.

As my mind cleared, I remembered Julie, her smile, her curious gaze, her delicate hands. I had become Julie-addicted over the past two days. What was next? I laughed to myself and decided to simply be. I put on my tights and sneakers and took the stairs to the lobby. She was already there, and by the look of her face she wasn't an early riser either. There was no makeup, and her hair was in a high ponytail.

"If I wasn't flying back today, I'd just skip this morning torture," Julie laughed, rubbing her eyes.

"Yes, the sunrise idea always seems much better in the evening," I replied.

The street outside was deserted, but as we moved closer to the Promenade, there were a few crazy runners already.

"I envy people who can start their mornings so early," I said, watching the runner passing by. "I've read a few books about entrepreneurs suggesting waking up at four or five in the morning. I honestly tried, but it was torture. Seven or eight in the morning works just fine for me."

Jullie shuddered. "I am so bad at early wakeups. Sleeping for ten to twelve hours isn't a problem for me, so I set my sweet point between eight to nine hours so the world won't think I'm skipping my life by sleeping."

We soon reached the waterline. It was so quiet, and waves were tiny and splashed at my feet. The light shimmered on the horizon already.

"When do you leave?" Julie asked.

"Tomorrow morning," I replied.

She tilted her head to the side. "Is it warm in LA now?"

"Yes, it's a bit warmer than here."

"I wish I lived in a warm place," Julie sighed. "I hate the cold, and I hate snow. Sometimes we talk about moving somewhere down south, but usually it's just talking."

"I understand. I wouldn't want to move somewhere with real winter. If I want to see snow, I just drive to the mountains."

Julie nodded slowly, never taking her eyes from the horizon.

"What are your plans for the evening?" she asked after a few moments of quiet.

"There's going to be a party at the end of the conference. I need to be there to discuss potential collaborations. But I'll leave as soon as I can and will visit my grandmother. Who knows when I will be able to see her again? We video chat, but it's not the same."

"She seems like a tech-savvy person."

"It was not easy," I laughed. "But she's trying. Recently, she discovered Instagram, and she keeps sending me these travel photos, paintings, and animals."

Julie smiled. The rising sun colored the sea in shades of warm pink, red, and yellow, and all these colors played on her skin. Again, I caught myself staring at her. But this time, I didn't hide it.

Julie had such delicate features, and her lips parted. She felt that I was watching her and looked at me. Her gaze scanned my face and stopped at my eyes. Her eyes were warm pools of caramel. She wasn't scared of looking back at me; in fact, she was open. I wondered if she guessed what I was feeling. I stopped myself before I did something stupid and turned away to the sea. It was I who got scared and shy. We stood in silence.

My heart finally stopped hammering down my ribcage and calmed. We walked down the shore, sun blazing in full force now.

Chapter 8

*W*hen I looked into Ann's eyes, everything paused. There was just me and her, and then she looked away. The warmth spread in me when I caught her looking at my face. There was something so familiar in Ann and alien at the same time. I needed more time to know her, but I wouldn't see her again after today.

I checked the time and sighed. "It's time to go back, I need to get packed before leaving for the conference."

"Yes," Ann agreed with a wry smile. "Thanks for dragging me here."

"The worst part was rolling out of bed," I laughed.

Blue was woven in Ann's features, and she was looking solemnly at the sea. I didn't know how to say goodbye. There was no chance we could stay in touch living so far away, as we both knew it'd end eventually.

We crossed the street to the hotel and entered the lobby.

"See you later?" I said, more like a question.

"Hope so, though I will be with the sponsors today. But I'll try to make it to lunch."

"Thanks for spending these evenings with me, and the morning." I smiled.

I'd miss her, her direct behavior, her huge blue eyes, her smile, our talks. I'd miss silent moments of how she studied me. There was a chance I wouldn't see her at the conference; she'd be leaving with another group and spending the day in negotiations.

She tilted her head looking at me, and then she hugged me. That was unusual for me, as I didn't really hug people other than my family and Mark. But I leaned into her. Ann's hair smelled of cinnamon, and it grazed my face. I inhaled deeply and hugged back. We stayed like this for seconds or hours. I didn't want to let go, my body pressed to her.

And then she stepped back and smiled. "Bye, Julie," Ann said.

"Bye," I murmured, but she had already disappeared behind the door to the staircase.

Chapter 9

ANN

I slowly went up the stairs, unlocked my door, and slid to the floor. I touched my bracelet and stared outside. I needed to get ready, but I was numb. I didn't mean to hug her. But when she was in my arms, I could feel her heart beating next to mine, I could feel her breath on my neck. I almost kissed her, and it took all my will just to say goodbye. I needed to breathe, slowly in and out, in and out.

I gave myself five minutes, changed and ran to the shuttle. Today my task was to convert new leads, so I plastered a smile on my face and did the job while my heart broke a little. Each time I saw brown hair, I turned to look closer to see if it was Julie. But every time it wasn't her.

I missed lunch and was starving. There were a few representatives at the conference my company wanted to work with, and it was my job to form a connection with them. They kept talking and told me all the different nuances of their companies and how they were excited to collaborate with us. So, the next time I checked the clock, it was 4 p.m. She would be leaving anytime now, leaving me.

I excused myself and went to the central hall, but she was nowhere to be found. The crowds had already begun to thin, some people going to the airport directly from here. A few groups were leaving to continue somewhere more private with some beer. I poured myself a glass of water and was heading back when I spotted her at the door.

I froze, looking at her back. As if she knew, she turned, and our eyes met. Julie smiled, and that smile was like a sun. But then she stepped outside.

That was it. She was gone.

I spent a few more hours at the conference and took a taxi to Arlozorov Street.

Mary opened the door, and her smile was so warm and familiar I almost cried right there. Her dark eyes met mine, and she ushered me inside.

She took me to the balcony and pointed to my usual spot, which contained a cozy armchair, burgundy velvet so shabby, as it was twice my age. But it was one of my favorite places on earth. We had spent so many hours here talking, discussing my parents, my relationships, and my career. It was a warm evening, but I draped a blanket around my shoulders and exhaled shakily.

Mary glanced at me and disappeared inside. I heard her making tea. Around me, pottery figures decorated the walls, and old carpets with African ornaments covered the balcony tiles. Candles were everywhere, but only a few were lit. A string of lights covered the perimeter.

Mary appeared and gave me the cup. It was always the

same: huge red mug with white polka dots. I assumed she had a set of those because I remembered breaking two of them. She held the same cup in her papery arms, her fingers showing old calluses.

"Now, tell me," Mary said.

I took a sip, tasting herbal tea. "I met a woman."

Mary's eyes glinted and she gestured for me to proceed.

"But she lives in another country. Ukraine, can you imagine? She works at the same company as I do," I explained, running my hand through my hair. "Every time my eyes found hers, I had to make myself look away, but all I wanted to do was stare. I felt the pull and a crazy desire to touch her. Her skin, her eyes, they have some power over me. I stumbled with the words, and I was so scared a few times I almost ran away. I almost kissed her for God's sake, and we met only two days ago. I feel that I know her or knew her in another life maybe? But in this life, I know nothing about her, I wanted to talk to her all the time, to find out every detail of her life. And she has a long-term boyfriend." I miserably lifted my gaze to Mary from my drink.

She beamed and leaned forward to hear more. "And how was she with you?" she asked. "Did she want to spend time with you?"

"Yes, I think so." This time, I was beaming. "She suggested we go to watch the sunrise together, and we did." I took a deep breath. "But never have I felt this way before. Her face is constantly in my head now."

I took another sip and tried to steady my shaking hands. Mary reached and took my hand in hers.

"Do you think she had any interest in you? Do you think she feels what you feel?" she asked.

"She doesn't feel the same way for sure. It's like a wave that wants to sweep me off my feet. She enjoyed our time together, I think. She said that we could be friends, but we both don't believe in long distance friendships."

"And do you just want to be friends with her?"

"No, of course not," I sighed, my eyes stinging.

Mary's brow shot in the air. "Will you try? Not everyone is given such a gift in this life. I knew a girl who said the same words about a boy she met. They were from different worlds, and it took her immense courage to try."

I looked at the sky; the moon lit the clouds with silver. I squeezed the blanket tighter around my shoulders. "I don't know what to do. She doesn't know I'm gay."

"She doesn't need to be gay to be with you. The only thing she needs to do is choose you. You are sitting here afraid to move but think about what she'd need to sacrifice if she chose to be with you. She'd need to risk her beliefs, the beliefs of her family and her country. Not everyone in this world is open minded, unfortunately. Will she do it? We don't know. The question here is: Are you going to try?"

I was scared. I was sure now I could still forget what happened, just proceed on with my life. In a month, the feeling would become a memory. But did I want that? If I chose to give it a try, Julie had the power of lifting me to the sky or making me fall. What if she refused me? Would I survive the blow? Of course I would; it would hurt like hell, but I'd live. The major question was if I'd forgive myself if I didn't try?

"Don't think so hard," Mary laughed. "You already know the answer."

Her silver hair was long, and she wore leggings and a tunic. Mary was seventy-eight, but she didn't look her age. She took my hand, moved closer, and looked at me.

"You are so lonely. Don't try to prove me wrong, I know you are. Your job and surfing keeps you busy. But this girl may show you the feelings you've never had. I don't believe you'd be connected to a weak person; you just wouldn't click. So I assume she might want to try, and she might want to fight."

Shakily, I smiled. "That's why you had three husbands?"

She didn't reply immediately. "I think I was searching for the feeling you are describing, but I never found it. Maybe in another life?" Mary said, leaning back in her chair and touching her hair. She was a flirt back in the day.

Mary's eyes grew darker as she watched the sky outside.

"The girl who had these feelings was your mom. And you know how connected she is with your dad."

Oh, I knew. I grew up in that love. You could see their connection, the support they gave each other; their thoughts were aligned. And they shared this love with me … till they stopped.

"I hate what they did to you. And I pray for them to change their minds to see that the problem is with them, not with you." The corners of her mouth pulled down, making her face look her age. "I just can't understand how a mother can abandon her daughter," she sighed.

"It's okay." I took a sip of my tea. "I'm used to it now."

It had been four years since my mom told me to go away. Till my mid-twenties, I tried to become what they wanted me to be. I was building a career and going out with a guy. He was nice, but back in my teens I felt that I had no interest in men and after giving dating a try with a man I knew I couldn't do it, not for them, and I broke up with him.

After I came out to my family, only my grandmother supported me. My mom and dad laughed off the idea and said it was my own kind of rebellion. But it was not. They spent years trying to persuade me to believe I was normal, as if I could change the way I was. And I almost believed them; I tried to be the daughter they wanted. Eventually, they just could not accept it. They said I was a disgrace and they never wanted to see me again. It broke my heart and spun me into a string of constantly changing partners.

A year ago, I realized they would not give me the love and acceptance I craved. I stopped seeing anybody, instead focusing on work, and spending my time alone traveling, reading, and surfing. I was learning to love myself, and I was comfortable alone now. Three days ago, I was happy with my life, but today I was contemplating diving into something that could break me again. I was contemplating the rejection I might face again.

But would I try? I took a deep breath. Yes, I would.

I smiled at Mary, and she hugged me.

"I will always be there for you," she promised.

I felt a little braver now.

Chapter 10

JULIE

*M*ark met me outside the airport and held me tightly to his chest.

"I missed you," he murmured into my hair as he kissed the top of my head. He was a mountain of a man.

"I watched all the movies I wanted, met with Andrew, cooked, and then sat on the couch realizing I had nothing to do. So I sat waiting. Thank God it was only a few hours ago," he laughed, that signature deep laugh I loved.

I traced his hair and stood on tiptoes to kiss him.

"I missed you too," I said.

"How was the trip? Was it dead boring making you want to run away as soon as possible back to me?"

We were crossing a parking lot. The air was crisp, and I could see that it had snowed lightly before. Patches of dirt were covered in white.

"Actually, it wasn't so bad," I said, chuckling at the feigned pained expression on Mark's face. "I enjoyed the workshops. I think we could use the strategies they suggested, and I can't wait to share them with the team on Monday."

I cranked the heater in the car and hid my palms beneath my legs where the seat heating spread.

"And do you remember I told you I met a Benzon speaker at the bar?" I asked.

He nodded.

We were rushing on the highway, and all around was a different shade of grey. Here, I could see more snow, but still not enough to cover the greyness. I missed the sun and sea breeze already.

I told Mark about Ann, how we sat at the bar, and the sunrise. It was this morning, but already it felt like a lifetime ago.

I didn't tell him that she evoked such feelings in me I could not yet decipher, some kind of warmth and closeness. I didn't tell him that it broke me a little that I would not see her again. And I did not say that I would love to talk with her again. But there was no way, as we just lived too far away, and our worlds were too different. I cringed at the idea of video chats; I needed to feel a person sitting across from me. Zoom and Messenger did not provide that intimacy.

I tried this with Darina, my friend who moved to Dublin. In the beginning, we talked a lot and texted. But as the time went by, we found less time and less things to say. Now we did it every month just to check on each other. Well, that was life. But I needed a direct touch with a human, not just an image on the screen.

"Oh my God, you are tanned!" said Tanya, my fellow designer and a goddess of coffee making when I met her at the office kitchen.

"No, I'm not. There wasn't enough sun and time to

tan, unfortunately," I said mischievously with a laugh. It was a work trip, after all.

Tanya was a ball of energy, tall, with chin length blond hair and a sharp nose. Her eyes always darted excitedly across the room, trying to find something new. Her latest hobby was stained glass making. How she juggled work, her little daughter, and all her creative endeavors, I had no idea.

"Tell me, how was it?" she asked. "I'd kill to see the sun, but now I need to wait patiently for my New Year's vacation."

"But it's only in two weeks!"

She had been planning a trip to Thailand for months.

"It's two more weeks of waiting," she huffed. "So, tell me."

"I actually enjoyed the trip." I told her about the conference, about my walks on Promenade, about the warmth and sea color. I left out the part about meeting Ann; it was personal somehow.

I looked at my watch after a while. "It's time for the meeting."

We grabbed our coffee and went to the meeting room. There were only four people on my team.

Diana, whose place I took in the conference, smiled at me; her son was better. I talked about the trip and dove into a discussion of design techniques they had explained in the workshops. My manager was pleased. She nodded, and we dug deeper on how to implement these new tools.

It has been more than a week since I came back from Tel-Aviv. I agreed to meet Tanya at the coffee shop in our office building before work. My morning latte made me wake up, and I tried to enjoy the Kyiv winter greyness surrounding me. The coffee shop was so busy and loud. The noise of the coffee machine, the barista banging the pitcher to create a foam, all this activity made me active too.

"The movie you suggested was awful. Sorry, Julie," Tanya said, sipping her cappuccino. This was old news; we liked completely different movies but kept suggesting watching one movie or another to each other. "The plot was obvious, and the actors were slow. I think I'd play the lead better than the main protagonist," she added.

"You sure would," I laughed.

We grabbed our coffees to go and went up to the office.

At my desk, I turned on my computer with numb fingers. It was so cold outside that it took twenty minutes for me to melt. I wrapped my hands around the cup, finding it was still lukewarm as I waited for my Mac to boot. I opened my inbox first.

In the midst of familiar names and threads was an email from a Benzon employee whose name I had not heard before. Subject line: *Invite*. I clicked on it, scanned the letter fast, and almost spilled my latte on the keyboard.

The contents said:

Join us at the Future of Benzon, 12 January in Barcelona, Spain.

You are invited to an event dedicated to celebrating our 10-year anniversary. It is intended to foster conversation and learning.

Come along to our beautiful office in Barcelona.

Please reply to this email to discuss travel details.

Best regards,

Maya Rodrigez

My jaw dropped, and I looked around me. The office was almost empty; Tanya was scrolling an Instagram feed. Was it a joke? How could I possibly be invited to a major company event? I was just a web designer in a small Kyiv office.

Ann.

It dawned on me. Of course she had done it. She had enough power in the company to ask for a random employee to be invited. A heat radiated through my chest as my hands started tingling. She made it possible for us to see each other again.

I smiled and went to the internal corporate website to find her email. It was easy: ann.weis@benzon.com.

I opened a new email tab and put in her email address, subject line: *Thank you*.

And typed:

Hi Ann,

I received an invitation, and I guess it's your doing.

Thanks for giving me the sun in January too. Looking forward to seeing you again.

Julie.

And then I hit send.

"Why are you beaming?" asked Tanya, noticing my expression when she looked up from her phone.

"It looks like I'm going to Barcelona in January," I said, still in shock.

"No way! How did you manage that?"

I opened the invitation email and showed it to her. She read and asked, "Do you know how I can get one?"

"Have no idea." I shrugged.

"Maybe they choose random employees from every office?" she wondered.

"Maybe."

It was a bit offensive that she thought I was not good enough to be invited. But who was I kidding? It was not about being good, it was about being important. And I was not that important.

"Oh, wow," Tanya remarked. "You're going on vacation to Barcelona."

"It's not a vacation," I corrected. "It's a business trip."

She scoffed with a wink, "Sure."

And she was right; it would be packed with entertainment and activities. From what I heard about what they did five years ago, it was massive.

And I would see Ann again.

Chapter 11

I checked my work emails after breakfast. The sun poured in my kitchen and glinted on white countertops. Green hills of the golf club not far away kept my view fresh all year around. I unlocked my phone and tapped on the Mail icon. As I scanned twenty emails I received, my eye caught one from Julie Kovalenko, and my heart started beating faster.

Subject line: *Thank you.*

So, it must be okay, right? My finger hovered before opening it. She knew. I smiled; one email was enough to make my day. I had become an addict, a really vulnerable one.

It was easy to arrange the invitation. I marched into the office where people were compiling the magic potion for corporate events and asked who was responsible for attendees. They pointed to Gabriela. I invited her to lunch at the office dining hall and explained that I met a bright Benzon designer at the conference and would like to talk more with her about her vision on the upcoming project. It was absurd, as I could have talked to her via Zoom, no need to drag her to Barcelona. But Gabriela didn't question me and just asked me to send her Julie's name.

"No problem. It'll be done," Gabriela said, chewing a giant vegan sandwich.

It was easy. Today was the last working day before Christmas and Julie with her email glued a smile to my face for the whole day.

I used to love Christmas time. My parents always made it happy and magical. Every year we watched the Grinch and when I became older on the 25ᵗʰ, my mom and I always chilled on the couch and watched romantic Christmas movies. My dad said we were too sentimental, but he made us hot cocoa anyway.

I remembered it very well. The Holiday was playing, and Jude Law was so sweet. We huddled under the huge plush blanket, and my dad brought us three huge cups of steaming cocoa, topped with marshmallows. I remembered the warmth of the cup and the huge tree in the corner. I remembered their smiles. It was perfect, until it wasn't.

Since they stopped talking to me, Christmas was the time I missed them the most.

This year the plan was this: Christmas Eve with my neighbors, Jack, John, and Ian. They knew my story, and they became my family to replace the one I had lost; they cared about me. So we'd be eating till we couldn't breathe and on the 25ᵗʰ, I was going surfing.

I finished wrapping the presents just before I needed to leave. That was my fault, though, since I always left gifts for the last minute.

I replied to Julie's email: "*You're welcome. See you soon.*"

Short and sweet.

I kept running through the rooms trying to find my keys. The Grinch must have stolen them, I thought, when my phone pinged. I almost dropped it when my foot caught the carpet.

One new message in Messenger. I opened it, and it was Julie. She had found me on Facebook. In her avatar photo, she smiled mischievously, a close-up portrait. It was probably taken in the summer, her skin tanned and freckles more visible than when I met her.

"Merry Christmas, Ann!

I hope you are spending time with special people. In the Ukraine we celebrate Christmas on January 6th. But more celebrated is New Year's night.

Hope you have a magical day today! Sending you a bit of snow.

And I look forward to seeing you again soon."

Attached was a photo of a snowy alley in the night. It was lit by old-fashioned lamp posts, and it looked like some kind of park.

I typed back. My heart skipped beats, and I was smiling from ear to ear.

"Hi, Julie! Merry Christmas to you too! I am so happy you reached out. Heading to my neighbors' now for a ton of food."

Her reply came quickly:

"Send me pictures!"

"I will."

John opened the door and welcomed me in. He wrapped his enormous arms around me in a light embrace. John was in his late forties. He was fit, his muscles tight under the shirt. His stylish curly Afro haircut highlighted big hazel eyes, and a wide cheerful smile. He released me and looked at my face.

"What are you so happy about? I am sure it's not little old me you are so happy to see." He squinted.

He noticed everything.

"I met a girl, and her name is Julie."

A huge smile crossed his face. "Jack!" he roared. "Annie finally met someone!"

I heard the clatter of the dishes and Jack ran from the kitchen. His face was streaked with flour, and he wore a red apron with "Best Dad in the World" printed on it. Jack was shorter than John by a few inches, but he was massively built, a great tower of a man, with a well pronounced round belly. John always teased Jack that because he needed to taste all the food he was cooking, Jack was getting rounder and rounder.

I felt my cheeks burning hot.

"Nothing has happened and maybe nothing will happen. She lives in another country."

"Canada?" Jack asked.

"Ukraine."

Jack and John glanced at each other.

"Is it in Eastern Europe?" Jack asked.

I nodded, growing uneasy. "Yes."

The timer pinged in somewhere inside the house, and Jack put a hand on my shoulder and led me in. "Tell us everything."

We walked into the kitchen; it was enormous and styled like a magazine photograph. Copper pots were shining, and at least twenty of them were hanging up in the aisle.

A boy knelt at the oven, peering inside.

"Hi Ian," I greeted.

"Hey," the boy said, not looking up.

Ian was always shy; he always hid in his room when I would come by. He was comfortable only with Jack and John, and all others were intruding strangers. He was nine, and I had thought he was finally starting to melt towards me. At least he didn't run to his room, but he had been hovering close to Jack the last couple of times I visited.

"We are making cinnamon-sugar apple pie," Ian said proudly.

"Well, it's me and Ian. John just hampers our progress sometimes," Jack said, peering into the oven. "I think it's ready."

Ian put on huge oven gloves with an alien print on them. Jack opened the oven, and a sweet cinnamon smell hit me. John took a picture on his iPhone and gazed at Ian.

He caught my eye. "At least the boy won't starve to death. He loves to cook."

It was such a warm family image that it reminded me of my mom and dad. I pushed the thought away.

Soft Christmas music played, and they had already set the table. A lush Christmas tree stood in the corner. John collected vintage Christmas tree decorations, and I could spend hours studying them.

"This one I bought last year in Prague at a flea market, it's dated from the 1960's," he pointed to an old-fashioned glass satellite, a ball with four arrows. It used to be shining silver, but now it was dulled with age.

"Everything's ready," Jack called, Ian standing proud at his side.

It was magical. A red runner crossed the huge oak table. Gravy, ham, and vegetables were steaming, making my eyes water. We sat at the table and took each other's hands. Amazingly, Ian didn't cringe away from me, and his small warm hand squeezed mine. John saw it and beamed at me. He said grace in his low voice, and we dug into the food.

"So, tell us everything." Jack looked at me. "Who is she? What does she do? I'm sure she's smoking hot."

Ian rolled his eyes and gulped a mouthful of ham.

"I met her at the conference in Tel Aviv. But there is actually nothing to tell." I smiled. "Yet. We talked in the bar, went to a sunrise, and she flew back home. But I can't stop thinking about her."

"Are you going to see her again?" John asked.

I told them that I arranged an invitation for her to Barcelona. "And I don't know what will happen there, but I want to see her again, even once. She has a long-term boyfriend." I exhaled, frowning.

Jack and John exchanged glances. Ian looked warily at me, his childish face a grimace of concern.

"Does she know that you're gay?"

"Nope," I replied. "And I'm scared."

Jack put an arm on my shoulders. "Don't be. You are one of the kindest people we know. And if she can't see it, you are better off spending Christmas with our boring selves."

Ian nodded, and I made an effort to catch my dropping jaw.

"I don't know her." John grinned. "But it's time for the world to set your lonely soul with somebody equal. Everything will be alright; trust your instincts. And this Julie girl should dump her guy for you."

It was a scary thought, and I wasn't allowing myself to look so far forward. I worried about the decisions Julie would need to make if, and only if, she chose me. And there was not much of a chance of that happening.

I ate so much I couldn't move. This was a real Christmas when you felt so full somebody had to roll you home.

I grabbed my glass and went outside. There, in the

darkness of the night, I shivered and tightened my jacket around me. The sky was so clear I could see a few stars and planes dotting the darkness. I inhaled deeply and tried to lighten my mind with more wine.

I heard the doors sliding, Jack stood silently by my side and looked up. "I want you to know that we are always here for you. And I worry that you spend so much time alone. I hate your parents for taking your trust in people from you. And I hope Julie will prove you wrong and you'll trust her. But what if she rejects you?" He shifted from one foot to another. "The last time was a blow, and I'm not sure how much more you can take."

"I know you worry, but I need to try."

"Of course, you need to try, it's just that I want a better life for you." He searched my face. "I want to see you smile."

"You make me smile."

"We are old fools you like to spend time with, and only Heaven know why, but I know you can't build a life on your career and surfing," Jack said.

I didn't know what to say. "I'm scared," I finally admitted, my voice low and trembling. "What if she is not interested in women at all, or in women's bodies? Every time I looked at her, I wanted to touch her lips, to stroke her skin. What if she shies away from me?"

Jack exhaled and rubbed his forehead. "Annie, you decided to try, so you will find out. But I hope with all my heart that she won't hurt you." He took my hand in his. "Oh, you are freezing. Let's go inside."

I glanced one last time at the stars before going towards the light and warmth.

Chapter 12

JULIE

The balmy air hit my nostrils as soon as I stepped out of the plane. Thank God my other colleagues were flying on a different plane. The tickets for them were bought in advance, and that flight was full. I didn't know them and wouldn't like to try and have a polite conversation with them.

I took a taxi to the hotel; there was only one hour left before the start of the program. Then we'd have short city center tour before going to a restaurant. Benzon booked a venue not far from Rambla. It didn't sound fancy, but for a free trip it sounded great.

The day was almost hot. January in Barcelona was not always pleasant, but compared to the snow at home, this was heaven. This time, Benzon booked a much more luxurious hotel for the employees. This was all for VIPs and me. I laughed as I looked around the fancy room. The headrest of a dark blue bed ran high, almost to the ceiling. A linen wallpaper with a sakura tree adorned a wall opposite the window. A barely traceable scent of a bergamot coated the room, while a big white sphere of a lamp reflected on the walls in a million tiny lights. I was going to enjoy these two days.

I ran to the bathroom. The marble floors were so polished, you could use them instead of a mirror. By the sink stood so many bottles of expensive lotions that my eyes went wide. The shower was separated by a glass wall. It all screamed money and style, and I had never been in a hotel like this.

Usually, Mark and I rented Airbnb apartments, nothing fancy, as they were cheaper than hotels, and we cooked there, saving money on restaurants.

It took me five minutes to understand how to turn on the shower; it had numerous handles and levers, I stared at it, and finally chose the tropic rain setting. And those towels, I could have sworn they were combed by hand to make them so soft, and somebody splashed expensive perfume on each of them. So this was how rich people took showers. I surely liked it.

As I stepped in the room, bare feet touching the heated floor, and checked the clock on the phone, I was horrified. That divine shower had taken all my time, and I had only ten minutes left to make myself look presentable. I put on a dress, boots, my jacket, and a touch of lipstick before rushing to the hall.

There was a big group already, and I saw that all newcomers were checking in with the lady in a white suit.

"Julie Kovalenko," I said.

She found my name on the list and smiled. "Welcome, Julie. The tour will start soon."

I stepped to the side and looked up. A huge shining chandelier hung from the ceiling, the walls were draped in cloth wallpaper of a dark burgundy, and everything screamed of money. I was not sure if I liked the style; it was similar to castles from the 19th century; but this was all new for me.

I studied the people around me. Benzon employees were mostly in their thirties-forties, it was a strange choice of a hotel for this age group. Everybody looked around in awe. Maybe they wanted us to experience something new. I was sure all of them rented stylish apartments and hotels in a more modern style when traveling.

I scanned the lobby and eventually spotted Ann. She was talking to a woman, and both were sitting on a hideous velvet couch. Ann's eyes were focused on the speaker, her dark hair had grown a little longer and was almost touching her shoulders. Her leather jacket was folded on her knees, and she was wearing her usual black t-shirt and jeans.

As if Ann felt my gaze she turned her huge eyes in my direction, and the warmest smile tugged her lips. The woman she spoke to noticed and turned to look at me as well. Ann excused herself and walked towards me. I caught myself, but I was beaming. She reached me, and I fought an impulse to hug her.

"Hi," she said.

"Hi," I replied.

I couldn't take my eyes off her. Her blue eyes were deep oceans, and I was swimming farther and farther in those deep waters. Her skin was so pale that her lips were practically blooming. Her lips parted in a sharp inhale, and I caught myself. She noticed that I was looking and smiled.

"So happy to see you," Ann said quietly.

"Let's get ready. It's time!" roared a huge man at the door. He was in his early 40's, tall, his black hair pointing in all directions, and a neatly trimmed beard had a life of its own on his face.

I glanced at Ann, and she pointed toward him.

I'd been to Barcelona three times already, and I had visited all the must-see sights, as everyone at the party had as well, I assumed. Mostly the people around me were probably well-traveled. And there were five people from the Barcelona office in the group. I figured this tour must be exceptional for the organizers to include it.

After an hour of the tour, I saw why they did it. It was hilarious and completely different from everything I had ever experienced before. We looked at Basilica de la Sagrada Familia from the back and were taken to secret gardens and streets that were mazes. The group stopped at unexpected places and veered into bars. Tapas and drinks were already waiting for us, and after a quick food break, we continued. In two hours, the group was so lightheaded from the drinks that every joke from Raphael the guide was two hundred percent funnier. Even Ann, who was a quiet person, laughed so hard her eyes became watery, and her cheeks were turning pink from all the giggling and fun.

Our final stop was at a restaurant, and people from the group were lifelong friends by now. Raphael handled the crowd professionally, speaking to everyone but not being obtrusive. The jokes were intelligent and respectful, still making everyone hug themselves from laughter. At the end, everyone hugged him and took pictures.

"I am staying, don't worry," Raphael laughed, posing for the hundredth picture. "Who's going to entertain you later?"

He possessed a charming quality that made thirty people love him in just a couple of hours. The group poured into the restaurant. Unlike the antique hotel, this place was modern looking. A few walls were left of the original old brick, and all kinds of paintings were hung there. It was like a small art museum, and I noticed a two-star Michelin sign at the entry.

People wondered around, some gazing at the paintings, some going straight to the bar. In fifteen minutes, the Benzon founder would speak and then the night would go to unknown drunk directions for all the attendees.

We perched on a sofa. I could not stop stealing glances at Ann's face all evening; something drew my gaze to her. I was sure she noticed, but she didn't say anything.

"Do you come here often?" I asked.

"I guess so. They send me to Barcelona on business trips a few times a year. Do you see that guy in the red shirt?" She pointed to a tall handsome guy with a steel gaze. "He is the director of the Barcelona office. Smart, but slick as a fox. Superb for a company, but not so favorable to the women. He knows how to charm them, then acts like nothing has happened. A few valuable women left Benzon because of him. So now it's a tradition to make all newcomers aware of his reputation."

"Are you warning me?" I questioned with a wry smile. The guy was looking around for prey already, like a shark.

"No," Ann said as she played absentmindedly with her bracelet. She shrugged. "I had an idea you weren't interested."

"Did he …" I trailed off, as I didn't know how to ask if he hurt her. "Did he make a move on you?"

"Oh, he tried. But his charms didn't work on me. He doesn't force or bully anyone, and he isn't a monster or anything. He just knows how to charm a woman. For him, it's only entertainment, and for a woman who looks only for entertainment, she'll get it. But for a woman who seeks more, he is dangerous." Ann quickly glanced around. "I'm not sure he'll find somebody tonight, as the women who are here today are not new to the company."

The bell chimed, and we were called to attention. Everyone turned to the middle of the room, and the founder and CEO, Tom Adams, gave a speech on our achievements as a company, pointing to the most profitable offices. The Kyiv office was one of the fastest developing ones.

"It's time to feast!" he ended, and everyone clapped.

Dinner was a buffet with lobsters, oysters, and various kinds of meat. In the corner was a man who sliced jamon, so very Spanish. I got full very fast, as the food was amazingly delicious.

Ann glanced at her watch; it was almost 10 p.m.

"Do you want to leave here and go to the sea?" she suggested. Her eyes were shining from the Sangria.

"Yes," I replied eagerly. I knew no one here, and I was ready to finish with the official part.

As we stepped into the darkness outside, I exhaled. Inside, I was constantly aware that I was expected to talk to somebody about work and what I did, but right now I just wanted to relax. But it also seemed that everyone wanted to do the same, so no questions were asked.

Ann opened the Maps app on her phone. "The sea is down there," she said after a moment, pointing to the left.

Chapter 13

ANN

*T*hank God we left the party. The tour was surprisingly good, but now as alcohol flowed, more and more people became intrusive.

Since it was January, the streets were not crowded, and tourists were scarce. They mostly hid inside restaurants and bars, as the temperature drop in the evenings made it impossible to relax outside.

We were walking slowly, and I was checking the map a lot since I had no idea where we were.

"Oh, I remember this place," Julie exclaimed, pointing to a cozy bar. "I've been here with Mark."

"What does he think about you coming here?" I asked. Every mention of him made my heart sunk, a deep hollow echo in my chest that reminded me that Julie was in a relationship.

Julie was looking around, searching for familiar signs. "He might be a bit jealous about me traveling around without him, as it's unusual for us. But as these are work trips, so he's fine. And he thinks these trips will influence my work."

I kept my eyes on the sidewalk, trying to keep my frown from showing. "Does he travel on business a lot?"

"No, not at all. He is an attorney in a big agricultural company. He stays in one place, and tasks go to him. He was happy that I found a person to spend time with on these trips." Julie glanced at me. "A friend." Then she looked quickly to the side, as though being shy of what she said. She tucked a loose strand of her hair behind her ear.

A slight shiver ran down my arms as I listened to her talk so warmly about Mark. He cared for her, and they spent a lot of time together. I felt that the more I found out about Julie, the less of a chance I would get to be with her.

"Who are the people you spent Christmas with?" Julie asked, switching the conversation.

I sent her a picture of me, John, Jack, and Ian, a selfie. I also sent a couple of pictures of their gorgeous Christmas tree and food. Jack knew how to serve the table so it looked like it came from an interior design magazine, and he collected thousands of likes on Instagram.

"They are my neighbors. I told you about them," I said, and Julie nodded in recognition. "Actually, they are more like family now. Jack and John struggled to adopt a kid. They were so happy when they got Ian; he was six and remembered his parents, who left him. Ian's parents decided that they didn't need a kid anymore, and they did everything to prove they couldn't be good parents. Ian had crazy mood swings in the beginning, from tantrums to complete withdrawal. As time passed, he started to forget that life. There was no love there, so I am surprised how he saved that kernel of kindness and brought it into his new life. Now he is inseparable from Jack and John. Especially Jack; he copies everything he does."

Now we were walking down the seaside path. It was

deserted, with only a few runners and the vast darkness of the water. Hotel W glinted like a huge sail in the darkness.

"It's so unusual to me," Julie remarked. "Gay marriage isn't allowed in the Ukraine. Actually, I don't know anyone gay back home."

Back home? But she was talking to one now. Did she suspect that I was gay?

I cleared my throat. "They are struggling to get more rights in the US as well. And not all people are kind and supportive, even now. Jack and John have come a long way, but because both of them were African American, it was even more difficult. And Jack, when he was much younger, before he met John, was beaten so badly that he spent weeks in the hospital. They are so natural together now, but it took immense courage to get where they are now."

"In the Ukraine, gay couples are hiding. People aren't ready for them to come out, and it's sad," Julie added with a sigh. "And since Ukraine is a part of the former USSR, LGBTQ is difficult for them to comprehend, especially for older people."

"What about you?" I asked after a moment of quiet.

"Love is love," she replied simply, looking out to the sea. "No matter what the gender."

Julie's dress waved in the light wind, her hair dancing around her face, her lips relaxed. I kept watching her, happy to be close, afraid of the next move. My eyes kept falling to her slender neck and her collarbone. I wanted to trace the skin there, to kiss every inch of it. My heart beat faster as I imagined it, making my breasts harder. It was torture to be that close and not being able to do anything. I was so afraid of scaring her, while also slowly suffocating myself with need.

I asked Julie about her Christmas instead.

"I would say the most celebrated winter holiday for us

is New Year's night. Christmas is on January 6th, and according to tradition, you need to cook twelve meals for Christmas Eve. Not many people do it, though."

"Twelve!" I exclaimed. "That's crazy. My version of solo Christmas is Chinese takeout. But it only happened once. Jack and John saved me from takeout food. Jack is a fabulous cook, and he always cooks so much I always have casseroles in my fridge. I guess he just cooks for four."

"They sound like caring people. It's great that you have them." Julie smiled.

"Back to your Ukrainian Christmas and the twelve dishes," I said, grinning wide.

"Usually it's my grandma who cooks all twelve. Younger people usually don't follow the tradition. January 6th for us is the day to spend with family. New Year's night is the time for parties, drinks, and food. We have a few traditional salads." Julie suddenly stopped. "No, forget it, we have one traditional salad."

I couldn't stop myself and burst out laughing, Julie was so deliberate with explaining the salads.

She put a hand on my shoulder and said, "You don't understand; it's really important." She also started giggling. "Wait till you hear what's inside that salad."

"What?"

"Mayo." She folded her finger. "Boiled potato, pickles, boiled carrot, and boiled eggs." She continued to fold fingers. "And I am not sure you have it in the US, but it's like a hot dog, but big."

Julie watched my horrified expression and laughed again. She shrugged. "So, you cut all the ingredients in a cube shape and mix."

"It sounds awful," I groaned, wrinkling my nose.

"Wait, I forgot about green beans." Julie doubled over with laughter while I made a gagging sound. "You must try it one day. It tastes pretty delicious compared to how it sounds."

"No way," I protested, still cringing. But the thought of trying that awful salad with Julie didn't sound so bad.

She was still smiling, but her gaze went to the dark horizon. "We were spending New Years with Mark's friends, and I don't know." Julie rubbed her wrist nervously. "I don't feel comfortable in their company. They are his friends, not mine," she sighed. "I would prefer to spend the night with just the two of us, or with my brother and his wife."

"I'm sorry."

Julie waved her hand. "It's not important."

We followed the lights of the seaside path, slowly walking away from the city center. The night became chilly with the wind blowing from the sea.

"It's freezing," I said, shuddering.

"Yes," Julie agreed with a shiver. "We probably should be heading back."

I opened the Maps app again; it showed forty minutes by foot back to the hotel.

"Do you want to take a taxi?" I asked.

Julie turned the screen towards her and glanced at the map in my hand.

"It looks like we can explore the city at night. Let's go."

She took my hand. Hers was cold, but my heart fluttered from the touch. Julie looked down, and then right at me. Once again, I was drowning in her eyes of liquid caramel. This time, she didn't release my hand, just squeezed gently. She turned and took me to the right.

"It's the wrong way," I laughed.

"Really? I am awful with maps and directions."

I led us through the dark alleys. Google Maps always showed the shortest way, and it usually was not the safest and most pleasant one. Some streets were so dark and deserted that I kept speeding up my pace. But Julie at my side noticed things I would never pay attention to. She was looking all around at beautiful signs of the bars and the school closed for the night.

All I could feel was her hand in mine. It was warm now since we were moving much faster and were hidden from the sea wind.

As we were getting closer to the hotel, more bars were open and busy. In one of the alleys, a young couple kissed passionately, his arm squeezing her breast as she moaned quietly.

Julie glanced in my direction. I looked away, my cheeks burning, hoping the night hid it.

She told me about Kyiv, her places of power there, how it all was covered in snow now.

"But the snow in the city is beautiful only for the first few hours. Afterwards, it gets grey and turns into dirty piles shoved to the side of the walk. I could live without it," she sighed.

We approached the hotel. It was warm in the lobby. A fireplace crackled in the center of the hall, the light glinting on the various antiques set around the building. The golden clock with the statue of a hunter and his dog chimed midnight on the mantelpiece.

"Let's take the stairs. I am on the third floor," Julie said.

"Sure. My room is on the fifth."

We found a grey door with a staircase sign and went up slowly. When we reached the third floor, Julie turned towards me.

"Thank you for showing me the way back. And for the evening."

Her eyes grazed my face and stopped for a second on my lips. I took a strand of her hair, liquid silk in my fingers, and tucked it behind her ear. She froze but looked directly in my eyes. I traced her jawline and placed my hand lightly onto her cheek, just for a second. She inhaled lightly, and I caught her lips parting.

I dropped my hand and through the roaring in my ears, I heard myself saying, "Good night, Julie."

"Yes," she caught herself and opened the door to the corridor. "Good night."

She glanced one last time at me and disappeared. I walked slowly to my room and dropped on the bed. My heart pounded so fast I couldn't catch my breath. I still felt her soft skin under my fingertips. I touched my fingers to my lips and closed my eyes.

Chapter 14

I opened my room door and stepped inside. What the hell happened just now? Nothing really happened, but why did I react like that to Ann's touch?

The warmth had spread through the bottom of my belly when she slowly traced my cheek. The need deep inside. When I looked at her lips, they were so full and raw that I felt something I hadn't felt for so long, I almost forgot what it was like: desire. My heart hammering, I took small, deep breaths. I didn't want to think what it meant, that her touch had woken me up from the sleep I didn't know I was in. I crossed the room to the window and opened it wide. Cold air enveloped me and the only thing I knew for sure: I needed more.

More, but it confused me. Did I want a woman? What about Mark? Strangely, but I didn't feel as if I was betraying him. And nothing happened. But what if it did happen?

As I imagined Ann's face, her direct gaze, pale skin, her lips grazing mine. The image sent shivers down my spine, a tingling warmth inside.

Stop. If I imagined these scenes with a man, it would be a betrayal. But it was with a woman, a gorgeous one. And I'd never felt anything remotely like this towards a female.

I breathed in shakily, the chilly night air touching my face through the open window. It was a new feeling. Was it a welcome one? I made myself believe that it was not cheating on Mark. It was something I wanted to try.

Didn't every woman secretly fantasize about having sex with another woman? Being on my deathbed and being asked what the few things were that I regretted, I didn't want to reply that I didn't try when I had the chance. But I was rushing forward. I was not sure Ann was on the same page with me. I closed my eyes and her face appeared, her moves so gentle. It might have been that she simply tucked my hair, but the way her hand lingered. Something told me that she felt something too.

My fresh fantasies aside, I thought I would want us to stay connected even though we lived on different sides of the Earth. I was not sure it'd work, but this time I wanted to try. So many things I wanted to try with her. Again, my mind went to that touch, and I shook my head.

Since I didn't really have friends and Ann as far as I understood walked through her life quite lonely, we might be able to save each other. We might be friends. *Friends with benefits*, my foul mind whispered.

When we were walking this evening, I discovered the connection between us. Being close to Ann, I was myself, not trying to prove anything. Back home, I didn't have the chance to be that way. But what now? After the episode on the stairs, I did not want to ruin everything. What if I was mistaken?

Those thoughts were rolling in my head in the shower

and in bed. The thing I understood finally after tossing in the sheets for hours was fear. Fear of losing Ann. This new light I had just recently met. I wanted to stay close, if she'd want to keep me close.

Chapter 15

ANN

I woke up with a start. An alarm shrieked from my phone. I dragged myself out of bed and peered outside. The old, narrow street was lit by the morning sun. I hoped I didn't scare away Julie yesterday. I would find out pretty soon, I supposed.

I had no idea what entertainment Benzon had for us today, and I didn't really care. All they said was to wear something comfortable. We'd need to move, run or something. It was not that I didn't wear comfy clothes. I put on my usual outfit: a t-shirt and black jeans, white sneakers. That was easy.

Not so easy was the fact that I needed to dress fancier in the evening. They asked everyone to bring a cocktail party outfit for the closing evening. That was today. Activities in the morning till 3 p.m. From three to six was free time to rest and squeeze into the tightest dress I had ever worn.

I hated when I needed to dress up. Usually Benzon didn't point out what you should wear. Jeans and boots always worked for me, even when I spoke at a conference.

But this time, they stressed the importance; even the HR manager I had asked to invite Julie reminded me to bring the dress, knowing my love of comfy jeans and leather jackets. Now it was hanging in the closet. Black, of course, and the size of a pillowcase. But it was for later. Now was jeans time.

I ran down the stairs and to the hall. There was a group gathered already. I approached the hostess and gave her my name. She smiled, noted something in her list, and asked me to wait. I tried not to search for Julie in the crowd. What if she wanted to avoid me today?

I walked to an old fireplace and made a point of looking closely at the bunch of statues on it.

"Mornings are not your time, right?" I turned to look at Julie and found she was holding a cup of coffee for me.

My hand was slightly shaking as I took the cup from her. She glanced at it and smiled reassuringly, and just like that I knew this would be a wonderful day.

"You are my savior," I said, taking a huge gulp of cappuccino.

"I didn't know what type of coffee you drink, so I made a safe choice. Is it okay?"

"Perfect. My mind starts working slowly. I hear it." I tapped my temple and took another sip. "Thank you. Let me guess, you went to the sea?"

"Yes, but since the sun isn't rising early, I started when it was dark, seven in the morning"

"You are crazy. How do you do it?" I groaned.

"I guess part of me is a morning person when I am away from home," Julie said before being interrupted by our hostess.

"So, everyone is here," she announced, looking down at the clipboard in her hands. "Do you want me to tell you what we are going to do today or leave it a secret?"

A few guys shouted, "Tell us!"

They were still tipsy from yesterday's drinks, or they had taken advantage of the tiny bottles from the fridge in their room.

"It's a Port Aventura Amusement Park!" the hostess said excitedly. "Maybe you've heard about the Red Force ride? 112 meters high, zero to 180 km/h in five seconds by Ferrari." Her eyes were shining from the excitement.

I groaned and scanned the crowd around me. People were cheering. Why did everyone love these parks? I would need to hide or spend time in the cafeteria. Julie turned to me, and she was beaming. Her face fell when she noticed my expression.

"What's the matter? You're white as a sheet," she stated.

I rubbed my forehead and whispered, "I hate roller coasters. Honestly, I am terrified of them. Why is this park even open? They should be closed for the winter."

The hostess walked past us and heard the question. "Port Aventura is usually only open on Christmas and New Year's during the winter. This year they extended it to the middle of January," she explained.

"Awesome," I said feebly, giving a weak smile. The woman eyed me suspiciously and went to the hotel counter for documents.

"Now she will keep an eye on me," I whispered to Julie.

She laughed. "Just eat cotton candy, walk around, and smile a lot. She won't know."

We packed into a sleek bus and like school students were driven to the park.

"What about the grand fun I was promised?" I grumbled on the bus to Julie.

"I've seen the video of the Red Force; it is quite grand and terrifying." Julie was so amused, lights crackling in her eyes. She was clearly a fan of the rides. "We don't have roller coaster parks in Ukraine, and I always need to hunt them down where I travel."

"Oh, good for you." Now I was grumpy because the day wasn't turning as great as I imagined. "I went twice, first with my parents. I was so excited. I was ten, I think. When I stepped from the ride, I was so nauseated and scared I refused to go onto any other. I didn't feel the adrenaline, I felt pure terror. We decided to try again when I was fifteen, with the same results."

"You look so strong, but you are afraid of roller coasters," Julie noted, shaking her head.

"It's my kryptonite," I laughed. "I am okay with cars. You know, ones where you bump into each other."

"Boring," Julie chuckled, but she smiled kindly at me.

The park wasn't crowded. When we all poured from the bus, the hostess said that we would be here till 2:30 p.m. Thank God it would not be for long.

"And let's meet at 1 p.m. at the Red Force, everybody." She pointedly looked at me. "We are going to have a Benzon ride together."

My heart dropped. Nobody protested; everyone was excited. Perfect. I was the chicken today.

"Snake," Julie murmured to me, watching the hostess. "We have two hours to come up with an idea on how to get you out of this."

"Maybe I should say that I have a problem with my blood pressure or something?"

We strolled away from the group. The lines were short today.

"I can stay with you in the line and wait for you while you ride. Let me buy popcorn," I told her.

Julie looked at the map, and she decided to try all the scary ones.

Every time she exited the ride, she was so happy. Her cheeks were rosy, hair a crazy mess from all the wind and speed. She was truly an adrenaline junkie.

I laughed as she explained the ride, moving her hands to show the directions the car took.

"And the feeling of the loop when you are upside down ..." She was breathless as we made our way through the park.

"You are the first person I met who enjoys rides so much and is almost thirty," I laughed.

She grinned back. "I didn't have a chance to ride them when I was a kid. Now I am making up for it."

I scanned my watch, seeing 1 p.m. creeping closer.

"Did you come up with an idea how to skip it?" Julie asked.

"You know, I have a crazy idea." I swallowed loudly. "I will do it."

"What?" She stopped walking and stared at me. "Your face paled from the kids ride I took, and the Red Force is the scariest, highest, and fastest ride ever. I think it might be the fastest one in the world."

"I know, but maybe it's time to try it again. The third time's the charm."

Julie had inspired me with all her excitement and giddiness. I needed to try at least. Nobody had died there, and I hoped I wouldn't be the first one. My hands started to shake.

Julie stopped me. "Are you sure you want to do it? We still can come up with a way you can skip." She touched my shoulder and looked directly at me. "Nobody is going to judge."

"Nobody cares," I chuckled and took a deep breath, trying to calm my hands. "Oh, hell, let's do it."

We approached the ride, and my jaw dropped. The

structure was 112 meters high. I tried to count how many floors it was. Thirty-seven? Even Julie stared at it frozen.

"Wow," she said. "We can do it, though. I'll be with you."

We. She was scared, but excited. I was just terrified; my heart hammered at least 200 beats per minute. My throat and chest locked as I tried to take a breath.

"You okay?" Julie asked. "You look ill."

I nodded. Our group was standing near the entry. As we came closer, the hostess checked her clipboard and looked me up and down. She registered dread on my face but said nothing.

"Let's wait for a couple more guys and then we will be ready," she told everyone.

I stood aside, trying not to vomit from the fear, my blood roaring in my ears as I stared at this monster of a ride. It was massive, and I heard shrieks of people. It took all my self-will not to bolt to the nearest alley.

Finally, the last two people arrived. She had a distant, unfocused smile, and he looked sideways. Were there places to make out even in the adventure park?

"It's only thirty seconds, you know. One blink and it's over," Julie said.

We took our seats towards the back. I was so nervous I was going to faint. Good, at least I would not need to endure this hell for long. I stared forward at the seat in front of me, paralyzed. *I am going to die here*, played on a loop in my head.

Something warm touched my hand, I looked down and through the fog I saw Julie's hand squeezing mine.

"Breathe," she told me. She was calm. "You are brave—"

And it started. Momentarily, I was pressed deep into

the seat. Julie screamed but didn't let go of my hand. A great force made it hard to even take a breath.

As we rushed up, I glanced down. It was so high my poor hammering heart skipped a beat. Now we were on the top, and the wind was freezing here. In the next second, we were falling.

Now, I screamed. Everyone screamed. It made it easier. Julie was not holding me anymore; she clutched me. And we were down. My heart had never beaten so fast in my life.

I turned to Julie, feeling like we were running on pure adrenaline. Time stopped as I drowned in her pools of caramel. She was breathing hard, and I felt her grazing my hand up and down with her thumb. I looked down, but she quickly removed her hand.

"You did it," she said breathlessly.

I was still stunned from the force, the speed, Julie's touch. There was something personal in it, caressing. She was looking directly in front of her and breathing hard. I had a crazy urge to cover her lips with mine, to feel her heart beating next to mine, to catch her breath.

Stop. The ride made me experience many raw feelings at the same moment: fear, adrenaline, and desire.

As we climbed out of the car, I thought that it was not so bad. One person had made it bearable. My legs were heavy and filled with cotton, but I smiled.

The bus brought us back to the hotel right on schedule. I needed to get ready for the evening party, but I was exhausted and drained. And I needed to pack all my stuff that was scattered around the room. My flight was at 5

a.m. the next morning, and I thought that it would be best to leave the hotel at three. I figured I should rest a little.

I set the alarm for an hour later in case I fell asleep and buried myself under the covers. The energy was still pumping through my veins, and I couldn't calm myself down enough to rest. So I just closed my eyes.

I heard the faint noises from the street outside, but all I saw was Julie's face. Her glinting eyes when the ride was over, her slender hand holding mine, her finger caressing mine. I hoped I hadn't imagined it. The warmth spread at the pit of my stomach, between my legs. I let my thoughts wander. Suddenly, my alarm screamed. I had dozed off, and my dreams were oh so sweet.

I took a hot shower. The water was running down my neck, between my breasts, down my belly. I felt it, I felt the need. The need to explore her body inch by inch, her skin on mine, those eyes on fire.

Today was a cocktail party I needed to dress up for. I put on a black lace bra, and the dress was so tiny I felt naked. And the heels? I hated heels. After trying to create any semblance of order with my curls, I gave up. They were unruly. Last touch—burgundy lipstick.

Chapter 16

JULIE

I put on my lipstick I always used for special occasions. The liquid silver dress hugged my body, and I curled my hair into waves. As I studied myself in the mirror, a girl from a James Bond movie peered back at me. I liked the result. But I didn't remember any of Bond's girls having freckles. Oh well.

As the elevator door opened, I was back in the 20th century. The style of the lobby with its deep colors, the carpet of dark red, the golden statues, and the looming fireplace. The crowd was shimmering, with men wearing tuxedos. The women were elegant, some in sleek dresses that ran to their toes. And Mark said I had chosen a too fancy dress.

I eventually reached the hostess, who wore a crimson gown with cleavage so deep I tried not to stare. Soft music was playing in the background, and we were in the time machine. People openly gazed at each other's outfits. Only phones were out of place; two girls in the corner were taking selfies.

I heard the stair door open, and I froze at the sight of

Ann. She wore a strapless black dress, her lean legs highlighted by the heels. Her dark lipstick matched her perfectly. I realized I haven't actually seen her out of jeans and t-shirts and her leather jacket. As she crossed the hall to the hostess, men followed her with hungry gazes.

She reached me and smiled. "I love how you look," she said.

"You look stunning. These guys can't stop staring at you."

"This definitely is not my style. I feel a bit self-conscious," Ann said, trying to hide herself by crossing her arms.

"You look amazing, don't worry," I reassured her.

Thank God this time we didn't need to drive anywhere. They escorted us next door to a restaurant of the same style and name as the hotel.

The Benzon CEO took the microphone, tried his voice, and scanned the crowd.

"Tonight, I am not going to tell you about the achievements and growth of our company. That was yesterday. All I want to say is thank you. Thank you for your work and your teams. People are the core of our success. So, I hope today you'll enjoy the dinner, and tomorrow we will be ready to move forward. I hope these two days were a satisfying refreshment from the bleak weekdays," he chuckled. "To Benzon." He raised his glass.

The crowd cheered.

"I am sure most of these IT people are wearing evening outfits for the first time in a couple of years," Ann remarked as we stopped at the table with lobster.

"That's probably the point, for people to feel something new. I think it's the first time ever for me to be at a party like this, one so glamorous," I said. "I mostly wear casual or active types of clothes, and there are no occasions to dress fancy, only prom and someone's weddings. And now look at me." I gestured to my dress and giggled. "I look like a girl from a James Bond movie."

"Yes, you do," Ann agreed, scanning me from head to toe. "Let's see everything they have here. I saw a barman making fancy drinks."

We grabbed plates and covered them with the fanciest food we could find and moved to the bar. What was the point of a corporate party if we stayed sober?

During the evening, we met Benzon employees from all over the world. After a few drinks, everyone was so accommodating. Guys from Buenos Aires kept inviting us to visit their city.

"We are so far away from everything that we always miss all the conferences and events because they are usually in the US and Europe. And it's simply too far for us to travel. But our city is a gem. You should visit," Manuel said.

Everyone here was talking about their cities and offices. I was a positive Kyiv advocate.

Being dressed all fancy, at the end of the party it became a usual networking celebration with employees from everywhere: New Deli, Tokyo, Barcelona, LA, NY, Buenos Aires, Tel Aviv, Prague, and London. Most people here had worked for years at Benzon, and some even opened the offices a couple of years ago.

Everyone shared their ideas of company growth and were open to discussions. I could easily forget the dark walls, 18th century paintings, my tight dress—which had started to itch, and imagine that we were sitting at a campfire sharing stories.

All evening, I caught how men paused to look at Ann, her slim waist highlighted by that tiny black dress. It didn't show anything, but it gave plenty of room to imagine the body that hid under the fabric. And as time went, my gaze kept falling to her cleavage whenever she bent over for her drink. How that damn dress highlighted her full breasts, curvy thighs, and fit bottom.

And Ann deflected those glances. She just dismissed those men. But my eyes? She kept catching me, a tiniest smile on her lips making me blush. But as the night came closer, her gaze became hungrier. Oh, she hid it perfectly, made sure no one paid attention, but her gaze kept sliding down my lips, neck, lingering on that silver dress of mine.

Sometime later, I dug my phone from the purse. It was 11:30 in the evening. A few people started yawning because of the jet lag.

I was leaving tomorrow, but I didn't yet have a chance to ask when Ann's plane was leaving. And I wanted to spend more time with her before she was gone.

I turned to Ann. "Do you want to change and have a stroll through the city?" I asked.

She nodded with a smile. "Sounds perfect."

We slowly moved through the restaurant, saying goodbye to people we had met. The atmosphere shifted to calm and friendly, and I was a bit sad to leave. It was the same sadness that you felt when you were leaving summer camp. You enjoyed the company, but there was a good chance you would never see those people again. At first you thought that even if you were living far away you would be BFFs, but it never turned out that way.

The hotel hall swayed a little; the cocktails were amazing, but strong. Ann took the stairs, as always, and her high hills echoed on the staircase. It was not that easy for me to move in that dress of mine, and when I reached my floor, Ann was already waiting for me.

Her face betrayed nothing, but her eyes were blazing. They locked on mine as I reached her. I swayed to the side, and she caught my bare shoulder. Ann glanced briefly to her hand still on my skin and looked directly into my eyes.

I froze, my heart hammering. Ann slowly traced her hand to my neck, my chin, her fingertips barely touching me, but all my senses were focused on that touch, sending pleasant shivers down my core. She moved closer, but inches from my face she stopped, asking for permission.

I couldn't breathe as I swiftly closed the gap and touched her lips, ever so gently. Her lips were soft as silk. She tasted like the strawberry daiquiri we drank together just moments before leaving the party.

The fire roared inside me, going down, warming my core. I touched her neck, her skin, her shoulders, the hem of her dress, traced her chest. I wanted more.

"Do you want to go into my room?" I asked, my voice shaking.

"Do *you* want it?" She was looking at me, her lips red not from the lipstick but from my kiss. I dragged a thumb on her lower lip, nodding, and she smiled lightly.

"Yes," I whispered.

My heart hammered when I opened the door. What was I doing? I didn't know. But what I knew was that I could not leave now. And I didn't want to leave, oh god, I wanted her.

When we were inside, Ann tossed her heels to the side and stood in the middle of the room, just watching me, fire in her eyes, lips parted. I slowly reached her, put my arms around her, and unzipped her dress. It fell to the ground, revealing her perfect body. She wore a lacy bra and panties, the lace barely covering what was underneath.

She kissed me slowly, our tongues grazing each other. Ann slipped her hand under my dress and cupped my breast, making me moan lightly. She touched me with such a hunger, but still so gentle. I melted like butter under her fingertips.

Ann kissed my neck, the hollow of my throat, and then she lowered the straps of my dress and it fell to my legs in a cloud of silver. I was not wearing a bra, and Ann slowly traced the bare skin of my breasts, and a light brush on my peaked nipples sent shivers down my spine. I almost growled from the sweet sensation.

She kissed my collarbone, her hand in my hair. I wanted to see her too, to get rid of those scraps of black lace, so I unclicked her bra and what I saw was beautiful. I touched her, I kissed her, I licked her, and she slightly moaned in my arms. Never had I seen such beauty; all my thoughts were focused on the woman in my arms, and she was trembling.

But her hand was steady as she traced my belly button, my thighs, between my legs. She paused there and made a soft sound when she understood that I was on fire. Ann held my hand and led me to the bed, gently laying me down and tugging down my panties. I was breathing hard when she touched her lips to my thigh, when she started feasting on me.

Oh my God, she knew how to touch a woman. With every stroke of her tongue, I came closer to a cliff, and when I lost it, I whimpered Ann's name, barely breathing, my body covered in sweat and the pleasure I'd never experienced.

Ann's eyes were blazing. She watched me with her huge eyes, a smile on her face. I couldn't take my hands from her breasts; I kept caressing her, squeezing. She was gorgeous. I touched the hem of her panties, and she shivered in my arms. I went down and put my hand inside them, making Ann inhale sharply.

She was so warm, so wet there as I moved my finger in

familiar strokes. It was easy to touch her, as easy as touching myself. Ann moved her hips along with my strokes, moaning my name, and when I put my fingers inside her, she screamed, hot liquid spreading down my fingers. I covered her lips with mine. Ann touched my hair, my back.

"I want you in my life," she murmured.

She slowly stroked my belly, moving lower and lower.

"I want it too. I want you, but how—" I moaned because her fingers started moving faster.

"Shh," she whispered, kissing me.

I was not sure how long we spent in that room, touching each other, exploring our bodies. Ann took me twice more to the peak, and I fell asleep exhausted in her arms.

I opened my eyes in the darkness. A shadow was moving. Ann was putting her dress on, fumbling with the zipper.

"Where are you going?" I asked.

"I have to leave for the airport."

"Now?"

"My flight is at five in the morning."

"Oh," I breathed. "Am I going to see you again?"

She crossed the room and kneeled in front of me.

"I remember you said something about wanting to see me more often a couple of hours ago." She smiled and kissed me slowly, tenderly, a memory of last night rushing to me.

"I do."

She kissed my cheek, and whispered into my ear, "We are going to see each other soon, I promise."

"Okay," was all I could say. My heart was aching, I

didn't want her to leave. The string between us stretching, pulling.

Ann zipped her dress, grabbed her heels, and turned to me at the door.

"Bye, Julie."

I couldn't let her go, not just yet, so I tossed the blanket aside and ran to her. I was completely naked when I wrapped my arms around her.

"I will miss you," I murmured, kissing her again.

She was so sweet under my lips, but I had to let her go. Neither of us had the power to stay away, so I finally released her.

"Bye," I said.

Her eyes lingered on my breasts, and she grinned. "You are so beautiful." And with that, she was gone.

I crossed the room back to my bed. I stood and stared at the heap of crumpled sheets. What happened that night, I could not understand. Did I cheat on Mark? With a woman? If it was just a one-night stand, I might have tricked myself into believing it was not infidelity. Just to try what it meant to touch and be touched by a woman.

The problem was that this was *the woman*. It was Ann, and I had a feeling that we would have more chapters in our story. Would we sneak to other cities to spend time together? It would not work; she and I didn't believe in remote relationships. Especially romantic ones. It would fade away sooner or later. At that thought, my heart sank, a silly heart that was already in Ann's possession.

I didn't notice the moment I fell for her. Now with every breath I took, it all became more complicated. I cheated.

The feelings I had from that night were new to me. I had never been so raw and open with a man, even with

Mark. Now I was awake, as if her touch made me wake up from an ancient sleep. What should I do next?

My eyes went to the white pillow where Ann had lain just minutes before. I could forget everything that happened. The night was magical, but I could give a cold shoulder the next time she reached me. I was sure she would not insist and I would never see her again.

I laid in bed and buried myself under the blanket. The sheets still had a smell of Ann's perfume. I inhaled slowly. If I chose it, I could never see her again. As I laid a hand on her pillow, I decided to see her again one more time, and then I would make a decision.

The alarm cut off my dream, the dream of sweet pleasure. I wanted to go to the sea for the last time before my flight. I needed to get out of the room. As I pulled on my jeans, I noticed the pool of silver at the floor—my dress—and I was hit by the memories.

With shaking hands, I grabbed my phone and room key and ran out of the room. The elevators were stuck on high floors.

Ragged breaths escaped me. I couldn't stay inside anymore. I opened the staircase door. One landing down, I turned around and stared at the place where Ann kissed me, her lips gently touching mine. My heart hammering, I turned and ran, ran out of the hotel, down the streets, till I reached the water. I stopped right at the water's edge. I could not breathe; my lungs filled with cotton, and tears were rolling down my cheeks.

Cheater, cheater, cheater, my mind kept saying.

I had betrayed Mark. Who was I kidding thinking I just

wanted to try and see what it was like to have sex with a woman?

I was falling in love with her. Was I gay? Last night was the most sensual night in my life, I didn't know my body could feel what it felt. Was I bisexual? Or was it only Ann? I was an ordinary woman falling in love with another person. But her being a woman changed everything. Apart from her living in another part of the world, this relationship might break all that I had built with such care: my life, my work. Loving a woman in my country was not a blessing, it needed to be hidden.

You are a lustful cheat, a voice in my head screamed. *Mark was always so good to you*. And I betrayed him, I slept with another person. And it was not only one night. I knew I could drop my life as I knew it for her. I wanted to stay close, to support her, to talk to her, to erase the constant loneliness from Ann's eyes.

But distance would not let that happen. There was no future for us. My world, my country, would not tolerate the love of two women. And I had betrayed the man I loved. And the problem was that the next time I saw her, I would fall in her arms again, and I would betray Mark again, and again.

I needed to choose: the life of cheating, loving Ann, and going back to Mark, or leaving Mark. This thought was like a dagger to my heart. Oh my God, what had I done? How could I fall in love while being in a happy relationship?

Was it all happy? Were you really happy? my heart whispered.

I touched the water; it was cold and stung my fingers. Good. I needed this coldness to stop the flow inside me.

This crash may crash my life, crash *me*.

My fingers had become numb under the water. I

decided one thing: I was going to see Ann once more. I would say what I was feeling, and I would see where it took me.

Till then, I would go back to my usual life, back to Mark.

I pulled my hands out of the water and wiped my cheeks, salt from the sea mixing with my tears. The beach was deserted, grey water splashing at my feet, mirroring my mood.

Yes, last night was perfect. My body was still sore in the parts of neglect. Ann's lips on me made my toes curl from pleasure even when I thought about it. But all this was painted in shame, the shame of cheating. And the shame of returning to my usual life, as if nothing had happened while this night had turned my world upside down.

I walked slowly on the rim of the water. As I took deep breaths of the salty air, my mind cleared a little from the fog and darkness.

It was not beautiful to meet somebody when you already were with somebody. The betrayal weighed on me. The waves were licking my feet, the wind gently blowing through my hair, playing with it.

Chapter 17

ANN

The plane hummed as I looked out the window, the infinite blue on the pillow of white fluffy clouds.

It had taken me five days, only five days, less than a week, to fall in love. That night was the best night of my life. This power, it gave me wings and fear. What was next for us? Would there be an *us*? How could we manage it living on different continents?

All of these thoughts filled my head as I tried to focus on the movie playing in front of me. After multiple attempts to follow the plot, I finally gave up and pressed pause.

What was a simple feeling for me was not so simple for Julie. She had a family, a home, a boyfriend. What place would I take in her settled life? I was not sure there was even a place for me. But it was for her to decide. And I had left her to untangle all this herself, the confusion of being attracted to a woman, last night.

I dragged a hand through my hair. I needed to contact her, to help her.

It's always like this with women. They think too much, my grandmother had once said.

The scenes of last night kept replaying in my head. The silk of her skin next to mine, the sounds she made when I took her to the edge, my name on her lips, her touch on my breasts, my legs, between them. I closed my eyes and listened to the hum of the plane.

Chapter 18

I grabbed my bag from the baggage belt. Here, everyone primarily spoke my language. I was back home. I crossed the green corridor, stepping out of the sliding doors and into the crowd of waiting people. I saw Mark's face searching the crowd, and when he caught a glimpse of me, a warm smile appeared, and he waved. He held a sign: "Natasha." I laughed.

"Sorry, but Natasha could not come. She asked me to take her place. She said a shabby guy would be meeting me at the airport," I told him.

Mark grinned and scooped me into a hug, holding me a moment longer.

"I was waiting for Natasha, but you will do." He kissed me. "I missed you."

"I missed you too." I inhaled his familiar smell, guilt pounding in my heart.

"Tell me everything. You didn't call me much."

I told him everything, except for last night. I told about the tour, the bar, the night walk with Ann, the roller coaster and how she was afraid, the fancy party, the people I met, my morning at the sea. I said nothing about how I betrayed him. *Liar,* my mind kept whispering.

"This Ann girl sounds lovely. Was she by your side for almost the whole trip?"

Thank God he was driving, I looked out of the window to hide my eyes, the crimson on my cheeks.

"Yes, pretty much all the time," I said, an image of our entangled bodies flashed through my mind. I needed to stop it.

"Are you going to keep in touch with her?"

"I'm not sure, Mark. She is one of the most interesting and kindest people I have ever met, but I am not sure an online friendship will work."

"Yes, it sucks." He meant my friend in Dublin. "Now that you are back from the sea, take a look around."

He was talking about the snow. For the few days I was away, it had covered everything in a thick layer. When we reached our street, it was dark. The soft glow of the old streetlamps painted everything in light shades of yellow.

Mark and I always wanted to live in the old part of the city. We rented a spacious apartment off the beaten path. It was a flat that used to belong to a potter who had moved to Germany, and as he was a good friend of Mark's father, we got the place. It had three bedrooms, and one of them had been converted into his studio.

As I unlocked the door, the familiar sight made everything that happened in Barcelona a dream. It was so far away, that hotel room enveloped in the sweet noises of ours, the touches that awoke me, it was not real. This was real. My life here, familiar.

Ann's face appeared in my mind, her laugh. I quickly pushed the sight away. I didn't want to think about what I had done.

I unpacked, took a shower, made myself a hot cup of

tea, and perched on the windowsill. This moment could be described as hygge: me in Mark's sweater, huge blue fluffy socks, soft leggings. As I peered outside, the snow started falling. All was nice and cozy but for the claws that were gripping my heart, slicing it bit by bit.

I called my mom.

"Hi," I said, taking a sip.

"Hi! I hear you are back home, always sipping," she laughed.

"It's cold here, and I need warmth."

"Yeah, how are you? Tell me about Barcelona."

"It was good." I paused and took another sip. "Can I come over tomorrow evening?"

There was a moment of silence till she replied.

"Is everything alright?"

"Yes, don't worry. I just miss you and Dad." I tried to sound cheerful, but my mom did not believe it for a second.

I needed to talk to her. All these thoughts threatened to blow my head off, and I wanted her to say that I was a good girl who did nothing wrong. She never said this, though. She always said what she thought, but it helped anyway. Mostly, but sometimes it hurt like hell to face the truth from her.

"When are you planning to be here?"

"Around seven, after work."

"Can you bring those heavenly Pavlova they sell across from your office?"

"We decided to stop eating them, remember?" I laughed.

"No, it was you who said this nonsense. I can eat whatever I want, and you can watch me eating. Don't buy yourself one."

Those Pavlova from Happy Baker across the street

from my office building had one goal: to add a few inches on the waists of everyone who visited their bakery, and you could never stop with just one.

"They put something addictive there. Drugs, I am sure," I mumbled.

"It's sugar, honey. Oh, I have to go. Dad will be home soon," Mom said. "See you tomorrow."

I put the phone down and glanced through the window. Snow subsided, and now only a few snowflakes were flying in the air. I pressed my cheek to the cold glass of the window. What was she doing now? Her eyes kept appearing in front of me. Her lips on mine, her hand holding mine as we were finding our way back to the hotel. Her curves in the dark, her smile in the sun. I closed my eyes.

"Are you okay?" Mark sat beside me.

"Yes, I am just tired. It was a long day." And night.

Liar, came a whisper in my head. *Cheater.*

He wrapped his hand around me and kissed me. Ann's face appeared again in my mind; as I kissed Mark back, my thoughts kept running to her. How rotten was I to kiss my boyfriend and think about another person? Guilt pumped through my blood now.

Mark did not notice anything. Thank God people can't read each other's thoughts. But mine were so loud now that I could have sworn he could hear traces of them if he listened closely enough.

"Next Saturday is Andrew's birthday. Do you want to go?" he asked. Mark always asked, and I always went.

"Sure." This time, it would also be a distraction.

"Oleg and Katya are going to be there with their baby girl," Mark said. I knew what he was doing, and a warm smile crossed his face.

Mark loved babies; he was a natural. That was the talk

I always avoided. He wanted kids. I didn't. Maybe one day it might change, and as they say *never say never*, but for now, I knew I didn't want kids.

It hurt like hell when Mark didn't take my decision seriously. He said I put my career over everything, and I was not even a businesswoman. He kept saying we could make it work. We would do everything 50/50. I did not want it.

Recently, he had stopped pushing me. I think he decided to give me time. But he could not stop admiring them everywhere we went, especially when his friends' wives started popping kids out one by one. He felt as if he were missing everything, and he was genuinely interested in becoming a father. I avoided this topic as much as possible, steering him away. But this was a bone of contention between us.

And even long before I met Ann, I knew this could ruin us eventually. Now, I was the person who might ruin us.

"Great," I mumbled. "I'm happy to see them."

I didn't come off as convincing, and he flinched at my tone but didn't say anything. Mark kissed me on the forehead and left to watch his show.

I grabbed my book. It was *Shadow of the Wind*. I had decided to reread it before the trip. Barcelona was so gothic. Not the one I encountered just yesterday, but the feeling I had this morning on the beach was similar. Dark.

I was back in my life with his friends, my work, his arms, and my family. But all I wanted to do was to crawl to Ann's side. I closed the book; there was no point trying to read now. I finished my tea and joined Mark at the TV, as if nothing had happened. As if at the same time yesterday I was not trembling under a woman's touch.

❧

Tanya was waiting for me at the coffee shop.

"How do you even walk in that hat?" I asked instead of greeting.

She wore an oversized woolen hat with a huge matching scarf. The hat was so massive it constantly dropped to her eyes.

"Wait till you see my mittens," she beamed and hugged me. "How was your trip?"

"It was actually nice."

"Again this *actually*, as if being sent for free for a couple of days' vacation could be bad," Tanya snorted.

"The program was not as fascinating as they said it was in previous years," I said, and she huffed, making me smile. "There was a tour through the city, a very unusual one, and the guide was so funny. He practically melted the hearts of the group and broke the ice perfectly."

"That does not sound really interesting," Tanya grunted. "One cappuccino, please."

"Latte for me," I said to the barista. "Next day, they took us to a roller coaster."

"What are you, twelve?"

"You know I love roller coasters, so it was great for me."

But not for everyone, I thought, remembering Ann's face that was as white as a sheet and her scared, huge eyes.

"Have you heard about the Red Force? It was in that popular travel show," I asked.

"Yes, but there's no way I'd ride that ride. I am too old for it," Tanya retorted with a dismissive wave.

"They kinda didn't give us a choice. They said it was a major team building activity."

I remembered Ann's hand in mine, adrenaline pulsing through my veins, how I wanted to calm her. At that moment, I realized that I wanted to care for her. I carefully tried to banish thoughts of her, but they kept crawling back into my life. I shook my head lightly.

"Crazy," Tanya said.

"After that was a fancy old-fashioned party, a way for everyone to show off in fancy dresses. But eventually it was a pleasant evening." *And night*, I thought as the image of Ann's slender wrists, her fingers on my body crossed my mind. "Everyone relaxed with cocktails the barman made. In the end, everyone became buddies, you know, like in a summer camp, when you say goodbye at the end and think you'll stay in touch forever."

"No one ever does."

"Exactly."

We grabbed our coffees and made our way up to the office. I was absent just a few days, so all was the same here: the laptop, my mug, stack of papers, sticky notes exactly where I left them. But my heart and mind were far away from where they were the last time I was here. All I was trying to do since I returned home yesterday was to lock my thoughts and stop thinking about her.

My manager called me to her office and asked how it went in Barcelona. She was still stunned how a designer from her team got an invitation to the VIP management party.

Finally, when I got to work, I could stop the constant blabber in my head.

At lunch, Tanya asked no more questions, and we talked about the latest TV shows and our plans to go to the theatre.

The clock hand rushed to 6 p.m. I said goodbye to everyone, put on my jacket and my hat, and crossed the street to the bakery.

"Five Pavlovas, please." Two for Mom, two for Dad,

one for me. But I was not sure the eventual divide would be the same.

I joined the crowd going to the metro station. Some were rushing home, some were catching the rare, beautiful winter evening. Snow kept falling. I couldn't remember the last time it had snowed so much. It kept covering everything with a fresh white layer.

Fifteen minutes later, I exited the station. Nine- and sixteen-story buildings were lit by people coming from work. Thank God my parents lived close to the metro station; I was not a fan of crowded buses during rush hour.

As I slowly picked my way to their house, I felt calmer. This was the street I grew up on. I took an elevator to the fifteenth floor. It was an old one, brown inside, with confessions of love written on the walls and a few curse words and dirty images. It rumbled and shook so hard everyone was amazed that it still worked.

I pressed the bell and heard it ring inside. My mom opened the door, and the familiar smell of incense hit me. My dad was a yoga fan now, and he always lit the scented sticks.

"Hi, come in, come in," Mom rushed me inside.

As I glanced in the mirror, I saw my cheeks were flushed from the cold. I took off my coat and hugged Mom.

"I need to tell you something, I did one thing, and I am struggling to understand if it was a terrible mistake or a beautiful truth," I said, looking at her, still standing in that tiny entryway.

"Go to the kitchen and take those Pavlovas out."

The kitchen was small, like in many typical flats in Kyiv, a perfectly cozy place for two to eat. But mostly whole families were raised here and lived here, so it got crowded.

A yellow vintage teapot stood on the table, steam rising from its spout, containing green tea with jasmine, my mom's favorite.

"Where's Dad?"

"He'll be home in an hour or so. He is staying late at his office."

I hugged her again and held her close. My mom gently stroked my hair and when she stopped, she said, "Sit, pour us some tea, and tell me everything."

I did as I was told.

"I met someone at a conference in Tel Aviv. Do you remember I went there in the middle of December?"

She nodded.

"This person was in Barcelona and …" I took in a shuddering breath. "I cheated on Mark."

Nothing changed in my mom's face. She held my gaze and stayed silent.

"It's a woman."

She smiled a little but hid it fast and put a serious face on. "The main question here is how you feel about her. Was it a one-night stand? Did you want to experiment?" she asked.

"That's what I keep asking myself. And the problem is that I guess the answer is no. I can't stop thinking about her. Her name is Ann. She is a fierce and independent woman and an advocate for women's rights. She is gentle, she listens, she feels me. There is a constant pull to her."

The tea water in the cup I was holding had ripples from my shaking hands.

"I don't understand myself and what I want. I was perfectly happy with Mark, and now this."

Mom raised an eyebrow. "I wouldn't say that you were perfectly happy. Every couple has arguments, but your fundamental beliefs and wishes are different. Take your views on kids, for example." Mom pushed a loose strand of hair from her eyes. "Where does Ann live?"

"Los Angeles."

"It's so far away." My mom took a deep breath, thinking. "How did it all happen? How did she treat you?"

"I think Ann first felt the pull, our connection. She just talked to me in the hotel bar, and then it turned out she was a top speaker. She stayed close, and we talked a lot. Ann arranged my invitation to Barcelona. We were there together almost the whole time. On the first night, she touched my face. That simple touch allowed me to understand what I wanted: her. And the second night, we were in the fanciest dresses, and she kissed me. And one thing led to another …"

To some, my relationship with my mom might seem too open, too relaxed. I could tell her everything.

"How was it?" Mom asked. She smiled; oh, they were so open minded, my parents. "It looks like it involves your heart and soul."

"It was the most passionate and tender experience I've ever had," I whispered, a wave of sadness covering me. "I miss her, and I want more of this, us. But I am here, and she is across the ocean."

"Are you going to see each other again?"

"I hope so," I said. "But I don't know how and when. I haven't heard from her since the moment she left my hotel room. And I don't see how it can evolve into something bigger. It's too complicated. And I am with Mark …" My voice trailed off.

"Would you leave Mark for her?"

"I don't know." Big, salty tears were sliding down my face. "I am torn between my feeling towards Ann, my betrayal of Mark, and the impossibility of this relationship."

My mom took my hand in hers. "Give it some time; it's still so new. You came back only yesterday. No one is asking you to choose now. If you don't see each other again, there would be different choices you will have to make. But from what I see, you need to see her again, even if it is only one more time. Give it time and pay attention to your relationship with Mark."

"You don't like Mark, do you?" I asked.

"He is a perfectly nice young man, but sometimes I think he doesn't see you. Sometimes he doesn't pay attention to your needs. Sorry, it's not my business," she finished as I started to get defensive of Mark.

"Aren't you worried that your daughter could be gay?"

"She can be whatever she wants as long as she is happy. And she's probably bisexual."

I laughed. I was blessed to have such supportive parents. I remembered Ann's pain written on her face when she talked about her parents. It was so much easier when I spoke to Mom. Nothing changed; it was still my decision to make.

As I finally took a bite of Pavlova, I relaxed a little. "I wanted to ask you, have you ever cheated on Dad?"

A mischievous smile appeared on my mother's face. "I almost did. It was ten years ago, and we met at work. He didn't work in my office, he was from a partner company, and sometimes he held meetings in our building. We met in the office corridor once, and he looked so intently at me. Next time, we met in the office cafeteria, I smiled at him and walked away. And once he found me in a copy room; I guess he waited till it was empty. He was tall, in his 50's and with smoldering dark eyes. He asked for my number, and I gave it to him."

"No, Mom, why?" I groaned.

"He was enchanting to me. So new, so handsome and

mysterious. I had been with Vlad for twenty-five years by that point. Of course I fell for the stranger, for this idea of newness."

My mom had said she almost cheated, but still my heart was pounding. She was perfect with my dad, and all the rough edges had smoothed over the time. They lived in synchronicity.

"He called in a few hours. He said that from the moment he saw me he could not stop thinking about me. And he asked me to meet him at a restaurant. A restaurant sounded like a real date to me, and I didn't want to do it. I said that I could meet him for a coffee. Oh, I was intrigued. That day, I put extra effort into choosing my clothes and makeup. He was waiting for me with a bouquet of red roses, classic. Later, I dumped them in a trash can. No way could I go home with those roses. We talked, he complimented me. I said I was married. He said he didn't care. After an hour and a half, I went home, but he just couldn't let me go."

My Mom blushed and looked away.

"Of course I was flattered by the amount of attention. I was vulnerable at that time, mid-forties. I was not sure of my looks, always doubting myself and my appearance. He was like honey to my raw soul. He sent me messages praising my beauty, asking me to meet him again. I rejected him twice, and the third time I surrendered. We met in the park, and it was late spring. I was enjoying his company, and with every passing moment my attraction grew. He suddenly stopped and looked at me with his piercing eyes. He asked if he could kiss me."

My hand flew to my mouth. "What did you say?"

"That was the moment that changed everything, Vlad's face was in my mind. I realized that moment that I need to choose. Either I stayed true to myself and the person who had loved me for twenty-five years, or I threw it all away by kissing this stranger. It wouldn't end with the kiss, I knew that. My body was taut with want, but want of what? As I realized later, the want was not for this man but for the feeling of being treated like a queen. I couldn't hurt Vlad like that. I stepped away from this man and said no, he couldn't kiss me. And that was the last time we met, and I asked him not to contact me ever again."

"How did he react?"

"Hurt was written all over his face. I didn't know what he imagined about me, that I was the *one* for him or something. He took my hand and begged me to stay. I said goodbye and almost ran away. I could imagine myself in his arms, I could imagine his hands touching me, and I knew how it would feel. But the cost was too high for that moment of pleasure."

"How did you feel afterwards?"

"Relieved that I caught myself in time, that I didn't make a mistake. I'll always choose Vlad. That meaningless fling would have hurt us both, it might have even destroyed us. I knew what was at the stake. But still, it was so difficult to say no to the sweetness of a new feeling. When I came home, I told Vlad everything. At first, he just hugged me saying nothing, kissed me, and then he made love to me, looking me in the eyes. It was so tender and passionate. I didn't remember when the last time was that he touched me like that. Afterwards, he said that it was his mistake that the man's flattery was so important to me. He said that he had taken me for granted when I needed support. From that moment on, he never stopped seeing me."

"Thank God you didn't do it. I can't imagine you separated."

"Never say never, as they say. As long as it works, it

works. We both know and cherish it," Mom said with a shrug.

"The thing is, I didn't think about Mark at all when I was with Ann. And when she kissed me, I didn't see his face. All I wanted was her. What does it say about me and Mark? Or am I so lustful that anyone will do?"

"Do you really think that?"

"No."

"You've never been interested in anyone but Mark. You chose him, and you stayed close. I think if it was any other man or woman, you wouldn't pay attention to them. But something in Ann triggered you, pulled you with such a force that you could not resist her and everyone else pales in comparison to her. So you should choose, do you stay in your comfort zone where everything is set, or do you step into the unknown?"

There's nowhere to step yet, I thought sullenly, staring at my tea.

"Show me her photo," Mom ordered.

I opened her Facebook profile on my phone. She was not active on social media, with just a couple of surf photos, but her primary picture was an amazing close-up portrait. I showed it to Mom.

"Oh, wow, she is beautiful. She is the complete opposite of Mark," she laughed.

I showed the photo of Ann on the surfboard, watching the sunset. The picture was so serene that I lingered on it and smiled.

Mom looked directly into my face.

"Are you going to contact her?" she asked.

"I don't know."

"Maybe you should."

I covered my face with my hands. "I don't know what I want. I hate that I cheated, but I don't want to let go of her. If it goes any further, somebody would need to move somewhere. And Mark ..." My voice shook, "I will break his heart."

"Okay, let's imagine you won't see Ann ever again, not even once. How would you feel?"

I paused, trying to imagine it all over, never really having ever started. An invisible hand squeezed my heart for just a moment.

"I would feel a regret, regret of not even trying, of not finding out more, confusion."

"Then you know what to do," Mom said.

"I didn't realize you hated Mark so much," I tried to laugh, but it came out fake and died fast.

"It's not about Mark, it's always about you. And yes, I think you deserve a better partner. I'm sorry." She took my hand again. "I love you, you know."

Right on cue, the key clicked into the lock, and I heard the front door open. We went to the hall to meet my dad.

"Hey, you're still here." Dad enveloped me in his familiar tight hug. "How was Barcelona?"

He kissed my mom, a quick touch on the lips. They were always my model of a great relationship, and I could not imagine them being separated. Till it works, it works, as Mom said. And it had been working for them for thirty-five years.

I stayed with them for an hour telling Dad about the trip. He always loved roller coasters, and when I showed him a video of the Red Force online, he was almost jumping from excitement. I guess I got that love from him. I didn't say anything about Ann. Telling my mom was one thing, but I was not ready for anyone else to know about her. I was close with my dad, but I would tell him later, if there was anything to tell.

As I hugged them goodbye, Mom whispered into my ear, "You know what to do."

I took the old rickety elevator down; it really was a threat to use it. And as I stood outside, near the house I grew up in, I took out my phone and opened the Facebook app, scrolled to Ann's profile, and tapped Messenger.

"I miss you," I typed, staring at the words. My finger hovered over the *Send* button. I heard Mom's voice and hit the button. Then on the whim, I typed, "And I can't stop thinking about you." She was not online. I stared at the screen. What did it mean? That I was taking a step further, and it would probably ruin my cozy old life as I knew it.

I took the metro back home. When I exited the station, big snowflakes were falling from the sky. I didn't like the cold, but the snow was beautiful.

The square near the Golden Gates station was deserted. Office workers were already home, and there were no tourists this time of the year. Only one couple huddled under the streetlamp. The house of Baron Steingel loomed in the dark, with its dark figures looking down from the walls with unseeing eyes. It had been deserted for many years but still had a magical glow about it. I loved imagining people who lived there and their stories.

My phone pinged. With shaking hands, I fished it out of my bag and unlocked it. There was a message from Ann: "I don't know what you did to me. All I think about is you. Sometimes I think that you are not real. Are you?"

I took a picture of the Baron's house and sent it to Ann. "Actually, I am a ghost, and this is my house."

"Can I move in?" she replied, making me laugh. "I want to see you," she added.

"I want to see you too, so much. I hate the distance."

And silence, no reply. Instead of going directly back

home, I took a detour to a coffee shop and bought myself a cup of hot chocolate. The steam rose from the cup in the frosty air. I heard the ping of my phone, my heart rushing in my chest. Slowly, I unlocked it and read the message.

"Would you like to spend a vacation in Los Angeles?"

I stopped in my tracks. This was it. The decision I would need to make. But who was I kidding? The moment I would be in Ann's vicinity, I would fall into her arms, craving her touch. I imagined the moment when she was right by my side, her eyes the color of ocean, I would drown there. Drown in her.

"I'd love to. When?" A swishing noise of the outgoing message was a noise of my mind chiming *cheat*. I tried to silence it.

"When could you take a vacation?" Ann's message appeared.

"The earliest I think would be the end of February."

"Amazing. Will your boyfriend be OK with it?"

I shuddered. This question had other questions woven in it. *Are you still with him? Does he touch you? Do you kiss him?*

"I'll find out soon."

But I thought Mark would be alright with the idea of me going on vacation without him. It would be the first one. And thank God I had a US tourist visa. I'd had it made last year, and I had even used it a couple of times.

A smile tugged on my lips. She wanted to see me. I crossed the street to my home and flew up the stairs. We lived on the fourth floor. The house was built in 1910, and after having just one renovation it still was in good condition.

I opened the door. Mark was watching TV but paused it and came to greet me. He looked tired, with dark circles under his eyes. He hugged me and kissed my forehead.

As I shrugged off my coat, I asked, "Is everything okay?"

"We are hitting the deadline on the project, and it is far from finished. And my boss is making our lives hell now. It's nobody's fault we are so late; the deadline was just too soon for such a big case." He rubbed his eyes. "And I have to wake up at five tomorrow to get to the office early."

"I hate that they make you work like horses." His management kept taking big cases and setting unrealistic terms again and again. Mark and his team were barely completing them in time. "You said you wanted to quit the firm."

"Yes, after this case I will start the job search, but right now I simply don't have the time and energy."

"Let's go to bed," I proposed.

"Yes, how were your parents?"

"Excellent," I replied, beginning to take off my clothes. "I am glad I went to see them." I took my pajamas from the drawer and headed to the shower. Mark stopped me at the threshold, his hands on my waist. He slowly lowered his head to kiss my shoulder.

"You are always running somewhere," he said. His lips moved up my neck and to my lips. The touch was so familiar. I kissed him back, but Ann's body was in my head, as she was laying heavily breathing on the white sheets. How bad was it to kiss a person and have an image of another one in your head?

"Go to bed. I'll take a shower, and I will be back here in a minute," I said.

I took my time in the shower, secretly hoping he'd change his mind or forget his plan. I couldn't stay away from him for a month till my trip to LA, but I didn't want to do it now. *Later*, I thought as I dried my body with a huge fluffy white towel.

As I entered the room, I could see that Mark was already asleep. His chest rose in a slow motion. I studied his face, so serene now. I knew every line of it.

It took me a few days to find courage to tell Mark about the LA trip. One evening, we were sitting in our kitchen. Mark was in a good mood, as the work project was finally coming to an end.

"Do you remember I told you about a woman I met at the Tel Aviv conference, Ann?"

"Yes, she was also in Barcelona, right?" Mark asked.

Oh yes. Next came the flash of a memory, her lips on mine, her fingers tracing my bare skin.

"We talked a lot in Barcelona," I continued, "and she invited me to Los Angeles."

"What did you say? Do you want to go?"

"Yes, I actually would love to go." I took a huge gulp of the tea to hide my face with the hope of covering up my eagerness. But at the same time, I knew what this trip could mean, and looking at Mark's open face, I hated myself for lying to him. This trip could, and probably would, result in me leaving him. And he supported me and wanted me to go. *Liar.*

"Then go. When are you planning?"

"The end of February."

"So soon," Mark said quietly.

It still was a month away.

"Yes."

"Sure, go, I am happy for you. I would love to see LA too, but I guess next time. Maybe Ann will invite us both. Does she have a husband or boyfriend?" he asked.

"No, she's single now," I said. Mark was always planning a few steps ahead, but this time it would not work.

"We could find her a nice Ukrainian boyfriend," he suggested, and I laughed, but it came out forced.

I was back to my usual life. Sometimes I talked with Ann on the phone. But it was still different; it didn't work this way with the long distance. All we did was wait. What would happen after LA, I had no idea.

On the weekend, Mark took me to the birthday party for his friend, and the first thing he did was lead me to the baby. Mark took the baby in his arms and cooed to her, played with her little fingers, and the baby smiled at him.

Katya, the baby's mother, stood close. "Mark, she loves you! Mariann isn't usually this calm with strangers. It's time for you to think about having one for yourself." She winked at me.

It took me a lot to smile back at her, and I bit my tongue and tried to hide my anger. Everybody thought that a woman should dream about this. Mark's friends knew about my position but loved to ignore it. "You will change your mind," they would say. They didn't even give me a chance to think differently. Every time they made me see red because of their ignorance.

Mark tickled the baby, and watching this union made me desperate to drink something strong. I spotted the table with bottles and moved there.

"Julie, wait," Mark said. "Do you want to hold Mariann?"

"No, thank you," I said politely, trying to send a warning message with my eyes to him. He didn't get it.

"Just try it. You'll love that new baby smell, and she's so adorable," Mark bounced the baby and held her out to me.

Katya looked at me expectantly. Mark was dazzled

with the baby love and the only lame excuse I could come up with was, "I am sorry, I need to run to the bathroom." I put a hand to my stomach and rushed through the crowd to the toilet.

As I locked myself inside, I let out a long breath. I had known it would happen; every time Mark saw a baby, he tried to prove to me it was the most amazing thing in the world. I was sure it was for some people, but not for me.

Every time I asked him not to do it, he promised and forgot about this promise instantly. Mark desperately wanted kids, and I desperately didn't. This was always the elephant in the room with our relationship. He thought I would change my mind, but as time went on, my decision only solidified. I hid in the toilet as long as I could, till somebody rattled the handle.

When I finally emerged, Mark had moved from the baby to his group of friends in the corner. I heard him discussing his latest avalanche of work. I reached the table with the drinks and poured myself a glass of gin and tonic. It was far from the last one I drank in that bar in Barcelona, but it'd do for now.

The rest of the evening I spent talking to the wives and girlfriends of Mark's friends. I always hated this segregation at parties: women talking to women, and men talking to men. I had almost zero topics to discuss with these housewives, as all their talk revolved around kids, weddings, and new homes.

Later, when we were in the taxi heading back home, Mark was angry.

"Why did you need to cause a scene?" he snapped.

"I didn't cause a scene. It's always the same." My head pounding, and I was tired. "You know perfectly well how I feel about babies, and you always try to engage me in playing with them."

"I only wanted you to hold her!"

"I'm sorry, but I didn't want it."

"For once, you could make an effort," he retorted, turning his head to the window.

I did not reply. There was no point in discussing it for the hundredth time.

"And you should drink less at these parties. You were clutching that glass the whole time. None of the other women drank that much," he added, still looking out.

"That is because I didn't know what to say to them! They were once funny girls I could laugh with, and now all they talk about is having kids, and one boasted about planning a wedding. They didn't drink because they were trying to get pregnant, or breastfeeding, or hoping they were already pregnant. Where did their aspirations go? Their career choices?"

"Oh, why do you even care? You are not a career woman yourself."

"They don't even travel anywhere."

"Oh, now you are a big traveler," he mocked angrily.

"No, I am not. All I am saying is that I didn't know what to say to them," I muttered.

"Maybe it's time for you to think about how to become more like them," he said.

Oh, that one hurt. It was like a claw gripped my stomach and squeezed. I only nodded.

"Sorry, Julie," Mark whispered and put a hand on my knee. "I didn't mean that. I just want us to have a baby. Next time you can skip these birthdays if you feel uncomfortable with the women there. But please think about what I am asking."

Mark looked intently in my eyes, pleading in his. I said nothing, as there might not be any other birthdays. He put his head on my shoulder, slowly kissing the nape of my neck.

"I love you, Julie," Mark said.

I looked out of the window. For the last few days it had become warmer, and the snow had almost melted. The taxi tried to maneuver huge puddles in the road on the way back home.

Time crept slowly, day by day I hid in my routine. I stayed longer hours at work. My boss was glad that I was speeding through my projects. At home, I became irritable, I snapped at Mark, and it wasn't his fault at all. I was restless and angry with myself.

If my heart was with another person, what was the point of me staying here with Mark? But I was a coward; I couldn't break up with him. And what if it was just a fling with Ann? What if my trip to LA was a complete disaster? The fact would remain the same: I cheated on Mark.

It was slowly destroying my sanity. One evening after work, I was so overwhelmed. There was wet snow falling as I was heading to the metro station. Suddenly, I stopped, and a person walking behind me bumped into my back.

"Sorry," I murmured. He said something unintelligible in reply.

I clutched my phone and veered into a side alley. It was quiet here, off the path of office workers rushing home after the weekday.

I froze and took in a few shallow breaths. Tears were sliding down my cheeks, cold instantly gripping them. I unlocked the phone and dialed Ann's number. She picked up after three rings.

"Hello?" She sounded calm.

"I can't take it anymore," I sobbed.

"Are you okay? Is everything alright? Where are you?" I heard a ruffling sound and the clicking of a door.

"Yes." I stopped. "No, not okay. I am tired, and I feel like an impostor. Every day I wake up next to him, every evening we spend together. I keep lying to him. I am tired of pretending. He sees I am not okay, and he thinks it's his fault. But it's not, it's me. I can't stop thinking about you, about what we did. And it's tearing me apart. The lie. Meanwhile all I want is to be by your side once again."

I was sobbing, my voice betraying me.

Chapter 19

ANN

*T*he last few weeks were difficult. And my greatest fear was that this relationship wouldn't stand the distance. We were too far, and this was too new. I missed Julie every moment. But for her, it was much more complicated. She was still living with the person only a month ago she thought was the *one*. My heart gave a happy jolt when she said she was thinking about me.

"I am sorry you have to do it," I said finally.

She was silent for a moment. I heard a distant car blaring; she was outside.

"I have to tell Mark. For him, everything is the same. For me, everything has changed—"

"Julie, wait, don't tell him anything. It's too early to decide. I don't want you to regret it in a few weeks," I said. The idea of her regretting leaving Mark scared the hell out of me, but she needed a way back; if I was only a short distraction, she must not ruin her life because of it. "There's only a week left, and then you will be here. It makes me so happy that sometimes I can't breathe. And the next moment, fear grips me thinking about what's next."

"And what *is* next?" she whispered.

"I don't know," I said, my voice shaking. "I ask myself that question every day, every second. We will figure it out. If you still want to, that is. I beg you, don't do anything that will change your life … yet."

All I asked of her was to wait.

"Okay," she whispered, barely audible.

"I am so sorry it's so hard for you. For me, it's much easier. I met a girl at a bar, and I have been mad about her since."

"Oh." I could hear a smile in her voice. "You know, I always thought that if I cheat on Mark, it wouldn't be just a fling, it would be a person I would like to spend my life with. It just doesn't make sense for me to cheat and never see that person again. What's the point? I always thought that if I met a person I fell in love with, I would leave Mark, and move on to a new life with this new person. In reality, my plan didn't work. It's so messy, and I feel as if I am constantly living a lie. And the person I want to be with is so far away. And this person appeared to be a she," Julie laughed. "It makes it more complicated."

"You are not a liar, Julie."

"I am," she replied bitterly.

Her conscience was made of steel, it was so powerful that it made her life hell now.

"Please, wait a week."

"Okay, good. I will. I miss you so much."

These simple words made my cheeks burn, and my heart beat faster. "You can't imagine how happy I am I met you."

"Let's do something amazing once I am in LA."

"That's the plan," I said.

We said goodbye and hung up our phones. I was standing outside, at the barbeque area of the office.

Only a week left and Julie would be here. I was elated and terrified at the same time.

The next six days dragged slowly. I cleaned the house, made reservations, and stocked the fridge. No one had stayed at my house before for so long. I prepared a room for her in case she wanted privacy.

Julie sent me a photo of the check in line. She was in the airport, so just twenty hours more. I was pacing the house, fixing the pillows when the doorbell rang. Jack stood outside.

"I made Julie a lasagna," Jack said, giving me the dish covered with foil. "She will probably be starving after the flight."

"Thank you." I hugged him.

"The house is sparkling!" he observed, peering in. "What are you doing?"

"Nothing. I am so nervous. Do you want coffee?"

"Sure," he grinned.

I pressed the button on the coffee maker as Jack perched on the bar stool.

"Ann, the girl is crossing an ocean to see you. Everything is going to be fine."

"What if she hates it here? What if she gets tired of me? We only spent a few days together before, in some hotels." I waved a hand dismissively.

"I am sure she is as nervous as you are, or maybe more. You are in a familiar setting, and she is flying from a different continent. It's only ten days, so cherish them." He rubbed his forehead and smiled at me. "You know, I think you both are so brave to follow your hearts. If it doesn't work, at least you both tried."

"I guess you're right."

"Are you going to come to dinner at our place?" he asked. "I would love to meet her, and John is so excited."

"Sure." I smiled. "But let's set the date and time later, when she is here."

"Of course." He took a sip of coffee and watched me pacing. "Do you want to watch a movie?"

As nervous as I was, we settled in to watch a movie. It was a new action picture about superheroes. I couldn't really concentrate, but it helped to waste time. When it finished, Jack gave me a hug.

"Go to sleep and come over for coffee in the morning before going to the airport," he told me.

"Thanks, but I guess I won't be sleeping tonight."

"Try, and I'll see you in the morning." Jack gave me a reassuring grin. "Everything will be great," he said, squeezing my hand and turning towards his house.

I took a slow deep breath, closed the door, and looked around. Tomorrow, this space would be filled with one more person. This idea warmed me. For now, I could only wait. I took a shower and buried myself under the covers. The phone pinged; it was a message from Julie saying that her transfer went smoothly, and she would be on time.

"I can't believe you are going to be here so soon. I can't wait," I replied.

I set two alarms and checked twice to make sure the phone was charged. I tried to sleep, and after twenty minutes of restless tossing, it was too hot, too cold, and I finally fell asleep.

When the first alarm rang, I jumped out of the bed. Today was the day. I was ready. I messaged Jack and asked if I could come.

"Sure," he pinged me back.

I put on my leggings, sweater, and sneakers and ran to their door. John greeted me.

"Ann, relax. You look like a student before an exam."

"I was never really afraid of exams," I said with a nervous shrug.

"So don't be nervous now. You did everything you could."

As Jack made pancakes, Ian sat on the bar stool, legs dangling. The sweet smell of cinnamon was amazing, making my stomach churn. I couldn't remember the last time I ate. John put a coffee mug in front of me.

"Thanks," I mumbled.

Ian was looking at me but staying silent, like he was reading my thoughts. There was something mysterious about the kid. Jack once told me that Ian could feel the feelings of another person. His gaze moved from me to a huge pile of pancakes in the middle of the table, and his mind reading stopped. Jack and John soon joined the table and asked about my plans with Julie. I hadn't set a strict timetable for us; I just had a few places I wanted to share with her.

"We'll see how it goes," I said.

"Take her to the roller coaster," Ian replied, his mouth full of pancakes.

I stared at him. "You know, she loves them," I said slowly.

"But you are terrified of them," Jack remarked.

"Yes, I am, but you guys also love them. Would you like to go if she wants to?"

"Sure," Ian replied, stuffing one more bite in his already full mouth. "I'll keep her company." Everyone stared at him. He was so calm as if talking about his old buddy.

"Okay, let's wait till she gets here, and I'll ask her," I laughed.

I glanced at my watch; it was time to move. I helped them clean the dishes, hugged Jack and John, and went back to my house. I applied a little make up, eyeliner and mascara, put on jeans and a shirt, and rushed to the car.

I prepared a bag of snacks for Julie. She might be starving after the flight. The traffic was light, and the drive to the airport took only thirty minutes. I parked the car and almost ran to the waiting area. Julie sent me a message saying that she had done the security check and was grabbing her bag.

Minutes later, I spotted her. Her hair was up in a ponytail, and she was wearing tights and hauled a carry on with a huge blue suitcase.

I rushed to meet her. She was looking around trying to locate me, and when our gazes finally met, time froze. She was here. *My* Julie. Her caramel eyes fixed on mine; the freckles dotting her nose had gotten dimmer in the Kyiv winter, but they were still visible. She smiled, and I couldn't stop myself, I placed my hand to her cheek, tracing her cheekbone with my fingertips. I was swimming deep in her eyes, as she leaned in my touch.

"Hi," she said.

"Hi." I put my arms around her. The smell of her perfume made me dizzy. I couldn't believe she was here. Julie was positively radiant. She relaxed in my arms.

We were grinning like fools and couldn't take our eyes off of each other.

"Let's go to the car. Are you hungry? I have snacks for you," I said.

"Yes, and let's grab a coffee here. I feel like my jet lag is playing tricks with my mind already." She scratched her nose. "Or maybe it's you."

I took her suitcase, and we ventured to find a Starbucks.

When we reached the car, she stopped and started laughing.

"What?"

"Of course you drive a truck, and a huge one."

Julie was looking at my black shiny Ford F150 Raptor. I grinned.

"I need to haul boards." I shrugged.

I loved the beast; it was massive, and I loved the looks of it. Last year, I upgraded it, and now it was a powerful monster. We put Julie's suitcases in the car and when we climbed inside, I gave her a cooler bag with sandwiches and fruits prepared just for her.

"Thank you. I'm starving."

She drank her coffee and devoured the snacks while telling me about the flight.

"I couldn't focus on anything during the flight, so I watched a couple of old movies: Forrest Gump and The Holiday."

"I love The Holiday!" I exclaimed. "It's my must watch movie every Christmas. It never gets old."

"Yes." Julie looked out the window at all the palm trees. "It looks like a resort here. And it's so warm."

She closed her eyes, the sun shining on her face, and again I couldn't take my eyes off her. Thank God I stopped for the red light; she was a dangerous distraction to have in the car. She opened her eyes and looked at me, her smile tugging at the corners of her lips.

I heard the honk from the back; the light had switched to green some time ago. I pressed the gas, and we giggled.

As the car hit the highway, we immediately got stuck in a traffic jam.

"It's like this almost all the time here, don't worry. We

shouldn't be here long. We'll probably be home in twenty minutes," I assured her.

"I don't worry," Julie said, touching my hand on the steering wheel. We were not moving at all.

I watched mesmerized by how she took my hand and how she entwined her fingers with mine. Her touch sent jolts of pure energy through my body. I had waited for her, and I would always wait for her. She looked directly at me, her liquid caramel eyes pausing my heart. Out of the corner of my eye, I saw movement.

"We need to move," she said, breaking the spell.

Damn it, the road. The traffic moved faster and moments later, we were speeding down the highway again. Julie left her hand on my knee, tracing circles. She was talking about work, how it and books had saved her sanity during the last week.

"With each passing day, it was physically painful to stay so far from you," Julie sighed.

As we drove on, I occasionally pointed out a store or a restaurant I liked. Finally, we reached the house.

"Don't tell me you live here," she gasped. Julie was staring open mouthed at the house. It was a white single story Craftsman style home with huge windows. A little meditation nook in the corner of a wide porch was adorned with creeper plants, a Buddha statue and snuffed out candles. I kept forgetting that she lived in a completely different world. The world of apartments, buzzing city centers, Europe.

We took her bags from the car and went inside. She immediately took off her shoes. The European habit I always thought we should start in America. I was showing her around when I felt a light touch on my shoulder. I turned to her.

"I have waited for this moment for a month." She

caressed my hair, my neck, slowly dragging her thumb on my lower lip.

I stepped closer and kissed her. Her lips found mine with urgency. My gates flew open; I had tried to contain my need from the moment I caught sight of her at the airport, but I couldn't stop it anymore.

Her silky lips caressed mine, and our tongues did the dance of lust. My hands roamed over her back and waist, and she pressed me hard into her, our bodies blending. I wanted every inch of her, ragged breaths escaping us as we gasped for air, but we were both too afraid to separate even for a breath. I tugged at her shirt, and she pulled mine off. I unhooked her bra, cupping her delicate breasts in my fingers.

Julie, with shaking hands, unfastened my jeans. I kissed her collarbone, the velvet of her skin under my touch. Her hand was in my panties, moving. I kissed her nipple, biting it lightly, and a moan escaped Julie's lips.

Her fingers moved with more urgency, my body responding to it with the fire of need. She lowered my bra with the other hand, her eyes falling to my breasts, hunger gleaming in her gaze. And when she looked at me with that gaze, her fingers circling magic in my jeans, the first wave hit me like a wall. I almost buckled; my legs were suddenly so soft.

After a few minutes in her arms, barely breathing through the pleasure pulsing in my body, I took her to the sofa, pulled off her tights, and kissed her belly button, gently moving my finger inside her. She was so hot, so wet.

Julie unhooked my bra and touched my breasts, tugging at my nipples. She gasped when I lowered my head between her legs and kissed her down there. Her moans became louder as I continued. The taste of her, I couldn't get enough, I needed more. And she kept begging me for more, crying my name as she arched her back and shuddered with a gasp.

We stayed on the sofa for more than an hour. I couldn't believe my body could react to another person's touch like that. Julie melted in my arms, and I crumpled under her touch.

"I can't believe I found you," I murmured, touching her lips.

She was exhausted but happy, lying naked in my arms. So vulnerable, I hugged her. Julie started to drift to sleep, the time difference catching up with her.

"Do you want to move to the bed?" I asked.

Julie opened her sleepy eyes. "Yes, but I'd like to take a shower first," she said.

I showed her where she could put her stuff. Clearly, she wouldn't need the other room. I wanted her close every moment she was here. I had previously freed a huge section of my wardrobe and showed her to the bathroom.

"Would you like something to eat after the shower?"

"Yes, I am starving," she agreed with a smile. "Again."

As Julie was taking her shower, I heated the lasagna Jack had brought over. I couldn't believe what I was feeling. The wave of complete bliss rolled over me when I was with her. The power Julie had over me scared me, but the moment I saw her at the airport, I decided to surrender, to enjoy that burning.

My body was attuned to her, but it was not only the physical attraction, it was her soul and mind that enchanted me.

Julie stepped out of the bathroom. Naked, with only a white towel wrapped around her slender frame. The water drops glistened on her shoulder. Her damp hair was gathered in a bun. She crossed the room and stood in front of me.

"I don't know what's happening, but I am so happy." She kissed me slowly, and then she traced my neck, my ear with her fingertips. "And it's all because of you," she whispered.

I felt the roaring fire again, deep down in my core. I fought an impulse to tug on the towel to see her again, completely open before me.

I was drowning in her gaze. But I knew she needed to rest, so I took a deep breath, trying to clear the memory of the sound of her moans in my ears.

"What's that heavenly smell?" Julie asked, studying the food.

She perched at the barstool, and I joined her across the table. Julie took in a mouthful of lasagna.

"Wow, it's delicious! Did you cook it?"

"No," I laughed. "I would have burned it to coals. Or I just wouldn't have started it in the first place; it's too difficult." I waved my hand. "The layers. My neighbor Jack made it."

"I remember you telling me about him and his husband."

"Yes, I think Jack's mission is to make sure I won't starve to death. They can't wait to meet you, by the way."

I looked closely at her reaction. I tried to hide how important it was for me how she'd interact with a few close people I had.

"Sure, sounds great," Julie agreed. "I'd love to meet them too."

I made her a cup of tea, but Julie's eyelids were becoming heavy. She was tired after the flight, and the time difference was really catching up with her.

"Let's go to bed," I suggested.

She glanced at the clock on the stove I had never used.

"But it's only 8 p.m. Isn't it too early for you?"

"I'll lull you to sleep and then read a book or something. Let's go."

"Let me change and dry my hair," she said, heading to the bathroom.

I cleaned the plates, mentally thanking Jack again for the food; he was my savior. When Julie exited the bathroom, I almost dropped the cup I was holding. She was wearing a black lace negligee, her hair laid on her left shoulder. The negligee was almost transparent in the places I was starting to love.

"Wow, I love your outfit," was all I could say. I couldn't take my eyes off her.

She looked at me under her eyelashes. "Let's go?" She took my hand and led me to the bed. This girl was making me crazy.

Julie's breathing got slower as she laid in my arms. I traced her hair line, the skin on her shoulder, her arm. I was afraid to move, but she was so fast asleep that cannon fire wouldn't wake her. I laid there and listened to her breathing, my thoughts getting calmer as I put my hands tight around her.

Later, I went to shower and put on my much less sexy pajamas: top and shorts. When I entered the room, the view took my breath away. There was a beautiful woman in my bed, and her brown hair was a halo on the pillow. The negligee's lace did a bad job covering her skin, and I could see her breasts rising and falling as she breathed. Her eyes were closed, and she looked so peaceful. Standing in the doorway I realized one thing: I was falling in love with Julie.

Chapter 20

I woke up at 4 a.m., and it was still dark outside. Of course, for a few more days my internal clock would be crazy. As my eyes adjusted to the darkness, I took in my surroundings and fixed my eyes on Ann. She was sleeping on her belly, her pale skin almost glowing in the dark. I studied her face, wanting to memorize every line of it.

The next time I opened my eyes, it was 5:43 a.m. This time, I was wide awake. I went to the bathroom to wash my face on tiptoes and quietly moved to the kitchen. I found my bag and fished out my phone. There were two missed calls from Mark and a few messages from Mom. I had called them yesterday from the airport saying that I had landed safely in LA. I typed a message to Mark that everything was fine, and I couldn't call because Ann was sleeping, and I didn't want to wake her with my talking.

My guilt was slowly rising, and I pushed it away. Then I replied to my mom. She was asking how it was going. Good, amazing, tender, raw, passionate? What should I reply? I settled on, *Good, Mom, very good*. And I added a heart shaped emoji.

I didn't want to roam the house alone, so I found my eReader and perched on the sofa with a blanket.

In an hour, I was starving, but I didn't want to make any loud noises, so I just grabbed a banana and sat back down on the sofa. The sun had risen, and the sofa was facing a glass wall with a green garden outside and glimpses of green hills of the nearby golf course.

Ann's house wasn't big, but it was stylish and light, and it stood comfortably between much bigger expensive-looking houses. Some were hidden by hedges.

I was still wearing the peignoir, so I couldn't venture outside, and all my clothes were in Ann's room. Just a few days before the trip, I had strolled into the mall and bought the sexiest lingerie I could find. My body was far from ideal, but this one highlighted the most interesting parts perfectly. I was rather flat chested, and my hip bones were sharp blades, with a nonexistent booty, but I was secretly proud of my flat belly.

Ann was more round on the edges, more soft, and her breasts fascinated me. They were a size C, round, fit, with pointed nipples that replied to my every touch, especially when they were trapped between my lips, and she had heavenly soft skin. I smiled to myself.

Who knew two months ago that I would be standing in a house on the LA hills fantasizing about the breasts of a woman I had fallen in love with? The love? I didn't fall into it. That was an English expression. I was simply feeling it. My strong internal compass pointed north, in the direction of Ann.

And now she was beside me. She silently moved my hair to the side and kissed my neck.

"Good morning," she murmured into my ear.

"Morning," I breathed.

Her hand moved down to my legs. She traced my skin and pulled up the negligee. As she was kissing my neck, with the other hand she lowered the strap and cupped my breast in her warm hand. Her fingers slowly caressed me between my legs, and with a gentle bite on my ear, she pushed two fingers inside me.

I gasped, the hot sensation pulsing in my veins. Her hand moved faster and faster, touching my most sensitive places. I couldn't control myself anymore and an animal sound erupted from me as I came. She covered it with her mouth. I felt the sweetness of her lips, her tongue playing with mine. Ann's blue eyes were oceans in the morning light.

My heart hammering, I peeled off her shirt and just stared at her naked parts. With my fingers, I traced her arm, her collarbone, with our eyes locked the entire time. My hand found her nipple next. I gave it the slightest squeeze. Her lips parted, and she inhaled sharply. Her back was pressed against the glass wall. I moved my hand down in her shorts; she was so hot there, blazing fire.

She tried to hold my gaze, but as I was touching her, she closed her eyes and moved with the rhythm of my hand. I stopped. Her eyes flew open, and she found mine, the powerful need pulsing inside.

I helped her shrug off her shorts. Ann was breathing hard; she was like clay under my fingers. I kissed her breasts, her stomach, the insides of her thighs, propping her legs to move wider. With my tongue, I touched her raw flesh down there. I was on my knees, and my hand found her breast.

Ann made tiny noises, but her moans grew more insistent with each second. She was trapped against the glass, her hot skin leaving prints, fingers lost in my hair.

The sounds she was making drove me crazy. I thought I could have come just by listening to her. Her body shuddered, and she froze. I stood up and kissed her shoulder, her cheekbone, and our lips met in the slowest move.

We slid to the floor, and I held her.

"Good morning again," I said.

She smiled. "Can every morning be like this?" Ann murmured.

"We can see to it."

Chapter 21

*D*uring my first three days in LA, we mostly stayed at home. We spent the time talking and exploring our bodies. We were like hungry teenagers who couldn't keep our hands off each other. I didn't need the rest of the world; I was comfortable staying in with Ann in this cocoon.

"Okay, we need to get out. You need to see LA!" Ann said as she stood in the kitchen in a bathrobe, her hair damp as she held a white cup of coffee.

"Thank you, but I am perfectly fine here."

"Of course you are," she laughed. "I have an idea. Let's go to see the sunset today. And tomorrow, I'll show you my favorite spots in the city."

"Do we really need to go anywhere?" I groaned.

"Yes, we can't stay in the house for ten days."

"I thought you liked it here with me." I pouted my lips. I knew she enjoyed our time together as much as I did. The evidence was physical, our bodies thrumming with desire at the end of each day.

She reached me and put her hands on my shoulders.

"Not really," she said, but there was such merriment in her eyes that I smiled. She touched my lips with hers so tenderly, slowly propping my mouth open, playing with my tongue.

The familiar tingle at the bottom of my stomach appeared. I wondered where all this desire came from; we were like endless vessels of need.

We moved to the garden. I was sipping wine, and Ann nursed her half full glass; she would be driving later today. It was an exceptionally warm day, the sun heating our faces.

"You know, I told my mom about you," I said.

Ann looked alarmed. "How did she react?"

"She was happy. It doesn't matter to her if I am with a man or woman as long as I am happy and cherished. And it appears she doesn't really like Mark."

"Why?"

"She thinks a couple should be more secluded, and Mark spends a lot of time with his friends, and I mean *a lot*. My mom and dad, they have their own world. No one is allowed in. I didn't have that with Mark, and it was okay with me. But now I am understanding what she means." My cheeks warmed. "And my mom is one person who completely accepts my decision about kids. She doesn't say, oh you'll want them later, you will change your mind. Actually, she says it's too much work and if she was in her thirties now, she probably wouldn't have kids. She loves us, but she says it's too much of a routine, with too much noise. But when she was young, she did not have a choice. Everyone had kids, and there wasn't any option where a couple could opt out."

"Aren't you offended?" Ann asked.

"Firstly, my mom is a woman and a separate person. Secondly, she is my mother. I respect that and always have.

My brother and I were relatively easy teenagers, but she still remembers that time with a shudder."

"You said your brother's wife is pregnant? What does your mom think about that?"

"Mom is happy for them, but she said she won't be too much help. When we moved out of their apartment, she and Dad started traveling a lot, and some kind of glowing aura appeared between them. She said she would help with any emergencies, but she wouldn't be a daily babysitter. Christina, my brother's wife, is completely happy with that. She already did a whole search to find the right babysitter."

"And what about your brother, is he okay with this arrangement?" Ann asked.

"Being raised in my family, he has a strong feminist streak, but sometimes it's not enough. I am not sure how it's in the United States, but in Ukraine, grandparents take an active part in taking care of their grandchildren. Mostly, they are happy to babysit, and if they are retired, sometimes they become full-time babysitters. My brother wants Mom to take a bigger part with the child rearing. And he can't understand her lack of excitement.

"I told him that it is his kid, and our mom has already spent twenty years on us. It's time for her to live a life without kids," I explained. "She showed me once the number of books on tantra and sexuality she is reading with my dad,"—I covered my eyes with a hand—"and how many sex toys they have. I hope I have the same libido when I am fifty-six. So, they don't need to go back to taking care of diapers again; they are finally busy exploring themselves."

"Is your brother also this close with your parents?" Ann looked intently at me.

"Not so close that my mom would show him sex toys,"

I laughed. "But he is close with Dad; they have the same personality."

Ann took a sip of her wine and smoothed her hair back. "Yours sounds like a happy, trusting family," she remarked, but her eyes were sad.

"Tell me about your parents. Why aren't you in touch?"

"It's simple: They rejected me when I realized I was gay. They wanted me to have a traditional family, with lots of babies and a husband with status." Ann dropped her face into her hands. "It crushed me. One moment I had loving parents, and the next moment they said I couldn't set foot in their house until I came to my senses and abandoned 'my gayness'." Ann put the last word in air quotes. "But how could I abandon it? I always knew I was attracted to women, and it confused me when I tried to be normal. I was completely alone." She rubbed her eyebrow, and there was desperation in her voice.

I reached out to Ann and hugged her tightly. She dropped a head on my shoulder.

"I am so sorry," I murmured, "I can't understand how people who should be the closest, the most protective, could abandon their child when she's most vulnerable."

"It has been almost five years and I still can't understand their actions and absence in my life."

"Have you met with them during this time?" I asked.

"Yes, a few times, and every time we meet, they pretend I'm not there." Ann rubbed a heel of her palm against her chest, her eyes fixed on the horizon.

"That is so rotten. As if you could change who you are." I wished I could alleviate her pain somehow.

"Yes," Ann said simply. "But finally, something that defined me brought something wonderful in my life: you."

I inhaled the strawberry smell of her neck and kissed

her lightly. "You are one of the strongest and most independent women I know."

"Don't you think that sometimes independence goes hand in hand with loneliness?"

I was silent, but it was exactly what I was thinking before.

"My grandmother, the one who lives in Tel Aviv, helped me a lot. She supported me and visited here often. Her latest husband was the sweetest person. His sister was gay, and he knew about the hardships she dealt with. I think she's proud of me." Ann sat back and smiled. "She was the one to encourage me to go after you."

"Say a huge thank you to her from me," I said.

"Maybe one day you can say it in person."

I beamed. "I would love to."

She smiled and looked out to the green fields. It was quiet for a moment.

I cleared my throat. "Ann, can I ask you a question?"

She looked at me, her brows furrowing. "Sure."

"This, you know, how important it is for me." I swallowed loudly. "My choice of being childfree. And I need to know …" I looked down. "Are we on the same page? Because I am not sure I could survive, if you …" I still looked at my fingers grappling chair arm. "If you want to have kids. I …" My throat closed, and I couldn't say one more word. And finally, I looked up at her.

Her eyes were huge, but that smile, it warmed me. She took my hand in hers, slowly peeling off my trembling fingers from that chair.

"I am gay, Julie—"

"But gay families can have kids now," I interrupted.

"I know. But since I realized I was attracted to women, I accepted that my life would be different. In those early days, when I still hoped I could be with someone, I just imagined a partner and me. And then I realized something was broken in me, and I was alone. And I was at peace with that. But I had never imagined having a kid in my life. I was too focused on myself and too protective of my space. I never swoon upon seeing baby pictures. I love quiet, I love my schedule, and I am not ready to give it all up. I never thought that I could have a kid myself." She actually shuddered. "But now, it is as simple as a day. I choose you."

"But what if I wanted kids? Would you do it?" I asked.

She leaned back on her chair, thinking.

"This is being childfree,"—she took her left hand—"and this is having kids." She took her right hand. "I am in the middle, not tilting into any direction." She pointed to the space between. "If my partner wanted kids, it would ruin my routine, but I would go with it. And I would not be the one to give birth." She lifted the right hand. "But if my person decides to be childfree,"—she nodded at me—"honestly, it's so much easier."

"What would be the decision if you were alone?"

"Easy, I'd go childfree."

Still, I was not convinced.

"But when years go by, won't you change your mind?"

"I want to be honest with you. Now, I don't think that I would change my mind, but some life-altering event could happen, and poof, all my beliefs could go haywire. But what I understand now, and what I feel I will understand forever, that it's always about choice. Here, the choice is between you and future imaginary kids. And I hope that I am not a person who can betray you that way. I can't promise anything, but I will do my best to choose you."

There was a blur of movement as I rushed to her, dropping on her lap, pressing against her warm body, my arms entwining around her neck, and my lips finding hers.

She laughed. "I choose you, Julie."

I dropped my head on her shoulder and closed my eyes. Minutes ticked by as I listened to her heartbeat.

"Okay, let's get ready. We need to catch the sunset," Ann said.

I groaned. "Do we?"

"I thought you were a big traveler and adventurer."

"I was."

She giggled and tugged at my arm, and we went inside to change.

We packed snacks. Ann ate mostly organic vegetables, so we wrapped celery and baby carrots with a dip and a few sandwiches. As Ann revved the engine and backed from the driveway, I looked around the neighborhood. She turned on some indie songs in the car, and we joined the traffic on the highway. We talked about books, and as it turned out, we both were avid readers, but Ann mostly devoured non-fiction, while I was fixated on fiction; romance was my weak spot. However, there was also a place for a chilling gruesome thriller in my heart.

It took us forty minutes to reach El Matador Beach. We grabbed our jackets and descended to the beach. The sky was already turning purple, and massive rocks were scattered on the beach like toys left by a kid who didn't bother to clean up after himself. The water turned all shades of violet and pink, and it was mesmerizing. Ann took my hand, and we walked towards the sun. There were a few people, and I was aware that it was the first time we were outside and could be a couple in a public place. California was a liberal state, and nobody gave us a second thought. But for me, it all was new. As we reached the perfect spot where the sun was slowly hiding behind the rocks, Ann stopped and stood behind me. She wrapped her arms around me and whispered, "Thank you for flying here to see me."

I turned around and looked at her. There was a calmness of the ocean in her eyes. I touched her cheekbone and slowly kissed her. There were people around us, but nobody cared.

The world erupted in a million shades of purple, and we silently watched as the sun hid behind the rocks standing in each other's arms. I wanted to pause this moment, to stay here. It would be imprinted in my memory forever.

She took my hand and led me down the beach.

"When did you realize that you liked girls?" I asked.

"I think it was when I was in my teens. And when I told my parents, they made me feel strange, broken; they said it was not human nature to be attracted to people of the same sex. And I believed them, I tried to hide that part within myself. I tried to find boys attractive. Oh, it would have made things so much easier, and I actually went out with a guy who my parents liked. The moment his cold, clammy hands touched my hips, I couldn't take it anymore. I broke up with him. Then the river flooded, and my body wanted a taste of life. And I found myself in beds with girls, often older than me. I explored their bodies inch by inch. My body found relief in their arms, but my heart and soul were lost. I never really felt anything towards them."

That hurt in two ways, one—I imagined Ann in the arms of another woman, and second, how lonely she had been. I squeezed her hand.

"Once, a woman named Madeline came into my life," Ann continued. "She was a talented surfer on weekends and a fierce attorney on weekdays. She fell in love with me. By that time, I was so lonely that I craved attention and touch. Just a few weeks into our relationship, she asked me to move in with her. I was twenty-six, she was thirty-five. Madeline was gentle with me, and she cared for me, but my heart was not in it. I started to wonder if something was wrong with me, if I could love at all.

"By day, we lived our lives. By night, my body was her toy, and my mind was shut. She tried to make me happy, she really did. But as time went by, her touches made me colder and colder. Eventually, I said we needed to break up. She cried, she begged, but I left. The pain on her face almost woke me from my dream in a cold sweat. Almost. Now Madeline is married to an older woman and lives in New York."

"Do you miss her?"

Ann shook her head. "No, I never really warmed to her. It was like when my parents left me, a shell grew around me. And no light penetrated it, no feelings got in. I learned how to live alone, and it was easier, safer ..." her voice trailed off, eyes on the horizon. "Till I met a woman in a Tel Aviv bar."

"You are not alone anymore," I said, touching her chin and turning her to look at me.

She stopped walking and looked silently in my eyes. I pressed my lips to her forehead, and I felt like one more wall of her inner cell was crumbling down.

The sun had hidden, and it was suddenly colder than before. As we reached the truck, I asked, "Where next?"

"I have an idea." Ann smiled mischievously. "I will take you to a movie scene."

I quirked an eyebrow. "Which one?"

"Oh, you'll see." There was a playful grin on Ann's lips.

As she was driving, I peeped into the cars moving along with us. They were all separate worlds: a tired man in a suit, a woman happily chatting with a teenage girl, and an elderly couple. Then I turned to Ann; she was a relaxed driver. I took in every inch of her face. She eventually noticed and took my hand in hers.

"Do you want to meet Jack and John tomorrow for breakfast? Jack sent me a message. It said something like, 'Stop hiding her.'"

I laughed. "Yes, sure."

"They have a son, Ian, and he's nine. He's a really quiet boy, so don't worry, nobody will throw a kid at you."

"I am okay with older kids. It was Mark who always tried to convince me to change my mind by asking me to hold a baby or play with somebody. In the usual world, kids are not interested in me, and we coexist in the same room pretty well," I said.

It was almost dark outside. Long ago, we had exited the highway and were now winding up the narrow road. I tried to make out the surroundings, but only trees lined the driveway.

"I hope you're not a serial killer," I said, squinting in the window.

"We're almost there," Ann chuckled.

And around the next turn, I saw what she meant. Shimmering lights of a Los Angeles night were everywhere, surrounding us. We climbed to an observation point, finding a few cars were here already.

"Now I understand what you meant about taking me to a movie scene." I grinned.

The closest car to us was quite far, and I could only see the dark shape of it; it was swinging lightly. I felt my face heating. Ann took my hand and gently pressed it to her cheek, and then she moved it slowly down, her velvety skin under my fingertips. She stopped my hand at the hollow of her breasts, and I kissed her, burying my other hand in her hair, moving her closer.

We made love in the car. Like in the movies, with Los Angeles glistening mere steps away.

Afterwards we climbed to the rear seats, Ann put her head in my lap, and I stroked her hair. The lights around us mesmerized me.

"What will happen with us?" I asked.

Ann took a sharp breath and studied me. "What do you want to happen?"

"I want to be with you, and not only for a week in a month, but always. And I want to stop lying. I will tell Mark everything as soon as I see him. It's time for him to find a woman who will give him what he wants."

"Would you do that?" Ann pressed. Her face didn't betray anything, but I saw the glimmer of hope in her eyes. She perched on an elbow and moved her face close to mine.

"Of course," I said. She wrapped her hands around me and pressed her soft lips to mine for a moment. "Did you think you were going to stay my paramour?" I laughed.

"I don't know. I decided to live in the moment while you were here. Because the longer I thought about us, the more I freaked out. I guess I was too afraid to let myself hope." She pressed her hands to the sides of my face. "And here you are, brave enough to talk about it, to dream."

"But I have no idea how to make it work, the logistics of us. We live on different continents, for God's sake! But I know that we should make it work," I said.

Ann's expression changed to business-like and she asked, "Where do you want to live?"

"Here," I blurted out without thinking.

"But you haven't even seen LA during the days you've been here," Ann laughed in return.

"Oh, it's a city on the ocean, how bad can it be?" I

scratched my nose. "Okay, wait, I replied too fast, but it was the first thing that came to my mind."

Ann tried hard to hide her smile.

"What are you so happy about?" I asked.

"Sorry." She tried to make a serious expression. "It's just that it's perfect." And she tickled me, and I laughed as she kissed me. The kiss became deeper in a second. Our bodies pressed together in the space of the car, my breathing quickened, and it was crazy how my body reacted to Ann's touch.

She stopped abruptly. "But what about your family?" Ann asked. "This place is far from Ukraine, and you are so close to them."

"That's true," I said as I was still trying to catch my breath, my heart beating fast. But really, what about my family? I would miss Mom and Dad tremendously. My brother would be busy with his kid soon. Zoom calls would work, but …

"I have an idea. Once you said you wanted to live in Europe for a year? That way it's only a couple of hours from Kyiv, and you could visit them often. And during that year you could understand if living abroad will work for you."

Ann mentioned a year as it was nothing, but for me it seemed like a long time.

"Do you see us together in a year?" I asked quietly.

Ann paused and tucked my hair over my ear. "Of course."

So simple. These two words reshaped my world in a moment, and then she smiled and looked at me.

"What do you think about Barcelona?"

"I was thinking about it too," I agreed. Really, Barcelona was a place I would love to spend a year in. I would not want to live there forever, but for a starting point it was great. "And there is a Benzon office there."

As Benzon was an international company with many offices scattered around the world, they relocated employees pretty easily. If you worked a few years in Benzon, you could relocate to any office or just work remotely.

"This sounds like a deal," Ann said, beaming.

"Deal." I pressed my lips to the hollow of her throat. Her pulse hammered against my lips.

Ann put a hand on my hip, and as I was only in my underwear, she slowly traced the edge of my pants. I moved my hand under her shirt and squeezed her breast lightly. Oh, she loved when I did it. Not only couldn't I keep my hands off her body, but she was really sensitive, responding to my touch.

As I kept stroking her, the silky skin under my fingertips, she slipped a hand in my pants. She was moving it slowly, building my needs. My body rocked with the rhythm of her touch. The noises I made were light cries of pleasure. Ann moved closer to my ear and lightly bit my lobe.

"So, are you sure about Barcelona?" she whispered. I heard her ragged breathing as I caressed her nipple. She moved her fingers faster, deeper.

"Yes! Yes!" My body shuddered. "Yes, I'm sure," I breathed out.

The next morning, I woke up to a light kiss on my cheek. Ann was already dressed. She put a glass of orange juice in front of me.

"Good morning," she said, lightly touching my hair. "We should get going soon."

I took a few sips of juice. "Should I be nervous?" I asked.

"No," she laughed. "They are probably more nervous themselves. They want you to like them."

I smiled and went to the shower. Ann said to be chill, but I was still a bit jumpy. They were important people in her life. I put on a casual dress that looked like an oversize t-shirt and put on my white sneakers.

"How do I look?"

Ann scanned me up and down. "Sexy."

I blushed. "Oh, wait, I almost forgot."

I rushed to my suitcase and fished out the bottle of Ukrainian wine and a box of custom-made sweets.

"Ready," I announced, straightening my dress as I entered the living room.

Ann squeezed my hand. "Don't worry, everything will be great."

It appeared that Jack and John lived just next door. As Ann opened the door and ushered me inside, a smiling man in his forties rushed to meet us.

"Oh my God, Ann, you didn't tell us that you found such a beauty," he exclaimed. "I'm Jack."

He moved closer to me and gave me a bear hug. He smelled like expensive cologne and bread.

"Hi, it's nice to meet you." I smiled.

A tall, lean man entered the hall with a boy hiding behind him. "So glad to meet you, Julie," he said, holding out a hand to me. "Finally. Was Ann keeping you a prisoner? This is Ian."

"Hello," Ian replied, lurking upstairs.

I gave the bottle and the box of candy to Jack.

"The candies are homemade and should be delicious.

The wine, well, we'll see," I said.

"Thank you. Let's go to the kitchen," Jack instructed.

They had the biggest kitchen I'd ever been in. You could have easily filmed a cooking show there. The copper cutlery was shining, the stove was the size of my bathtub, and the fridge was like a small room.

"It smells delicious," I remarked. The pan with sizzling bacon, the smell of melting batter and grilling sausages mixed with a fragrant coffee and the freshly baked bread made my mouth water.

"Jack is a chef at one of the top LA restaurants," Ann explained.

"The lasagna I tried at Ann's was amazing; it melted in my mouth."

"Did she starve you?" Jack asked, furrowing his eyebrows. "Ann always forgets to eat."

Ann rolled her eyes. "No, I eat just fine."

I laughed. "I guess she prepared for my arrival. The fridge was pretty stuffed."

"Thank you," she said, looking at John and rolling her eyes. "Please tell him that I am not starving."

John threw his hands into the air. "It's between you and Jack. Don't drag me into the food war."

I noticed how easily they all moved around each other. John poured glasses of the Ukrainian wine for all of us that I had brought. Jack swayed his glass, smelling it.

"I am not sure it's okay. I never drink Ukrainian wine at home. We import lots of Spanish and Italian ones, and I prefer those, as I am not sure the Ukrainian production technology is up to par. But an assistant in a wine shop recommended trying this one."

Jack took a sip. "It's not bad." He took one more sip. "Actually, I like it."

Ann and John agreed.

"You are just being polite," I laughed.

"No, it really is fine," John insisted, taking another sip and smacking his lips.

"I mean, it's not the best one I ever drank," Ann said, clearing her throat, "but it's okay."

"I should have brought vodka," I muttered.

Ann shook her head. "Nah, they don't drink anything stronger than wine. But they love sweets, especially Jack and Ian."

During this time, the boy was nowhere to be seen.

"He'll come out later when he's ready," John assured me when he noticed me looking around.

"What did you see already? Did you do any sightseeing? Where did Ann take you?" Jack asked.

"Well, we went to Malibu for a sunset. It was really picturesque," I said. A sweet tingle appeared in my chest as I remembered our hands linked together.

"And that's all?" Jack asked. "It seems that you two can't leave the house." He paused and looked at Ann, her cheeks turning crimson. "But you need to show Julie the city!"

"She must at least see places like Beverly Hills, Santa Monica, the Hollywood sign, and Hollywood," John told her, bending his fingers as he listed the sights. "And a few museums would be good, too. But don't get your hopes high for Hollywood; it's not the nicest district."

"And if you liked La La Land, Griffith Observatory is a must," Jack added.

"Yes, yes, we are starting with Beverly Hills today," Ann said, sighing dejectedly.

Jack took a heavenly smelling bread out of the oven and placed it in the middle of the table. John sliced it while Jack served bacon, sausages, eggs, tomatoes, and avocado.

"I'll go find Ian and ask him if he wants to eat with us," John said.

"So, how are you two together?" Jack asked, pausing to examine both of us.

I squeezed Ann's hand. Jack saw it and glanced at Ann.

"Good," she said, but her face was radiant, much better than only *good*.

"I am so happy for you two." Jack looked over at me, as though he tried to see something hidden, his gaze holding mine. "Take care of her. Sometimes she forgets to take care of herself."

"I'll do my best," I promised, leaning in.

"Sounds like a plan." A warm smile played on his lips.

John and Ian joined us. Ian was extremely shy, and he avoided eye contact and stayed silent during the whole meal. We switched to coffee and orange juice since it was only breakfast. Jack was the talker in the family. He told me about his job at the restaurant and said if we had any free time during our busy schedule we should visit.

"Ann, are you going to take Julie to Six Flags?" Ian asked. Everyone stopped talking and stared at him.

I tilted my head curiously, biting into a piece of bread. "What's Six Flags?"

"It's a roller coaster park," Ian explained, cutting into some eggs.

"It's so high and fast and the number of loops is crazy there," Ann said, her face paling slightly as she downed some orange juice.

"Maybe Universal?" John suggested.

"I've been to Universal in Orlando," I said. "And no, we probably won't go, as Ann isn't a fan of those parks."

"We can go with you. I'll keep you company," Ian said, chewing bacon, finally looking at me.

"Aren't you afraid of those high and scary rides?" I teased him.

He grinned back. "Try me."

I liked this kid. He was quiet and talked only when he had something to say.

John scratched his nose. "We can go, Ann. You won't be riding; you can just walk around the park with us."

Ann took a deep breath and said, "If no one is going to persuade me to try, especially you." She pointed at Ian with the fork. "I'll think about it."

"I won't," Ian said, his eyes glazing with excitement.

Jack and John showed me their house. It was huge, with light filling every corner. John worked in music production, and his office walls were covered with glowing magazine articles and diplomas. They had a pool in the backyard and an immaculate lawn with a flourishing garden. The place felt like home, with stylish touches coming directly from interior design magazines. I assumed Jack did it, with lots of cozy nooks to hide in and a huge library. When I went to the bathroom the size of my room back home and returned to them, I heard Ann talking about Barcelona. When I entered the room, Jack put an arm around her and kissed her forehead.

"I am so happy for you," he beamed.

Jack and John were amazing father figures. The protective care they radiated toward Ann was mesmerizing. They both hugged me tightly when we had to leave.

Back at Ann's house, she said, "Get ready for a lot of walking. We need to cover a large area today." She smiled.

I stepped closer to her and took her hand. "I'd prefer to stay at home with you." I touched the back of her neck.

She traced my lower lip with her tongue, the lightest touch sending pleasant shivers down my core. "Would you?" she whispered.

And I kissed Ann, crashing into her lips. Her hands moved fast to remove my clothes, and in a few moments, she led me to bed, gently pushing me to lie down. She was kissing me everywhere, her lips brushing my breasts and my ribs, stopping under my belly button.

"We should get going," Ann said with a playful smile on her lips.

I was breathing hard, my chest rising in fast movements. I craved her touch, moving my body closer to her.

"Later," I murmured. But she wasn't moving; her hand was hovering inches from my hip bone. "Please," I breathed out, and it did the trick. She propped my knees wider and feasted on me, making me whimper her name, taking me to the moon in a few minutes.

It took us an hour to get ready, but finally we were out the door and driving to Beverly Hills. We parked not far from Rodeo Drive and walked down the street. I gaped at the sports cars parked right in front of the luxurious shops with popular names everyone knew. Ann said she saw Richard Gere here once. Then we strolled through the residential area, looking at the houses and imagining who lived inside. We drove to the mansions in upper Beverly Hills, and my jaw dropped even more. The size of the houses, the style, it was like an open-air museum, but mostly hidden behind fences.

Later that day, we drove to Santa Monica, which was crowded because of the nice weather. Ann took my hand in hers, and most people didn't pay attention to us, but some gave curious looks and a group of tourists even pointed a finger at us. California was liberal and supportive of the LGBTQ movement, but the rest of the world was only starting to get there.

The pier was the same as the one in the Forest Gump.

But what I enjoyed the most was people watching. You could see all kinds of people here, like beautiful looking athletes, young people trying to find a way to Hollywood, groups of tourists huddling together, and teenagers on skates and bikes. There was activity everywhere.

For the sunset we drove to the Griffith Observatory. Once again, I was dropped in a movie setting. The sky was all shades of purple, and we took the side trail to hide from the crowd. Ann put her hands around me, and we stood there in silence, watching the sun going down. I couldn't explain the feeling of lightness and happiness inside me, but I knew the reason for it: Her arms were draped around me.

When the sun hid under the horizon, I turned to Ann and hugged her close. I felt the rise and fall of her chest as she breathed, her heart beating right next to mine. I couldn't imagine the moment I would need to go back home without her by my side, even if it was only for a few weeks.

We stood in each other's arms as the night descended on us. This moment was one of the few when I realized that I was irrevocably in love with Ann.

Chapter 22

J held her close to me. We were one, as simple as that. Our task was to save it. Now was the 'honeymoon phase'. It was easy and flawless, and the work would begin when this phase ended.

As we started descending back to the car, I said, "You know, I have this fear, since everything is perfect now. But my brain turns into protective mode, like I don't completely believe this is happening, that it will all end. She will go home, and you will never see her again. I know this is a shield, but I am still afraid."

"Yes, constant chanting to be careful, that it's too good to be true," Julie agreed.

"Well, it actually is too good," I said quietly.

"But I decided to shut that voice down. None of us knows what will happen, and constant worry only kills the joy of the moment."

"And did you shut it down successfully?" I asked, raising an eyebrow.

"I'm working on it. It's difficult to argue with my own fears." Julie brushed a hand through her hair.

"I was never really in a long-term relationship, so I am afraid as hell of the moment when what they call the 'honeymoon phase' ends," I admitted when we reached the car and climbed in. "I don't worry that my feelings for you will fade, no, but that you can—"

"Wait," Julie interrupted, pressing two fingers to my lips to silence me. "These phases aren't for ending things, they are for growing deeper into each other. Yes, the more time goes by, the more work relationships will require. But it's a work of getting to know each other on a different level and caring for each other. I don't really believe in a stigma of a 'honeymoon phase'. It's only the foundation of something much bigger." Julie took my hand in hers. "And I look forward to being your boring day-to-day partner."

This woman knew how to make me happy. After these words, a warm light grew into my chest. She was serious about me, about us. I still couldn't believe Julie had come into my life and pushed my fears away. I decided to cherish every moment we had, be it a month or fifty years.

"Can you imagine us growing old together?" she asked.

"You know," I said, scratching my nose, "actually I can, and quite vividly. We'll see, but it's the sweetest image."

"Save it for me," she pleaded with a smile.

But I would save this one as well. The warm light from a lamppost on the parking lot lit Julie's face with a honey glow, and her eyes looked deep into mine. The sun from the last few days highlighted her freckles, and brown hair framed her face with an auburn halo.

The next day, I took Julie to the beach. As I was tying my surfboard to the car trunk, Julie was dragging hers out of the garage. She was awkward, and having never really held such a big board, she didn't know where to place her hands and almost tripped. But with a brave face, she put it by my side.

"Here," she breathed.

I laughed. "Thanks, but I could have brought it myself."

"I know, but I'm here, and you don't need to do everything alone now," she said, going inside for a bag with snacks, hot tea in the thermos, towels, and wetsuits.

My hand froze while I was tying the rope, and I looked at my fingers.

I am not alone anymore. I had gotten used to doing everything by myself, living alone. And now, my gaze shifted to the second board at my feet. I had another human in my life. *I'm here, and you don't need to do everything alone now.* I smiled, hope blossoming in my heart.

Two hours later, I was watching her catch the smallest waves, so confident on the board.

"Are you sure you never tried surfing?" I asked.

"Yes." She was panting and focused on the coming wave. "But I think I have the gist of it."

"Really?" I exclaimed, watching her standing on the board and making it almost to the end, tumbling into the water. But she was a natural on the board.

A group of surfers huddled not far from us. They were wearing dark swimsuits, but their boards were so colorful, as the feathers of an exotic bird flying on the water edge. One of them waved and swam closer to us.

"Hi, Shawn," I greeted.

Julie swam closer to me. "This is Julie."

"Hi." Shawn held out a hand to her, and they shook.

"I see you have a newbie friend here." He winked. "I

remember Ann learning her first baby steps on waves," he said to Julie.

Shawn was in his fifties, and every weekend you could find him on the water.

"I noticed that you put your leg right on the edge, though. It makes you fall in the water at the end all the time. Try it now."

He showed Julie a place on his board where her leg should be. Julie looked at me briefly, and I nodded. She stood, and I saw what he was talking about. He moved her leg into the correct position.

"Let's try with this wave," he suggested.

It was slightly bigger to the ones before.

"I'll do it with you," I told her.

And she did it, slightly wobbly, but it was great. Julie was beaming, her wet hair plastered to her face. Her body was slick in the dark wetsuit.

"Nice one!" Shawn clapped and swam closer. "How do you two know each other?"

"Oh, it's a long story. We met in Tel Aviv," I said as Julie swam closer to me and took my hand in hers.

"Ooooh, I see," Shawn said, looking from our hands to our faces. "Finally, Ann." He turned to Julie. "Good luck with this wild one." He winked at her, his eyes crackling with mischief.

Someone called Shawn from the group of guys he had been hanging out with.

He nodded towards us. "I'll leave you both to it, then. Nice meeting you Julie."

"You too," she said.

I waved as he left. "Bye, Shawn." When he retreated further out into the water away from us, I turned to Julie. "Are you tired?" I asked her. "That was a lot for the first time."

She was tired, she admitted reluctantly. We swam to the shore and climbed out of the water. This was one of the few beaches with changing rooms, and in winter, only surfers used it. We took our bags with dry clothes from the car and went to change.

"Let me help you unzip," I said. Usually the wetsuits had a strip on the zipper to make it easier, but hers didn't have one.

Julie turned her back to me. I moved the zipper down and helped her out of the wetsuit. When her shoulder emerged, I kissed it, moving the wetsuit down. I touched her shoulder blade, slowly tracing the back of her neck with my lips. I moved my hand to her breast, her heart hammering under my palm. Julie pressed her back to me.

We were alone in the changing rooms. She took my hand and moved it down, pressing it between her legs. She was warm. I covered her lips as she moaned, her body moving in my arms.

"Shh, be quiet," I whispered in her ear. She clasped a hand to her mouth, trying to silence herself. I moved my hand to caress her body. She tried to stay silent as I moved my fingers inside her, touching her in the places I knew she loved. But in the end, it was stronger than her, and she cried as hot liquid spread on my fingers. I turned her to face me.

"You did amazing today," I said before kissing her. Julie kissed me back, still dazed. "Here's your clothes."

She slowly put them on. I smiled to myself at the way she had melted under my touch. It was satisfying.

We drank tea while watching the waves, and the weather was getting colder by the minute. Dark grey clouds were moving from the east.

"What do you want to do now?" I asked.

"Go back home, if you don't mind," Julie said. She looked sleepy, her eyelids growing ever heavier.

"Sure, it seems that we caught the perfect weather today."

As I was driving home, Julie drifted to sleep. That morning on the water had taken a lot out of her. I memorized every inch of her face when stopping at the stoplights. When I parked at the house, I touched her hair and her cheek.

"We're home," I told her.

She opened her eyes and smiled drowsily. "Thank you," she whispered.

"For what?" I laughed.

She shrugged. "For the day."

We climbed out of the truck and took the bags inside.

"Hey, why don't you go take a nap?" I suggested, nodding towards my room.

"Yes, I probably should," she agreed, rubbing her eyes. "Shower first, though."

I heard the water running while unpacking the food and wetsuits. When Julie opened the door to the bathroom, the steam poured out and she emerged pink-faced. She was wearing her lacy negligee that was unbearably sexy on her. Julie crossed the room and pressed her body to mine, her skin so warm after the shower. She brushed her lips to my cheek and whispered, "Good night."

"Good night," I laughed, as it was only 2 p.m.

She went to the bedroom and slowly closed the door behind her.

I took a shower and perched on the sofa. The darkest clouds covered the sky, and the rain would pour any moment now. I loved this weather, as it was the opposite from the usual LA sunshine. I made myself a cup of a chamomile tea and picked up a book. But I couldn't focus on it. My mind kept running to the bedroom, where the woman I loved was sleeping. I never really believed that I would meet a person I'd love with every pore of my body, with every corner of my mind.

I managed to live alone just fine. My days had a calming rhythm of familiarity. But there was one thought I forbade myself to dwell on. Was I lonely? A small frozen chamber in my heart. It had been reserved for another person, and it stayed vacant … always. Till Julie.

Julie was the person who opened the door to that closed, frozen chamber with a crash, and she filled it with laughter and flowers. She didn't know it. And she made the one thing I was always ashamed of, that I was a lesbian, a thing that filled me with hope and light. Her presence was a silent acceptance of my being queer.

The feelings I had for her made me strong and vulnerable at the same time. I was afraid about our future, the decisions she would need to make in her life so that we could be together. And even if she didn't talk about Mark, I knew they had a solid relationship. And if he didn't wish to be a father so strongly, I think they would be together for many years to come. But his need to be a parent made Julie realize that sooner or later she would need to let him go. He loved her, but she knew that if they stayed together, he would blame her for the life he didn't have.

I wanted to shield her from the pain. This breakup with Mark would hurt, even if she didn't show it. I would stay by her side through every minute of it.

The big raindrops started drumming on the glass. I watched the small rivers flow outside, the sound of the rain lulling me. I closed my eyes for a moment.

I felt a soft touch on my cheek and opened my eyes. I didn't mean to drift away; the open book still lay open in my lap.

"Hey," Julie murmured.

I blinked several times. "Hey."

The room had grown darker, as it was still raining outside.

"Can I lay with you?" she asked.

"Sure." I scooted over and opened my arms, finding that she fit perfectly.

"How's the book?"

I shrugged. "Not bad, a thriller, but the rain calmed me, and I guess I was also tired."

Julie turned her face to me and locked her eyes on me. "Ann?"

"Mmm?" I was touching her hair, the silk strands between my fingers.

"I want to be with you," Julie said. Her features were so determined; she wasn't smiling. "I never wanted …" She took a shaky breath. "I have never needed anyone like I need you. Now I know where my heaven is; it's by your side. And I am terrified that I need to leave in a few days. I know it's just for a few weeks and we will be together later, but I am afraid to leave you even for a short amount of time."

She looked so vulnerable, and I pressed her close to me.

"I know, honey," I whispered, "and I hate that you need to go, that you need to change your life because of me."

Julie drew back. "Now that I have you and know what this is,"—she gestured to the space between us—"I don't want my old life."

I smiled and kissed her gently, touching her upper lip with the tip of my tongue. Julie didn't move, her breath lingering on my lips. She was teasing, a playful smile on her face.

And then she kissed me back. I could feel her. She

untied my bathrobe and with shaking hands lowered my bra straps. Julie kissed my collarbone and paused at the hollow of my breasts. She slowly tugged down the bra and stopped. She just watched as her fingers slowly touched my nipple, the dark skin around it. Her lips parted, and she glanced deep into my eyes.

"You have a beautiful body. Do you know that?"

"Do I?" I quirked a playful brow.

"Oh yes," she whispered, kissing my belly, slowly moving down and down, till I gasped for air.

Afterwards, as I was trying to calm my breathing, Julie took a blanket and covered us both. The rain was puttering softly on the glass. Julie climbed back into my arms, and our breathing grew softer by each minute as we drifted to sleep.

I woke up to my stomach rumbling. Julie heard it and put a hand on my abdomen.

"I'm hungry too," she admitted with a slow smile.

"What do you want to eat?"

"What do you think about pizza?" Julie suggested with a childish happiness in her eyes.

An hour later, we were so full we could barely breathe.

"Oh, wow, American pizza is huge," Julie remarked, taking a sip of cola. "And greasy."

"It's not the Italian way for sure," I laughed.

I took my phone and checked the weather app. The next day was going to be a sunny day.

"Do you want to go to the adventure park tomorrow?" I asked.

"But what about you? You hate those."

"Oh, I won't be riding. I will wait for you standing safely on the ground. Jack, John, and Ian would love to spend more time with you. And they are crazy on those rides. I honestly don't know how they do it, but they go over and over on those loopy ones, where you often end up upside down. That family has bodies like astronauts."

"But won't you be bored?"

I shook my head. "Nope."

Her eyes glinted. "Let's go then."

I sent a message to John, and he replied with a confirmation.

"Let's see what this Ukrainian girl is made of," he texted back with a winking smile. I laughed.

"Beware, she is sturdier than you think," I replied back.

The rain subsided to a drizzle, so we decided to stay in and watch movies. Browsing Netflix, I stumbled upon Back to the Future, my favorite movie of all time.

"Have you watched it?" Julie asked, seeing me lingering on it.

"Of course, it's *the* movie, the movie of all movies."

"I agree." Julie grinned.

I pressed play, and we watched all three parts quoting lines, cheering and giggling. This felt like home. If this was what our future looked like, I couldn't believe my luck.

Later, I set an alarm for eight in the morning; it would be a crazy day. Julie wrapped her hands around me and whispered, "Good night."

I kissed her lightly and murmured back, "Good night."

I heard her breathing growing softer and felt her muscles relaxing. She fell asleep quickly. The thought of her leaving soon was pulsing with my heart, spreading the dread through my veins and tearing my soul apart.

I inhaled the sweet smell of her skin and tried to relax. I wanted to pause this moment, but let's face it, I wanted to pause every moment I spent with her. But all these moments were rushing with the speed of light, running from me. I had to let her go. And the moment of separation loomed on the horizon, dimming the time we still had here.

I looked at Julie's face in the dark. I needed to trust the future. It would play out as it should. But worry was creeping inside me, and I couldn't shake it off.

Chapter 23

JULIE

*A*nn's alarm was blaring throughout the room. I bolted upright as she turned it off.

"Sorry," Ann said, dropping her head back on the pillow.

I pressed my lips to her forehead. "I wanted to ask you, why are you afraid of roller coasters?"

"Oh, it's an old story. When I was a kid, I saw this video of a roller coaster car jumping off the track and crashing with full speed to the ground, full of people. The footage showed the people's necks snapping, and their heads rolling into unnatural positions. I barely kept my breakfast down after seeing it. Since then, I just don't trust these rides. I managed to ditch them almost all my life. The one in Barcelona was the first adventure park I had visited in years."

"What about today?" I asked.

"I understand now that these parks are better engineered and safe compared to the one I saw in that video. I'm not even sure that video was taken in the US.

Even so, I will hold your bag and enjoy the junk food they sell there."

My phone rang. I took it out, and the screen showed Mark's name. Ann noticed, the skin under her eyes tightening, but she tried to smile. "Go ahead, take it."

I crawled out of the blanket, my negligee hiding nothing. Ann glanced at me, and her eyes lingered on my body, the hungry grin on her lips. I giggled. Her stare made my core burning hot. I grabbed my phone and went to the living room.

"Hey," I greeted hesitantly, picking up.

"Hi," Mark replied, his voice strained. "Is everything alright? I haven't heard from you for a few days."

I just couldn't bring myself to call him. I knew what I had to do when I went back. So, I sent him messages saying everything was okay along with pictures of LA and the beach. I took a deep breath.

"Yes, sorry, we were busy." It sounded harsh. "Can you imagine I surfed yesterday? And it appears I am decent at it!" I added in a more cheerful tone.

"Of course you would be. You love the water," he laughed, his deep warm laugh, familiar. My heart was filled with guilt. He always gave me his constant support, and I would need to break it soon.

"How's work?" I asked, changing the subject.

He told me about the latest deadline and that it was crazy how much information they needed to gather before it. He said that all he did now was work, crawl back home late only to grab dinner and fall asleep, with every day being the same.

"I envy your vacation. The sun would do me good now." Mark's voice was tired.

"You need to start searching for a new job, like we discussed. There won't be any time later. After this deadline, there will be another. They won't give you a break, and you know it."

I was worried about him, and the news I was about to break when I got back would hit him hard.

"I will think about it when you're back." Every time he came up with an excuse, I thought he secretly enjoyed the amount of work they gave him; it gave him the impression of being a valuable asset.

"Mark, please, at least prepare a resume."

"Okay, okay," he sighed. I knew he wouldn't. He cleared his throat. "What are you going to do today?"

"We're going to a roller coaster park. Ann, me, and her neighbors: Jack, John, and Ian."

"You're going with three men?"

"Jack and John are married, and Ian is their nine-year-old son."

Mark paused. "Do you mean they are gay?" he asked, a tinge of amusement in his voice.

"Yes," I replied, my voice getting a bit protective.

We didn't have any gay friends at home. Mark was open minded, but he had never really talked to a gay person. Well, it appeared he lived with a bisexual woman, which was close. But he still had no idea.

Mark whistled. "And how are they? Did you meet them already?" he asked.

"Yes, and they are the sweetest couple. You would like them." I didn't know anyone who wouldn't.

He paused. "Julie, I miss you so much. Thank God you will be home soon."

I took a deep breath. Yes, I'd be back soon. But it meant leaving Ann, which was like a knife blow to my heart. I knew I would leave my heart with her and take my body back to the Ukraine to hurt the person I cared about.

"Don't worry, I'll be back soon." I knew I sounded like

a jerk not saying I missed him. I did miss him, but it was now more like missing a brother.

"Have a great day today. I know how you love the rides. Ride the scariest and send me pictures," he chuckled. "I'm going to bed now."

"Good night, Mark."

"Bye." He hung up. I dropped my head in my hands. This was difficult, the lie, and I knew the breakup would be raw. He was so used to me, so comfortable, that he would laugh off my love for Ann.

The bedroom door creaked slightly. I turned my head, and there was Ann standing in the doorway. She was wrapped in a towel, her face worried.

"How was it?" she asked.

"He misses me, but I don't really miss him. He wants me back, but I don't want to go back. He can feel something isn't right. He's working his head off for that stupid firm, and in a few days, I will break his heart."

Ann stepped closer and took a deep breath, her eyebrows drawing together. "I am so sorry."

"This is the right thing, I know, I can feel it." I put my hand to my heart. "But Mark and I have a history together, and it will be difficult for both of us. Later he will make sense of it, especially when he is holding the baby he has dreamed about. He will forgive me. And I just can't stay with him when I am in love with another person …"

I froze. I said it. Ann looked at me wide eyed.

She put a hand on the side of my face, gently pulling me up.

"I heard that another person is head over heels in love with you." Ann smiled. "I am sorry you will be hurt when you break up with him, and I wish I could help you. I can go back with you if you want."

"Thanks, but I need to sort it out myself."

"I knew you'd say that," Ann said, tracing my earlobe with her fingers.

"But you can help me now," I replied, tugging on the corner of her towel and dropping it to the floor. She stood completely naked in front of me. The view hitched my breath, her beautiful body, the softest forms. I couldn't stop myself from cupping her breast in my hand. She looked directly at me, not moving. My Goddess.

"You said another person likes me." I squeezed her gently.

"Yes," she murmured, "very much." Ann was holding my gaze.

I touched her inner thigh, slowly tracing her skin up. Her breathing quickened, and the rise and fall of her chest became more prominent. Her lips parted, but still she looked straight at me.

"You said you are in love with me," she whispered.

I moved closer and put my lips close to her ear.

"Yes, Ann, I am so deeply in love with you that sometimes I can't breathe." And I slid my finger inside her. She inhaled sharply. I put another arm around her, gently pressing her into my body. As I moved my fingers inside her, I said, "I want to be with you every moment of my life. I want to stay close."

Ann moaned lightly, and she trembled beneath my hands.

"Your body is the most exquisite thing I have ever seen," I whispered in her ear. "Your soul is kind and clear, and your mind is sharp." She was so hot, her body was moving in my arms, her breath ragged. I held her when she cried from pleasure, I held her when she stopped. I whispered, "I love you, Ann." And I pressed her closer with both of my arms.

"Julie," she said, her voice breaking, and she kissed me.

That kiss showed what she wanted to say. It was the most tender, open feeling. I felt her heart beating close to mine. And the wave of happiness that engulfed us made us stronger.

We were packed in Jack's enormous SUV. The back row of seats was reserved for us. The middle row was Ian's. Jack had prepared a basket of snacks for us, as well. I'd never been so at ease with the people I barely knew. Jack hugged me when we reached their house.

"When she is with you, she's glowing," he said, smiling and looking at Ann, who stood aside speaking to John. "Thank you," he added, his eyes filling with tears. He blinked fast and squeezed my arm.

When we climbed into the car, Jack snapped a photo of all of us from the front seat. Everyone was beaming, including Ian, and that boy always had such a serious old-man expression.

"Julie, tell us more about Ukraine," John suggested with a grin.

I moved closer to the front row; the car was so long it felt like I needed to shout from the rear seats.

"Your people are sure showing the world strength, loyalty and heroism," Jack sighed.

I nodded. "Ukrainians are completely different. They are protective, resilient and extremely strong-minded. Let's take for example the first meeting between people. Americans are open and mostly smiling, while at home people are more reserved. The difference is that at home when you meet a person, you don't trust them at all, and that person needs to prove that he is trustworthy. Here, I think people tend to see the positive in each other from the beginning, and then a person can lose someone's trust by doing something bad. Ukrainians are grumpier and more serious around strangers."

"I am like the Ukrainians," Ian said.

The car erupted with laughter.

"Yes, you are," I chuckled. "And their way of life is completely different. People mostly live in apartments they own. Some rent, but most try to buy them. Ukrainians love to show off, driving a car they can't afford, wearing name-brand clothes that are super expensive there and cheap here."

"What about the restaurants?" Jack asked.

"Because of high competition in recent years, many new coffee shops, cafes, and restaurants were opened. Each one tries to attract customers by maintaining the highest standards: The food, the design of a place, and the service is extremely high quality. And compared to the US, prices are much lower. So, in Kyiv, there is a huge number of stylish places, and I would say it's a nice place for gastro tourism. And there are a variety of bars. For example, there is one where bartenders and waiters are dressed as nurses, and shots are served in test tubes. If you want to order an extreme cocktail, one of the nurses can put a shot in a syringe and help you drink it."

"Sounds crazy," Jack laughed.

"I would love to visit Kyiv," Ann said, and I looked at her, trying to imagine her in my home city. It was an image I would love to see.

"What are your plans after this?" John asked.

"Julie flies back home the day after tomorrow." Ann took my hand in hers and squeezed lightly. "And then we are going to arrange her transfer to the Barcelona office."

She glanced at me with her huge ocean eyes, and I nodded.

"We want her to spend some time closer to Ukraine, so Julie won't be far from her family," she continued.

"We will give Barcelona a year," I said. "Then we'll see."

"Will your management be okay with your transfer, Ann?" John asked, always focused on business.

"They will be happy for me to go somewhere. They have been asking me to choose an office I would like to go to so I can help them with their growth."

Sitting here in the car going to the adventure park, the endless highway winding in front of us, the cars speeding along, the hills on the horizon; I kept forgetting that Ann was at the top at Benzon. She was an important figure.

"Julie, what about you? Will they allow you to transfer?" Jack asked.

"I am a graphic designer, and I can do my tasks anywhere. We don't have a lot of meetings and when we do, I can be connected online. One of my colleagues has been working from an island in Thailand for a year now. And my manager said that my colleague's productivity grew compared to him sitting in the office. So, I can either work remotely or in the office in Barcelona. I think I will stay with my current team."

"Ann always wanted to live outside of the US," Jack said. "I'm glad you're doing it."

The park was looming in the distance. A track the height of a skyscraper bent straight into the sky, a slithering ride curled in mind-bending arcs and an immense tower loomed in the middle, smaller loopy rides looking lost between the giants. Ann caught sight of me gaping and giggled.

"I can't understand you people," she said, shaking her head.

"It's your choice, but you are missing a lot of fun and

adrenaline," John chided, waving a dismissive hand with a grin.

When we entered the park, they showed me the craziest rides. While Ann was waiting down on the ground, Jack, John, and Ian created a tour for me, starting with the easiest and ending with the highest and fastest. There weren't a lot of people in the park, so we didn't have to wait in long lines.

In two hours, my head started pounding because of the pressure from the rides. Jack and John didn't seem to notice it, as they were always saying go-go-go. I remembered Ann mentioning that they had bodies like astronauts. I took an aspirin, which quickly helped, and we went on to the next one.

This one looked like a big hammer with seats placed in a circle. The circle rotated, and the hammer swung. It didn't look scary or fast. Jack and John decided to skip it and stay with Ann. I was pretty excited, so Ian kept me company.

We took our seats, and Ian's legs dangled in the air. He was small for his age. Jack waved, and Ann gave me a dazzling smile.

"You know," Ian said, "I have known Ann almost all my life, and I have never seen her this happy."

I turned to him, and he was looking intently at Ann.

"She always had this sadness in her. Daddy said it's because her parents left her. You know, my birth parents left me too." Ian shifted his gaze directly at me, his clear green eyes searching my face.

I nodded.

"But I have my family now. We found each other, and now I am not alone. But Ann, she was always alone. We take care of her, but it's not the same. With you, she is blooming and always smiling. Please don't leave her." He was so sincere.

"Why would I leave her?" I asked, furrowing my brows.

"I don't know, people sometimes leave. So please don't leave her," he repeated.

Ian cared so much. I stared at him, and my eyes stung. This boy knew things little boys should not know. He knew about being abandoned and the power of family and healing.

"I won't. I will stay close to her as long as she wants me to," I said.

"Promise?"

"I promise," I agreed with a nod.

Ian reached out a hand for me to shake. I stared at it, a small, pale palm. I took it, and we shook. His eyes never left my face.

"You are a good person. I like you," Ian said. "But my dad says I need to protect people I care about."

The seats shook under us, and we started moving. My jaw still hung open from this encounter. Ann caught my eye and burst out laughing. I assumed they saw us shaking hands. I liked this little guy; he was like an adult trapped in a child's body. Even now when we swung quite high, he was sitting firmly with the faintest smile on his lips.

I let go of the railing, took my feet off the panel, and let the force of movement sway me. In a moment, Ian did the same. He turned to me and smiled. For a few seconds, we didn't feel a gravity pull, and we both giggled.

When we reached Jack and John's house, full of the snacks that had been waiting for us in the car, it was dark already. Ian grabbed his tablet from the car seat and ran inside.

"Let me show you something." John beckoned Ann and me to the closed garage door. He pressed the key, and the door started moving up. Inside was huge. There was an empty space for the SUV, and a shining black Mercedes sedan stood in the middle. A smaller car was hidden under the cover in the far corner. John reached it and pulled down the fabric. It was a silver BMW vintage convertible. I whistled. I was not a car expert, but this one was a true beauty.

"It's your last day here tomorrow," he said, turning to me. "Take this rusty thing for a ride." He threw the keys to Ann, who caught them.

"But …" she looked at John wide eyed, "are you sure?"

"Sure, it needs some fresh air."

"Thank you," Ann said in a shaky voice. She pressed the keys to her chest and tipped her head to the side, watching him closely.

"Thank you, John," I chimed.

Jack stepped closer to John and hugged him. I noticed how John breathed in softly and burrowed his face in Jack's neck. His hands were slightly shaking.

We said good night and thanked them for the day.

"Tell Ian bye from us," I said, my chest expanding from the feeling of a connection with this family.

"I will." Jack winked.

We took our bags and went to Ann's house. When we were inside, I dropped my things and turned to Ann. She was standing in the doorway, looking at the keys in her hand.

I moved closer to her.

"I assume this is an important car?" I asked.

"It was John's father's car. He died last year from coronary artery disease. They built it together. His father had it shipped from Germany, and it arrived rusty and neglected. John spent years rebuilding it with his father. After his father died, John couldn't drive it. There were too many memories. It has been standing in his garage for a year."

"Oh." That was all I could say as I rubbed my neck. "Did you know John's father?"

"Yes, he was a wonderful man. It hit John pretty hard. Thank God Jack and Ian were there every minute for him. It helped him stay away from a deep well of depression. John doesn't remember his mother well, as she died when he was four-year-old. His dad was everything to him."

"I hope it will help John to see the car on the road tomorrow," I said.

The garage door stood open in the morning. Jack and John had left for work, and Ian was at school. It still amazed me how you could leave your things open and nobody would take anything. But this neighborhood was a closed one, so it was doubly secure.

Ann reached the car, tracing its hood with her fingers.

"I always dreamed of driving it. Wait till you hear how it purrs."

There was a note on the steering wheel. "*Have a great trip! We love you!*"

We packed sandwiches and blankets and then took our seats in the car. Ann was looking with awe at the panel. It was vintage, with beautiful old brown leather. She put the key in the ignition.

"Are you ready?" She smiled at me.

I nodded. The engine revved, making my eyes go wide. "Wow, it's loud."

For me, it sounded like a massive muscle car, and it was unusual for such a small convertible.

"Custom-made." Ann grinned.

We rolled out of the garage. The road was clear as we moved in the direction of Malibu. Ann pressed the gas pedal, and we were pushed back into our seats from the thrust of speed. This car was a true beast hidden in the body of a princess.

Ann was concentrating on the road; she was enjoying it so much. I was enjoying her, her dark hair disheveled from the wind, a smile on her full lips, and her pale skin glistening from the sun. She noticed me watching her, took my hand in hers, and kissed it. Then she dropped my hand and shifted the gear. Of course it was manual.

The ocean appeared between the hills. I was in awe of the dazzling blue, the roar of the engine, the wind in my ears, and the speed.

I closed my eyes. I couldn't shake the feeling that it would all end soon. Soon, I'd be back home, in the grey drizzle, and this would be just a dream. Ann was my sweet dream. I opened my eyes and looked around. I was still here. Ann was still by my side. I let out a deep breath.

We parked by the ocean. The parking lot was almost empty since it was during the week, and it was a bit chilly out, but the sun warmed my skin. We took the stairs down to the beach. Empty. Huge boulders were scattered here and there.

We walked in silence for a few minutes.

"I don't want to leave tomorrow," I admitted, stopping to look at Ann. "I have this crazy thought that all of this isn't real, that you are not real. And that the moment I leave you, it will all be gone."

"Don't," Ann said, pressing two fingers to my lips. "What we have is real." She touched my cheek, tracing my brow. "We will see each other in two weeks, and if not, I will come to Kyiv and stay with you. Now that I found you, I intend on keeping you close, here." She smiled and put a hand to her heart. "Always."

I kissed her, and she kissed me back. Our movements were desperate; we were trying to feel as much as possible before our separation. My hands roamed her body, her hair, and her sweet scent domineered all my senses.

I took her hand and led her to a huge boulder. Behind it was a small space between the hill and the rock. The sun was up high shining directly onto this small cove, making it warm. Here, we were hidden from the outside world. We dropped to the sand, finding it was cold, but our bodies were on fire. We were a mess of limbs, of sounds.

"I love you," I kept whispering, "I love you, I love you, I love you."

Ann covered my lips with hers. She kissed my body, leaving a burning trail after each kiss, and I could see our future together. Looking in her blue eyes, I knew that we could make it work. And I felt that this was real.

We tried to shake the sand from our hair and clothes. It would be barbaric to sit in the car this way, leaving the sand literally everywhere. We giggled while trying to get rid of it.

After our encounter, we strolled down the beach, just by the water's edge. Ann said that on Monday she would speak with her boss about transferring to Barcelona.

"He will ask how long I want to stay there," she said.

"A year?" I asked.

She raised a brow. "And then?"

"Back here," I replied simply.

Ann stopped walking and turned to me. "Really?"

"I love it here. And I don't want to take you away from the people you love. A year is quite a long time. I know that it's not the same when you visit as a tourist compared to living here, but I think I'll manage." I grinned. "Of course, only if you want me to," I added.

Ann was smiling. "I love how you see us together in the future."

"Don't you?" I asked.

"I see us growing old together," she laughed.

We resumed walking, hiding our smiles.

"I will speak with my team manager on Monday as well. I assume she will be fine with everything. As long as I am online for weekly meetings, and since the time difference between Barcelona and Kyiv is small, there won't be any problem. LA to Kyiv is more of a problem regarding time difference, but we'll figure it out closer to the date."

It appeared that Benzon probably would finance Ann's stay in Barcelona by providing her with a flat. The plan sounded easy enough, except the part where I needed to break up with Mark. I tried to hide this realization from myself. But a nail dug deep into my heart every time I imagined his face.

When we reached Jack and John's house, they heard the noise and stepped outside to meet us. There were tears in John's eyes, but he was smiling.

Ann parked the car in the garage.

"How was it?" Jack asked, stepping closer to us.

"Amazing." Her face was radiant. "It drives even better than I imagined. We might have left some sand on the seats though. Let me come by and clean it tomorrow."

Jack peeped inside the car. We tried to shake off the sand, but some had stuck. It wasn't really bad.

"How did you like it?" John asked me.

"I wasn't expecting it to sound like that," I laughed. "But thank you for letting us use it. It really made our day. Please do not hide this beauty in the garage; it should ride and shine."

"We might take a short trip on Sunday," Jack beamed.

Ann looked at John and stood on her tiptoes to hug him.

"I guess I will see you the next time I'm here." It was time to say goodbye. My flight was early tomorrow, so we would head to the airport in the middle of the night.

"It was a pleasure to meet you, Julie," Jack said, smiling. He stepped closer and enveloped me in a bear hug. He smelled of a pleasant men's cologne, bergamot. "Thank you for making Ann happy," he whispered.

"Oh, don't crush the girl," John laughed, and Jack released me. "I hope we will all spend more time together. There are so many adventure parks to visit." He grinned wide, dimples playing on his cheeks, and he hugged me.

I looked at them both, and my eyes stung. They were Ann's family, and they had accepted me from the moment they first met me. I didn't know that saying goodbye to this family would be so hard; my heart was pounding in my chest.

Ian was standing in the doorway. He moved closer and reached out a hand to me. I shook it, but I couldn't stop and hugged the boy. He froze but slowly put his hands around me.

"Remember what you promised," Ian said quietly. "I will be waiting for you to come back here."

I released him, the image blurring. In a few moments, tears would flow.

"Thank you, guys, for everything. And please take care of Ann while I'm away," I told them.

Jack clasped his hands to his chest. His eyes were a little red as well. Ann took my hand in hers and led me back to her house. As soon as the door closed behind us, I hugged Ann, pressing her close to me, tears sliding down my face to her shoulder. With my body shaking, Ann held me tight.

"Everything will be alright," she kept whispering. But I was afraid to leave. I felt as though something would happen, something that would keep me away from her.

Ann searched my face, her lips still swollen from the beach. She slowly kissed my cheek, catching the tears with her lips, brushing my hair with her fingers.

"You have sand in your hair," Ann whispered. "Let's take a shower," she suggested, pulling me to the bathroom. "Together."

Slowly, she unbuttoned my jacket, peeling off the shirt, tugging down on my waistband. In a minute, I was standing naked in front of her, but Ann was still fully clothed. Her eyes fixed on mine, then slowly moved down, taking in my details.

I reached for her shirt and helped her out of it. I unhooked her bra and slid it down. Her full form made me crazy, but still, I didn't touch her. Her nipples hardened under my gaze. I touched the button on her black jeans, unzipped the zipper, and slowly pulled them down. We stood there, breathing hard, not touching. I was mesmerized by the rise and fall of her chest, her ocean-blue eyes taking in my hips.

Ann stepped into the shower and beckoned me in. She turned on the warm water, the rivulets flowing between her shoulders, breasts, and legs. She took a washcloth, applied shower gel, and sweet vanilla scent filled the bathroom. Ann touched it to my arms, rubbing gently. She rubbed my back and my belly, avoiding my breasts and gently touching my inner thighs, but not more.

The need was building inside me like an avalanche, but still, she wouldn't touch me where I burned most. She slipped the washcloth in my hand, and I did the same, slowly tracing her pale skin. She was breathing hard when I was moving down her belly button, but I skipped the part she was longing for me to touch and moved to her hamstrings. A low growl escaped her lips. It took a few moments to wash down the foam.

Ann turned down the water, took a fluffy towel, and led me to the bedroom. She gently pushed me to the bed, with her knee she spread my legs, and eased her finger inside me. I gasped, a sweet sensation spreading through me. I started moving my hips, and she lowered her lips to her finger, going down on me, gently at first, increasing the intensity as her tongue circled, pressing harder.

What she was doing kept me breathless, and I was begging for more, and more, until the wave of an explosive orgasm covered me, my body shaking. Ann kissed my belly and sucked on my breasts and lips. I was panting. She put a hand to my heart; it was hammering in my ribcage.

She propped her head on my arm and asked, "How are you doing?"

I laughed and pressed her down. Now was my turn.

We stayed in bed for a few hours. I just couldn't let her out of my reach, and she kept her arms around me. We laid talking about the past, about the future; we were a tangle of limbs.

"I have a present for you," she said, going to the bathroom.

Ann soon emerged holding a small blue box.

"A little thing for you to remember me."

As if I could forget her. I touched the box, finding it was like smooth velvet under my fingertips. Inside was a ring; it was a starfish with a blue stone in the middle. The stone was the same color as Ann's eyes.

"This is a small part of the ocean to carry with you," she explained.

"It's beautiful, it's …" I was smiling, but tears started to roll down my cheeks again. "Damn it, I just can't stop crying."

I took the ring out of the box and slipped it on my pointer finger. It fit perfectly.

"Thank you," I whispered, looking at my hand, feeling better to have a part of her with me. Ann pressed her lips to mine.

"I will see you soon. I will come whenever you want me to be there."

I glanced at the clock. It was time for me to gather my things, which were still scattered around the house. I kissed Ann and put on my shirt and jeans. I pulled my clothes out of her wardrobe, along with the small presents I had bought for Mom, Dad, Alex, and his wife. They were mostly sports clothes, as my family loved practical gifts. I even found some baby rompers for my brother's son. I wouldn't see him much.

"Ann, have you seen my phone?" I called.

"It's somewhere in the beach bag," she said.

I found the bag at the door. My phone was at the

bottom. I unlocked it and froze. Seventeen calls from Alex, six from Mom, and nine messages, all telling me to call back immediately.

My hands started to shake. Had something happened to Dad? My finger hovered on Mom's ID, but at the last minute it shifted to Alex's number. I hit 'Call'.

"Oh, thank God, finally" he exclaimed. There was an urgency in his voice.

"Alex, what happened?"

"It's Mark. He was hit by a car when he was crossing the road, right by your house."

My knees buckled, ice gripping my chest. "How is he?"

"Not good, but he is conscious. He asked the nurse to call me before they rolled him in the operation room. She said his legs were severely damaged, and they are investigating his spine. There might be something seriously wrong with him. The impact was pretty hard, throwing him across the road."

"Where is he now? What hospital?"

"Central. I'm on my way there."

"Do his parents know?"

"Yes. But they will not be here until the day after tomorrow."

"Oh no, they are on vacation in Egypt ..." I remembered how happy his mom was when on her birthday Mark presented a small pink envelope containing the details of a booked trip to Egypt for them.

"Yes, and there are no flights till tomorrow night," Alex said.

"My flight is tonight, but it takes twenty hours to get to Kyiv."

"I know, Julie. There is nothing more we can do. I will find out everything I can at the hospital and will keep you updated. But hurry, he needs you."

"Yes," I sniffed. "Call me when you know anything."

"Okay, bye."

I slid to the floor, the beach bag at my legs, sand littering the carpet. I was staring at it, tears rolling down my cheeks. Ann exited the bedroom and was moving to the kitchen when she spotted me and my mess on the floor.

She ran to my side, falling to cup my chin, to find my eyes. "What happened?"

"Mark … accident … he is hurt … ambulance," I stuttered.

"Shhh." She pressed me closer. "Tell me."

I tried to explain the little I knew from Alex's call. And then it hit me, I jumped up and ran to my luggage. He needed me. What was I doing here?

I started shoving my clothes in the bag.

"We need to go to the airport," I urged.

"Your flight is in five and a half hours. We need to wait."

"He might die there while I wait!" I screamed.

The hurt slashed across Ann's face. She staggered a step back.

"Sorry." I stopped and dropped my bag, bits of shirts sticking from it. I stepped closer to Ann. "I am so sorry."

And then it hit me.

"Barcelona won't be anytime soon," I whispered.

She nodded. She had analyzed the news faster. While my mind was clouded in panic, she knew.

"And you won't break up with him."

I couldn't do it while he was hurt.

"I need to go back," I said.

Ann nodded again and sat on her bed, her huge eyes never leaving mine.

"Can I go with you?" she asked.

I looked at her. "I need to do it myself," I said, more gentle this time.

She nodded.

"Will you come back to me?" Ann asked so quietly, I almost missed it.

I rushed to her, almost falling when my foot caught my pants on the floor. I grabbed her shoulders and draped my arms around her, crushing her hard to me.

"Of course, I will come back to you," I said, sobbing. "You are mine now, and I am yours. But he needs me."

"Please don't go," she whispered in my hair, her voice breaking. "Please stay. I can't lose you." Her ribcage was heaving next to mine, and she was breathing fast.

I pressed her closer to me. There was not an inch of space between us, but I needed her even closer, under my skin. She needed to know.

"Ann, I love you, and you will not lose me. But please, please …" My voice was closing on me. "Please, wait for me."

"*Wait,*" she whispered back.

Ever since then I wondered, was this the first time the smallest chip of her heart broke? I had broken it. The trust. I was leaving her not to end things with Mark, but to help him.

"You are doing the right thing, and I will wait," she said, after hours or minutes in my arms.

She never moved; she stayed pressed in me, her breathing getting even, but her heart didn't stop hammering, never slowing.

Ann helped me pack my suitcase, staying quiet all the time.

"Do you want to sleep for a few hours before we go?" Ann asked.

"No," I said, leading her to the bed.

She stood there, and her eyes searched my face.

I leaned in and kissed her, and she replied, so tenderly, barely touching my lips.

"I am so afraid of losing you," she whispered.

"I love you," I replied, kissing her jaw, her neck.

"Please come back," she pleaded.

"I will," I murmured in her ear.

She found my lips, the salt of our tears mixing on our tongues.

"I love you," I said again, tugging her with me on the bed.

"I hope it will be enough," she murmured in the hollow of my throat.

The time rushed mercilessly, and I thought only minutes had passed when my alarm blazed. It was time to go. As I was pulling my jeans on, my raw body still buzzing from Ann's touch, I saw her black t-shirt crumpled on the floor. It had a faded Bugs Bunny print. Slowly, I picked it up.

"Can I have it?" I asked.

"Sure," Ann said, smiling. "Why did I think it was a wonderful idea to give you a ring? I could have just given you an old shirt."

Ann's face grew more serious with each passing minute, and she kept glancing at me.

As I was standing by the door, I looked around one more time, touched the wall and stepped through the threshold. We put my bag into the truck. I loved the beast; it had taken us to some amazing moments. Once inside, Ann put the key into the ignition but didn't start the car. She moved closer, her eyes so vulnerable, and I closed the gap between us, pressing my lips to her.

"I love you," I whispered. It was so easy to say it to her now.

"I love you, Julie," she said, pressing her forehead to mine, her hand in my hair.

She took a deep breath and looked in front of her, turned the key, and backed out of the driveway.

In the airport, Ann held my hand the whole time we stood in the drop-off line. Getting rid of the bag, we went to buy coffee. We still had half an hour. But it was difficult; the separation time loomed on the horizon. And now we didn't know the next time we would see each other. I was worried about Mark, since messages from Alex kept saying that he was still in the operating room.

The airport was almost empty, as there were not many flights this early. And as the time trickled through our shaking fingers, just like that, it was time to go. We reached the security check gate, and my eyes clouded with tears again.

Ann hugged me, our bodies finding each other, clicking together.

"I will see you very soon," she murmured desperately.

"Yes." My voice was shaking, and I turned my face to find her lips. The softness of her turned to hunger, but now our time was up. My heart hammering, I traced the line of her face, trying to memorize it under my fingertips. "Bye," I whispered.

"Bye."

I watched her while I took my things out at the security check. She waved and smiled, but I had never seen her eyes so sad. And then there was a bend, our eyes locked for the last time, and she was gone.

Chapter 24

ANN

I found my way back to the car, putting one foot in front of the other, stepping through the dense fog of my grief. When I climbed inside and locked the door, I crumbled, fat tears rolled down my cheeks.

She was gone. I knew it was temporary, but still it hurt like hell. The woman I grew to love with all my heart during the last ten days was flying away from me. It felt like a big part of my heart was being sliced away with a dull knife, each cutting stroke echoed in my chest.

She's gone, she's gone, she's gone.

I dropped my head on the wheel, my body shaking from the sobs.

Chapter 25

$\mathcal{A}$s soon as I cleared the security check, I found my gate. I still had half an hour before boarding. I shuffled to the farthest corner by the window and hid my face by looking outside. I couldn't calm myself down; my nose was running, and tears were sliding down my cheeks. I opened the photo app on my phone and scrolled through ones I had taken on the trip. I stopped at the selfie of Ann and me in bed, the morning sun glowing on our faces, happy. I knew she was not far, but soon I would be putting thousands of miles between us.

While I was looking at the photo, I touched my ring. I needed to be strong, for Ann, for Mark, for myself. Mark was unconscious somewhere in the operating room, and I needed to break up with him. The dull pain in the back of my head started every time I thought about it. It wouldn't be easy to do.

A woman announced the boarding call. I took a few deep breaths. There was no way to hide my puffy eyes, but at least I had managed to stop crying.

My seat was by the window, and the first thing I

wanted to do was cover my face with the blanket and hide inside my pain, wailing silently. Or I wanted to just drop everything and run back to her.

A man in his forties sat beside me. He was wearing a dark, expensive suit. Who wears a suit on a thirteen-hour flight? He opened his laptop and dove into some kind of report. Good, no polite talking from him.

I gazed out the window. There was a swarm of workers doing last-minute checks, loading the plane with provisions, and pumping the fuel in.

Finally, everyone was on board. I looked at my ring and typed a text message to Ann, a simple "I love you," and switched off the phone.

Three simple words, tossed around everywhere in the world. Meaning everything to one, meaning nothing to another. How could I write down in a text message what I felt?

I stroked the stone on the starfish and closed my eyes, seeing her eyes in front of me. The woman that turned my world upside down, who made me question my beliefs, my sexuality, and my needs. But with her, my puzzle clicked right and finished. Before I was lost, my wishes disregarded, and now, I found myself, found *me* in her arms. A wave of gratitude swallowed me, the wave of knowing that wherever I went, I would always be looking for her.

I closed my eyes when the plane climbed up, high into the white clouds. I thought about the last ten days and realized that only two months ago I didn't know that I would meet the love of my life soon, and that the love of my life would be a woman. I didn't know that it was possible to feel this kind of closeness, this unity. I could almost touch the energy pulsing between us. I didn't know this level of passion existed, this selfless feeling of doing everything for another person.

I knew we could make it work. This was not a flicker of a relationship, not a spark—it was here, and it burnt in the moment. It would grow to something even bigger and stronger, stronger than both of us. I knew what I felt. And I had asked her to wait for me.

I passed time watching thrillers, trying to take my mind off already missing Ann and worrying about Mark. How was he? When could he let me go?

When we finally landed in Frankfurt, I had managed to get a few hours of restless sleep between watching three movies I didn't remember any details of and eating lots of plane food.

I had a forty-minute connection, which was pretty short for such a big airport. As soon as we landed, I switched on the data on my iPhone. A message from Ann pinged, a reply to mine from thirteen hours ago. "You are my life now."

The warmth spread inside me. I sent her a message saying that I was rushing to my connecting flight.

I called Alex.

"Hi, how is he?"

"Yesterday the visiting hours ended, and they asked me to leave. He was still in the operating room, and since then I haven't heard any news from the hospital. I am on my way there."

My hands trembled.

"Do you think he's alright?" I asked.

"Yesterday they said that there was no danger to his life, that his legs were severely damaged, but they checked everything else, saying that as far as they could see, everything was stable. And I assume since there was no news, everything's okay."

"I can be in the hospital in four hours. I'll go straight from the airport."

"I will meet you there," Alex said.

When I rushed to the next gate, boarding had already started.

The two-and-a-half-hour flight was slow. I tried to read, but I kept rereading the same passage three times, so I listened to music. Images of Ann's eyes kept appearing in my mind, her smile and her lips on my skin. The latest album by a popular band played on repeat in her house, and scenes it conjured in my mind made me blush.

But what about Mark? I betrayed him already, I cheated on him, I was ready to break up with him, and now what? The guilt of my actions pressed me down like the changing gravity in the plane. I didn't want to do it, to face him, to put on a hypocritical smile while all the while I wanted to say goodbye and run back to Ann.

When we landed, I grabbed my bag and moved down the aisle, turning on my phone. Some messages from my brother immediately started pinging.

"He is semi-conscious, and he needs you," a message from Alex said.

"I will be there as fast as I can. I only just exited the plane. If you see him first, please say I am on my way."

I rushed down the corridor to the passport control area. Not many people were in line, and lots of windows were open. I got my passport checked in five minutes and rushed to the baggage claim. It was silent, and the belt wasn't moving. I stepped aside and eased myself onto a bench. I looked around at the familiar airport; I was home. My wanting to leave Mark didn't mean that I had stopped caring about him, and now he was hurt. *Cheat*, my mind whispered. I pushed the thought away. Where were those damn bags? The belt still wasn't moving. I prayed Mark was okay. I started hyperventilating, wishing Ann was by my side. But when would I see her again? My Ann.

Finally, the belt moved, delivering my bag in three minutes. I snatched it and rushed outside. The cold hit my nostrils; I had gotten used to the LA warmth. My hands were shaking uncontrollably, and I couldn't unlock the phone. Fat tears were sliding down my face again. I managed to get an Uber, as fortunately the driver was already there.

In the taxi, I tried to calm myself. During the flight, it all seemed unreal, as if it was not happening to me. And now seeing the familiar landscape and the streets, it hit me. I was in love with a person whom I had left miles away, and I was heading to help my boyfriend recover, how twisted was that? Mark needed me, and he needed me to be strong, not a crying lovesick girl.

It felt like hours; the car was crawling in the dense traffic in the center of the city. Eventually, we reached the hospital. I grabbed my huge trolley bag and rushed inside. At the reception area, a woman eyed my bag and said that Mark was still in the recovery room, and she asked me to sit in the waiting area. I called Alex, finding he was there already, in the waiting room. I stumbled toward him, catching other people's legs with my luggage, murmuring sorry, stopping in front of him. Alex was just a little taller than me, his light brown hair a mess, needing a haircut, but his eyes, just a copy of mine, scanned my red puffy face.

"Come here," he said, enveloping me in his arms. His familiar smell made me remember where I was, at home. But home now meant being far away from Ann.

"How is he?" I asked.

"They didn't say much, but both of his legs are broken."

Oleg, Mark's friend, was rushing to the reception area. I called out to him. He saw my face, and his expression fell. We told him we did not know anything yet. He hugged me awkwardly.

"He will be alright," Oleg promised. "You know, he was preparing a welcome home party for you."

"Oh," was all I could say, my chest tightening.

Two more of Mark's friends joined us, Igor and Victor. We all sat in silence, my head resting on Alex's shoulder. After what seemed like years, but in reality was only hours, the nurse called us.

"We took scans and operated on his left leg and hip. The bones were shattered in eight places. His right leg is also broken. He will experience some extreme pain, and his knee was displaced," she said. Each word dropped like a stone in my hollow chest. He was hurt, badly.

"What all this means is that he won't be walking any time soon. He will need to stay in bed. The recovery period will take a minimum of six months, and he will need constant care."

My body started shaking, and Alex's tightened his grip around me. If it wasn't for him, my knees would have buckled, and I would have fallen. I felt like I was falling already, along with all my plans for the future. Every sentence she said was like a hit in my gut. I just couldn't breathe.

"But the bright side is that his spine isn't damaged. The scans didn't show anything we should worry about. His legs took all the impact. And his head, while he hit it pretty badly, has no internal bleeding. Everything is fine on the scans. We will keep an eye on him, but as far as we can see, he is lucky."

I whimpered and covered my mouth with my hand. I was thankful to hear the word *lucky*.

"Will he be able to walk?" I asked the question everyone had in their mind.

"Eventually, yes, but it will be a long and painful process. In the beginning, he will only be able to lie in bed. He will need the help of a physiotherapist every day for the first months."

She said that he would stay in the hospital for two to three weeks, and then when he got home, he would need constant care for the first couple of months.

He needed me, and again I hated myself for thinking about myself in these moments, for feeling like I was trapped here. What kind of shitty person was I?

Igor kept asking questions. He had a medical education and was now working as a dentist. They kept repeating medical terms I couldn't understand.

"Can I see him?" I interrupted.

"One person can; he is still unconscious. But he will start to wake up soon, and it would be nice for him to see a familiar face. Please wait here, and I will call you."

And she left. We all stood there in silence.

"Do you want to change? I can take your bag to your flat, since I am not allowed to see him," Alex asked me.

Alex loved Mark. They had become close friends, and the accident hit Alex hard, but he was being calm for me, keeping up a strong appearance.

I pulled a few things from the bag, changed as fast as I could in the dingy hospital bathroom, hid the ring deep in my purse, and hugged Alex goodbye.

"Thank you."

The nurse appeared and called me. As we were walking down the corridor, she said, "His face is pretty bruised, so don't be shocked. The swelling will come down in a few days."

I nodded. We reached the white door with '112' on it, and the nurse pushed it open for me. I stepped inside.

The walls were white, and a big window showed the backyard of the hospital with trees and a small park in the heart of the bustling city.

Mark was lying on the white sheets. I gasped when I saw his face: bruises under both eyes, his nose was swollen, and the left side was dark purple. There was a big scratch on his forehead. The face that I loved, the face that had studied me every morning for the past three years, the face I kissed and the lips that kissed me back was all damaged to a point beyond recognition, and I couldn't imagine the pain Mark was feeling.

I heard the nurse leave the room, quietly closing the door.

Tears pooled in the corners of my eyes as I stepped closer to him. His right hand seemed to be the usual color, as all the impact had come on the left side. I touched his right hand, finding it was cold, so I put my hand around his, trying to make it warmer. Now I was crying in full force, tears sliding down my cheeks to the white sheets.

It seemed like I had started crying in LA and hadn't stopped till this moment. Maybe I knew? Maybe it was some kind of premonition that none of my plans with Ann had a chance of being completed. I felt that something terrible was going to happen. It *was* too good to be true.

Now Mark needed me, and I would be here for him. It was time to pull myself together. His left leg was in a cast that formed a huge bulk under the blanket. His right leg was partially covered, as the doctors had managed to adjust it. The room was bare, lifeless, and he would spend weeks here. I needed to bring something to make it cozier, to make it less lonely.

Mark started to stir, his right hand squeezed mine lightly, and eyes slowly opened and fixed on mine.

"You're here," he croaked.

"Of course I'm here." *Here*, and would be staying *here*. I pushed the thoughts of Ann away. "How are you feeling? Do you remember what happened?"

The nurse said he had a massive dose of painkillers in his system, so he would feel disoriented at first.

"I …" he started and looked at his left hand, which was bruised and covered in scratches. His eyes moved to his legs. "I feel numb. I remember a red car rushing towards me, the screech of brakes, and then the impact. I woke up in an ambulance," he said slowly, trying to remember. Mark lifted his undamaged arm and wanted to touch his face.

"Careful," I warned.

He winced, touching his nose. "What did the doctors say?"

"You will need time to recover, but eventually you will be as good as new. Let me call the doctor and he will explain," I said standing.

"Wait, how are you here?"

"Apparently you said to call Alex in the ambulance. He contacted me, and I came here straight from the airport. Oleg, Victor and Igor came to see you also, but they are not allowed in."

"You should have been here tomorrow." His eyes clouded. "How long was I out?"

"Alex called me when I was still in LA, five hours before my flight. So, roughly twenty-four hours."

"I don't remember anything, just that I was headed to the craft store to buy you those balloons, the golden ones you liked at somebody's birthday party, and then the red car, a clip from the ambulance, and then darkness." He looked around the blank walls, and his gaze wandered to my face. "Julie, I missed you so much."

Tears pooled in my eyes again. I pressed his hand to my lips.

"I will be with you, don't worry. We will get you up and running again," I promised. He was looking at me; the realization of the level of injury hadn't hit him yet. "And I missed you." This was only partially a lie. I missed him as a friend, and I dreaded the minute when I would need to talk to him. Right now, it was not a problem. The big conversation had moved to the future indefinitely.

I stood up and reached the door. "I will be back in a minute."

I found the nurse in the corridor standing with the doctor, a middle-aged man with grey hair. His tired eyes fixed on me when I reached them.

"He's awake," I told them.

"Good," said the doctor before going into Mark's room.

They asked him questions, but being on painkillers, he couldn't assess where and how it hurt yet. They explained the recovery process, with Mark's eyes getting darker when he realized the volume of the damage.

"When will I be able to run again?"

Mark had become an avid morning runner during the last year, and he was preparing for his first full marathon this spring.

"Probably not earlier than a year."

And now it sunk in. His eyes widened in horror and darted between mine, the doctor's, and the nurse's face.

"You will need to stay here in bed, immobilized for three weeks, and then we'll see. How your bones grow back together will determine when you will start physical therapy. Basically, you will need to learn to walk again," the doctor continued, and Mark's face fell. "But the good news is that your spine and all the nerves are well. You are lucky that only the bones took the hit."

They continued talking, but the nurse steered me away.

"Visiting hours end in fifteen minutes. Please come back tomorrow." She gave me a list of essentials to bring to Mark.

"Will he be okay today?"

"He needs to rest. We will give him more painkillers, and he'll just sleep."

They left us, the nurse pointing to her wristwatch and mouthing, "Fifteen minutes." Mark was staring at me.

"So, I feel nothing now, but the pain will be pretty intense after the medicine wears off, and three weeks of lying in bed. Shit." He tried to rub his eyes, but his face was sore, and he jerked the hand back.

I perched on the side of his bed.

"You'll make it," I said. Mark's eyes were lost and scared. "Mark, look at me."

His eyes were fixed on the window. He slowly moved his head and stared at me. This was the moment I realized I needed to stop wallowing in my own self-pity and help the man I still loved in a different way. He was lost lying on the bed, his body severely broken. I grabbed his good hand.

"Listen to me, you are going to be fine. I am so sorry this happened." I pressed his hand to my cheek. "But we will get you out of here. Thank God your spine and nerves are tough, so we will need to focus on your legs. I am here, and I will be here with you as long as they allow me to be. You are strong." I studied his face, trying to convey a message. "It's just temporary. And look at the bright side, your job was killing you lately, and now you have time to rest. You said you were working so much you didn't have a minute to look up, and now you will have the time. I know it's lame, sorry, but you always taught me to see the bright side, and I never saw it. So, it's my turn to help you see it."

His gaze was still a bit cloudy, as the medicine was working hard to dull the pain, but he was listening to me, a small smile tugging his lips.

"I guess you are right, nothing major, just broken bones. We will get over it." He tried to laugh. I hoped he believed what he was saying. "I need to call my boss," he said, the words slurring on the edges, work was always on his mind.

"Oleg already called him," I explained. Oleg was working with Mark on the same project. "One good thing about your dreadful job is that they have immaculate medical insurance. Your boss said to take your time."

I guess he didn't know how much time it would take.

"I think I could work remotely when I am a bit stronger."

"We will see later. Now you need to rest. The nurse told me that I need to leave at 7 p.m., the end of visiting hours. I'll be back tomorrow morning. And your parents are on the way."

Mark's face fell, and it cracked my heart a little.

"Oh, they were on vacation," he struggled to remember.

"Don't worry, you'll just sleep through the night, and we'll be here first thing in the morning. One more positive thing," I said with a wink, "you'll finally have a good night's rest. With all the drugs they are going to give you, you'll sleep like a baby."

His eyelids were heavy. I thought he was trying to stay awake, but all the news had sucked the energy from him. I kissed his cheek.

"I love you, Julie," he murmured.

"Love you too," I replied. He needed to hear those words from me. "Sleep well and get stronger."

Mark smiled and closed his eyes. I picked up my jacket and left the room, gently closing the door. The corridor was empty. I pressed my back to the door, and my strength left me. I tried to stay positive with Mark, but I was exhausted. Between the long, nervous flight and the news of Mark's accident, I was drained. I took a shaky breath and dragged my feet to the waiting area.

Oleg, Igor, and Victor were huddled in the corner, and they stood when they saw me.

"How is he?" Victor asked, their faces hopeful.

"He doesn't feel anything because of painkillers. His leg and hip are in a huge cast with metal nails going deep into his skin. The doctor said that it's his legs that took the hit. His spine and head are well, thank God. He has bruises on his face, but they are not serious and will heal fast according to the nurse."

I told them everything the doctor had told me, and we all moved to the exit. It was dark outside, the wind crawling inside my jacket. I desperately wanted to get home. My Uber finally arrived, and I said goodbyes to guys and climbed in. The warmth inside the car made me realize how cold I was, since I was still in my LA jacket that was too thin for the early Kyiv spring.

I had seen messages from Ann when I called for my Uber, but I didn't want to open them in front of Mark's friends. Now I opened my Messenger app, and there were two unread messages from Ann.

"I guess you are on the way to the hospital. Stay strong."

"How's Mark? How are you? Miss you."

I had landed five hours previously, but it seemed like a lifetime ago.

I typed: "I will call you in twenty minutes. I am OK."

"OK," she replied almost instantly. I opened the Photo app and started scrolling through our photos, the tears choking me again. I missed her so much already, and it had only been twenty-four hours since we parted in the airport.

Finally, the taxi reached my street. I asked the driver to stop in the middle of the road and climbed out. Only a day ago, the red car was speeding here, hitting Mark and nearly killing him. Now the street was silent, with only the light of my Uber blinking, the vehicle hiding the adjoining street. The warm light spilled outside from the apartments, showing glimpses of life inside. A woman by the stove, football match on the huge TV, a teenager by the window with the tablet, and a woman smoking on the balcony. I tugged my jacket closer and sped to the building entrance.

Once inside the apartment, I found my bag standing in the corner. I'd need to call Alex and say thank you later.

I then shuffled to the bathroom. What I saw in the mirror shouldn't have surprised me; I had a haunted look, red eyes, blotches on my skin from constant crying, and dark circles under my eyes. I washed my face with cold water, hoping it would help to subdue the redness.

My stomach growled, and I remembered that the last time I had a proper meal was on the flight from LA to Frankfurt. Well, the resemblance to a proper meal, as far as airplane food could be normal.

I opened the fridge and saw numerous boxes inside. Mark had ordered food from the restaurant for his dinner, as he probably hadn't been in the mood for cooking while I was away, so he ordered take out from our favorite Italian pizzeria. I noticed a bag on the table that had the restaurant's logo on it. The bag contained the focaccia. I took a bite and sat on the kitchen windowsill.

My hands shook, and I unlocked the phone. Ann's

happy face was smiling at me, the photo I looked at in the taxi. I took a deep breath and called her. She picked up after the first ring.

"Julie," she breathed. "How are you?"

"Hi." Her voice made my heart flutter. "I am fine, just bone-tired. I was at the hospital, he looked ..." I paused, "Ann, his body is broken, his legs ... there are more metal parts than his skin."

"Oh," she sighed. Ann knew what it meant for us.

"He needs me; I am his only thread to his previous life. I can't leave him now." I clutched my neck, as my throat was closing, making it difficult to speak.

"I know," Ann said. "I knew it all was too good to be true," she laughed bitterly.

"Damn, I hate it. I hate that Mark is hurt, I hate that I am here and you are thousands of miles away. All I want to do is to crawl back into your arms back to your house, in your bed, buried in your white sheets and for none of this to have happened. And I hate that I don't know how long I will have to stay here."

Finally, my tears subsided, and now I was just empty. Mark didn't deserve it; he shouldn't be in the hospital.

"Julie, you stay there as long as you need, as long as you think Mark needs you. I will wait for you. I was waiting my whole life for you. I can wait a few more months, and now it's easier. I know where you are."

"I love you," I whispered. This was the second time I had said it today, but this time I meant it with every pore of my body.

"I love you too. Do you want me to come to Kyiv? I can rent an apartment and work remotely."

"That is tempting," I admitted. "But I think I won't have a free minute during the next couple of weeks. I will have to get back to work, so running between the office and the hospital will keep me occupied. But I will call you every day, okay? Besides, I need time to figure all of this out."

"Sure, that makes sense." Ann sounded calmer now. "The house is empty without you."

I imagined the white walls of her bedroom, the view of the hills from the patio, Ann's back while she brewed coffee in the kitchen, and her slender shoulders. I missed it all.

"I just hope we will see each other soon," I said.

"Get some rest Julie," Ann said. She heard that I was tired, and I was; the day had stretched to forever. We said goodbye and hung up.

I dropped my head in my hands. I knew that all these calls, the messages, it would be crazy difficult. How did people stay in long distance relationships? The lack of touch and presence would drive me to board the plane and leave Kyiv and Mark to run back to Ann. But who was I kidding? I would never forgive myself. My phone started vibrating—Mom. I picked it up.

"I heard the news from Alex and was waiting for your call. It never came, and, well, how are you?" Mom was talking fast and worried.

"I just got off the phone with Ann, sorry. I was about to give you a call. I am fine but tired."

I told her about Mark, how he was so lost in that blank hospital room.

"I am so sorry it happened. Let me know if you need any help. How was your trip? How was LA?" She paused.

"You want to know about Ann," I laughed. "It was great. Do you want to come see me tomorrow evening? I'll tell you everything then, but now I am so drained and hungry I think I am going to pass out. I'll be in the hospital tomorrow. The visiting hours end at 7 p.m., so let's meet at 8 here?"

"Great, I missed you so much," she said.

"I missed you too, Mom."

"Okay, get some rest."

After we hung up, I shuffled to the fridge and heated the food in the microwave. It tasted like ash in my dry mouth. My body just needed to consume fuel. I devoured it in five minutes. The hot water in shower numbed my feelings and relaxed my body. I put on a t-shirt and shorts, set the alarm, and didn't notice when my head hit the pillow—I was already asleep.

The alarm dragged me from the depth of my sleep. I didn't remember what I had dreamt about, as the time difference and jet lag was getting to me. I hit snooze and fell back on the pillow.

I snapped a selfie and sent it to Ann. I was not a selfie person, but I hoped she would send me one. And minutes later it came.

"Good morning, sleepyhead," the caption said with a selfie of Ann with a book on the couch in the living room. She was gorgeous, and an image flashed in my mind: her naked body on that same couch, breathing hard, eyes closed. I glanced at her selfie again, her open smile, her eyes looking directly into mine through the photo.

My hand slipped into my shorts. I closed my eyes and imagined Ann, the curve of her hips, the tender skin of her breasts under my fingertips, quiet moans escaping her lips. I touched myself, my hand moving faster. My fingers were drawing familiar circles, pressure building inside. I came with a silent shudder.

Then I laid there, in Mark's and my bed, breathing hard and thinking about Ann. I sent her a message: "I don't know what just happened, but I finished myself off looking at your photo. Thought you'd like to know. It doesn't compare with the moments that I was with you, but since I am stuck here it will have to work."

Her reply pinged almost instantly: "Oh my God, tell me more. Show me."

I smiled. So, this was what long-distance dating was like. I put my hand back in my shorts and snapped a picture.

Moments later, a video showed in my messages feed. It was her pale skin and a black demi-cup bra. She moved it down with her finger revealing her breasts, her dark nipples slowly coming into view.

I groaned. "I want to touch you so badly," I typed.

"I will take care of it myself while you are away …" she replied.

My alarm blared again. The shrill sound brought me back to reality, the one in cold Kyiv, with a broken Mark and so far away from Ann. I took a shower, ate a bite of the stale food from yesterday, and got an Uber to go to the hospital. The grey city was looking back at me from the car window.

When I got to Mark's room, Victor was standing outside of it.

"Hey." He hugged me. "They are changing his bandages now."

"Have you been inside?" I asked.

"Not yet, but the nurse said he had a good night's sleep."

I liked Victor. He was thirty-four, no girlfriend, and was as free as the wind. The man liked to travel alone to godforsaken countries. The stories he brought from his travels always left us open mouthed. He and Mark had studied at the university together but took completely different paths. Victor freelanced and worked on projects when he needed money for his travels. Mostly he worked for half a year and traveled for the other half.

The nurse emerged from Mark's room.

"How is he?" I asked.

"It's too early to tell, but for now everything is going as it should. We will give him a smaller dosage of painkillers today so he will start feeling his leg. We'll see how he takes it. You can go in now."

Victor and I opened the door and stepped inside. Mark was pale, but when he spotted us, a warm smile tugged his lips.

"Hi," he croaked, his face lighting up.

We sat on the two sides of his bed, and I kissed his cheek. "I thought you had left already," he said to Victor.

"In three days," Victor replied.

"Where to, this time?" I asked, raising a curious brow.

"Bolivia," he replied and while he was talking about his plans, my phone pinged. It was Mark's mom. His parents had landed an hour before and were on the way to the hospital. She asked me the room number where Mark was staying. I replied, and she typed: "Will be there in 15."

"Your parents will be here in fifteen minutes," I said, looking at Mark.

I wasn't close with his parents, and since they lived seven hours drive away from Kyiv, I primarily saw them on big holidays. They were always nice and loved when we visited. But I felt the pressure from both of them regarding kids, as every time they saw me, they always asked about grandkids. Because of that, I often found excuses to skip the trip, and Mark went to visit them there alone. Preferring the quiet life of a small city, his parents didn't like to visit bustling Kyiv.

"I will give you two a private moment before they arrive." Victor smiled and left the room, always thoughtful.

"How are you feeling?" I asked Mark.

"I slept through the night, as you said." He was looking at me with so much tenderness in his eyes. "I don't feel any pain, yet." He touched the cast on his leg. "The doctor said my job for the near future is to lie here and heal."

"That does not sound bad." I grinned back. "I brought you your things, your charger, laptop, your book, and some clothes."

Mark took my hand in his good one. "I am so happy you're back."

I just smiled.

The door opened, and his parents walked in. His mom was a small woman in her fifties, his dad thin and tall; they were a peculiar couple. But as Mark said, they had a complete understanding of each other, and being high school sweethearts, they never looked in any other direction but towards each other. For Mark, they were the example of a good family.

Mark's mom, Elena, gasped when she saw his bruises and sinister looking metal nails. She rushed to his side, tears sliding down her cheeks.

"Oh my God, Mark," she sobbed. "How are you feeling, honey?"

She touched his face and his hair. Mark's father was pale, but he smiled at his son.

"You scared us."

I moved back to the door, giving them some privacy. Mark looked in my direction, and I pointed to the door and mouthed, "I will be outside." He nodded. I slipped outside and took a deep breath. Victor was standing by the window.

"Life is so strange sometimes. One day you are living

normally, and the next you can't even get up. He is lucky it's only temporary. Yes, it's a long way to go, but I can't imagine how people who cannot walk after a gruesome accident feel. It's like you don't have your freedom anymore." He was looking at the streets outside. "I know about wheelchairs, but …"

Victor was a free spirit who roamed the world, and it shook him to his core to see Mark this way. Mark, who was always athletic and strong, now lying chained to a bed.

"Sometimes I forget how fragile we are," he admitted.

What could I say? "We are," I agreed, and we stood silently watching the sleepy Sunday city outside the window.

Elena opened the door and walked to me.

"I am so happy to see you," she said, pulling me in for a tight hug.

Victor watched us and greeted Elena.

"I'll go say bye to Mark," he said, disappearing into Mark's room.

"Do you know where I can find a doctor or a nurse to talk to?" she asked.

I pointed to the end of the corridor to the nurse's station, and Elena squeezed my hand and went there. As I stood alone, I thought about how we had no control over our lives, one accident—and the life of a person shutters to pieces.

I stepped through the threshold. Mark was talking quietly to his father. His dad smiled at me and enveloped me in a hug.

"Hello, Julie." He released me and glanced back at Mark.

"Hello." I liked the constant calmness of Mark's dad, but he was a bit awkward around people, avoiding eye contact.

"Have you seen Elena?" He asked, looking down.

"She went to find a nurse or a doctor to speak to."

"Oh, I need to hear it too. Be right back." He nodded at Mark and shuffled outside, his back bent.

The bruises on Mark's face had deepened as bruises always did before starting to fade. He looked tired. All the visitors were a pleasant distraction, but they took too much of his energy.

"They assigned me a guy who will help me take showers and move for the next few weeks. All from the bed, of course."

"Have you seen him already?"

"Yes, he came this morning. I liked him. His name is Ivan, and he is in his late twenties. During this time, I think I'll grow close to him, sharing the most spectacular views of the intimate parts of my body." He winked. "You'll see him, he is a pile of muscles."

Mark winced.

"Do you feel it?" I asked.

"When I don't move, I feel a dull pain. When I move even slightly, it's sharp. Have you seen the length of these nails?" He pointed to his hip.

"They look gruesome," I laughed.

"Exactly. I am an ironman now." He smiled. "Literally, iron is stuck inside of me."

The way he was acting surprised me. He grinned and even joked about his condition. If I were him, I would have been staring silently at the opposite wall. But not Mark; he was strong. And he would fight. I perched on his bed, and Mark touched my neck, tracing my cheek. He looked me in the eye and smiled slightly.

I pressed his hand to my cheek and whispered, "Get better."

"Are you going to work tomorrow?" he asked.

"Yes, but I'll come here in the morning before going to the office. Do you need anything? Anything from home?"

"I see you brought a lot already, thanks."

Talking made him tired; he was blinking slowly and finding it difficult to focus on me.

"You need to rest. Do you want me to come back in the evening?" I asked.

He managed a stiff, sleepy nod. "Yes."

"I will go visit Alex and come back."

I bent over to kiss Mark's cheek, but he tilted his head and our lips met. His lips were dry, but the kiss lingered, the touch so familiar. When I moved away, a playful smile was on his lips.

"Get some rest, Mark," I laughed.

He winked.

When I stepped outside the room, I saw his parents at the end of the corridor talking to a doctor. I walked over to them and listened to the same information he had given me yesterday. When he finished, I said that I'd be back later today and hugged them goodbye.

It was so strange how my old reality mixed with my new one but giving a hug to Mark's parents made me feel that all the things that had happened in California were in my imagination.

Chapter 26

JULIE

*A*lex lived twenty minutes away from the hospital in a nine-story apartment building, so I decided to walk. As I was thinking about Mark and marveling at how he was coping, I stopped abruptly in my tracks, a woman bumping into my back.

"Sorry," I muttered, stepping to the side. My heart started pounding inside my chest with realization. It was me. I was the reason Mark fought, why he smiled and joked. He did it because of me. Our love moved him. And for him to get better, I needed to stay close. And I really wanted him to get well.

I took a deep breath and realized that I was trapped. If I chose to leave now, it would hurt him even more than I thought. So, I would stay, and then, when he was better, I would run into her arms.

∼

Christina, Alex's wife, opened the door. Her belly was huge. She enveloped me in an awkward hug; it was not that easy to hug a person with an eight-month-old baby inside of them. Her blond hair was up in a messy bun, and the dark circles under her eyes showed how long it had been since she had a good night sleep. Even though she was tired, her eyes were kind.

"I am so sorry about Mark," she said sadly. "How is he doing?"

She ushered me inside, Alex was in the kitchen putting plates on the table. Their apartment was an airy, freshly renovated three bedroom in Scandinavian style. Huge floor to ceiling windows opened to the city outside. Soon the white walls would be viewed as a clean canvas by the baby. And I was a little worried how Christina with her mild OCD would handle the disruption of her perfectly organized home.

Golden chicken roasted in the oven, and I realized I was starving, my stomach rumbling painfully. I told them everything the doctor had said. Their faces grew darker. Christina squeezed my hand and after I said he'd need to learn to walk again, her eyes reddened.

"Sorry, hormones," she said quietly, pointing to her belly.

"But you know Mark. He is resilient, and he is pretty cheerful now."

They smiled weakly in return.

"So, Alex, are you cooking now?" I wanted to change the subject. He shrugged.

"I get tired fast now, so it's time for him to learn, but the thing is that he might be a better cook than I am, so he'll stay in this role." Christina was looking at Alex and grinned. "Forever."

"I don't mind actually. With YouTube tutorials it's not a high science."

"Who would have thought, Alex—*the* cook?" I laughed.

And when he served us dinner, surprisingly it was really flavorful. The crispy roasted chicken with a salad sprinkled with quinoa melted in my mouth.

Christina was a career woman from head to toe; she enjoyed mountain climbing as a hobby, so their decision to have a baby put a lot of restrictions on her, but she still went to the office every day.

"Mom will be at our place in the evening," I told them.

"Damn, with all the stuff happening I forgot you just returned from LA. How was it? Did you meet any Hollywood stars?" Christina asked.

I met the star of my life, I thought. It was a sharp jab in a heart. Ann was so far away from this cozy, modern kitchen.

I told them about the city, the hills, the long beaches, the dark ocean, my surfing attempt, and the adventure park. I didn't mention Ann much. They would find out when the time came, and I hoped they would understand.

On my way back to the hospital, I called Ann. She was at Jack and John's. They greeted me, and Jack shouted that he missed me already. Ann excused herself and found a quiet corner. Her velvety voice was a balm to my soul. I told her about the day and said that my mom would be coming to see me that evening.

"Are you going to talk about us?" Ann asked.

"She will ask a lot of questions, I mean a lot, and details …"

Ann laughed.

"Good." She paused. "God, I miss you so much. It has been just a few days, but it feels like forever."

"I know," I said quietly.

After we hung up, I still heard her voice in my head. *Please, wait for me*, I thought.

When I reached Mark's door, the nurse was exiting his room, holding a tray with a used syringe.

"How is he?" I asked anxiously.

"His leg hurts. He tried to show a brave face, but winced even from the slightest movement, and the sweating won't do any good. I gave him a painkiller and sleeping pill so the night shouldn't be a nightmare for him. He'll be out in a few minutes." She gestured for me to step into the room.

When I went in, Mark's face was strained, and he was breathing hard. When his eyes fixed on me, he tried to smile.

"You're here," he murmured.

I rushed to his bed. The sheets were crumpled under his fingers.

"Is it bad?

"No."

"Mark?"

"Yes," he croaked. The beads of sweat were gathering on his forehead. "But it should get better in a few." He closed his eyes briefly. "It eases." He started breathing calmer.

"Good night, Mark," I held his hand; it was the one part I knew wouldn't hurt him if I touched it. "I will be back in the morning."

He was slipping away. "Love you," he murmured, his lips barely moving, and he relaxed, sleep taking hold.

I studied his face. The swelling was partially gone, and his face was taking its usual shape; only purple bruises on his cheeks and nose remained. A few days' stubble gave him a sexy fighter's look. He was handsome, and the nurses would swoon around him.

I smiled to myself, this was the man I loved, and I was going to let him go, day by day, even if he didn't know that yet.

Five minutes after I had opened the door to my apartment upon returning home, I heard the doorbell ring. My mom was early like she always was. She hugged me tightly, grazing my cheek with her golden earring.

"How are you?" she whispered. She was the first person who asked about me first, not Mark, and he deserved it, but my mom always focused on me first.

"I fell in love," I said simply.

"Oh." I felt the smile in her voice. "Tell me everything."

I ushered her into the kitchen, placed a steaming mug in front of her, and told her how we had planned to move to Barcelona for a year. I told her that I originally would have come back to break up with Mark, arrange my work, grab a few things, and head back to Ann. But now all my plans had gone to hell, Mark was in the hospital, and I couldn't leave him.

"He needs me now, you should have seen the look on his face, like I am the one thing that keeps him fighting."

"That's a lot of pressure he puts on one person." Mom frowned.

"But he never did anything bad to me, he never treated me with disrespect. I still think of him as a close person, as a dear friend. I can't just abandon him there in a hospital and run to enjoy my life. I will wait for him to get better, and stronger, so he can handle the news. Not now."

"That's the right thing to do." She was rubbing her forehead, her eyes fixed on the cup of dark tea in her hand. Then her eyes flared to my face. "But what about Ann?"

I let out a shaky breath.

"She misses me, but she understood and said she would wait for me." My love, so far away. "Let me show you some pictures."

I grabbed my phone and opened the Photo app. Our happy faces peered from the selfies we took on the beach, a few dreamy portraits of Ann. There was one of her when she was trapped deep in thought. I loved it best.

Mom watched the photos in silence, a small smile playing on her lips.

"You look so happy, and she is beautiful." She stopped at the photo where Ann kissed me lightly on the patio of her house. The evening sun was shining behind us, drawing a halo around our heads.

"So, are you saying you love her?" she asked.

I nodded. "And I hate this situation. I want to be with her, not stuck in the apartment I share with my boyfriend. I was ready for a new life."

Tears stung my eyes. It was unfair, unfair to Mark, unfair to me, and unfair Ann. We all should have been settling into our new lives now.

"This is the first challenge of your relationship, an early one." Mom looked at me. "I am so sorry you have to go through it. But you'll never forgive yourself if you abandon Mark now. Can I ask you a personal question?" She was suddenly shy.

"Was all this before not a personal dialogue?" I laughed. "Sure."

"How does sex work between two women? There is no, um, crucial organ, and how do you ..." She tried to show it with her hands. "Well, you know."

"You can get a crucial organ,"—I showed quotation marks in the air—"in a sex shop, all sizes, colors, and materials. And it just works with us. Ann noted from the beginning what I like, and she knows how to touch a woman because she, well, is a woman herself."

I knew my mom would ask these questions.

"So, is it with your hands?"

"Hands, mouths, toys, bodies," I explained.

"Oh, wow." Mom leaned back on her chair. "So it does work."

"Yes." I was smiling.

"And there is no chance to get pregnant, perfect," she concluded.

"Exactly, and I never gave it a thought, but it appears I am fascinated by breasts."

Mom glanced quickly at the photo open on the phone.

"And she has big ones."

"Oh, yes."

We started laughing. I loved that I was so close with my mom, that I could discuss my sex life so easily, even if it was with a woman now.

I took her hand in mine. "Mom, I will miss you so much."

"Oh, I'll come and visit, and video call often." She winked. "But I see how you speak about Ann. It's not a crazy infatuation, it's a steady and strong current. You both just need to wait a little."

Ann was smiling from the photo on the phone.

I nodded. "Yes."

I told Mom about Jack, John, and little Ian, about

surfing, about LA and the lifestyle they lead there, which was so different from ours.

"I would love to meet all of them."

"You need to get better with your English," I laughed.

"You're right. Maybe we could go take courses with Dad."

"How do you think Dad will react to me being with a woman?"

"Actually, he knows. When I told him that you went to LA to stay with a woman you met at the conference he said, and here is a quote, 'Poor Mark, she'll leave him.' When I asked what he meant, he said that he always knew that you were bisexual. I was stunned and asked how he knew. And he said, another quote, 'I know my daughter.'"

I felt warm feelings rush towards my dad. "How did he know?"

"I have no idea." Mom shrugged. "Ask him."

Chapter 27

JULIE

*T*he next few weeks rushed by in a blur. Every morning I went to see Mark at the hospital, then went to work, and evenings I spent with Ann. We developed a habit of being in each other's lives online. We shared everything, the meals we had, the walks we took, capturing everything to share later.

One Saturday, she called me in the morning. I was sleeping late, so it was night in LA. I woke to the sound of my phone ringing. Ann was also in bed, a soft glow from the bedside lamp lit her.

"Perfect," she said. "I wanted to try something."

She pulled off her shirt. I sucked in my breath; she was so beautiful. I wanted to touch her skin with my lips, trace her neck with my tongue, go down, down. Ann put her fingers in her mouth and sucked, and then she moved her hand in her panties. I watched, mesmerized, as her body started moving, her hips going up and down. She looked at the camera all this time, soft moans rippling through her.

I quickly took off my shirt and panties, my body

buzzing from the image on the screen. Ann paused to watch me.

"I love you," I whispered, touching myself. How she looked on that small rectangle of my phone made me crazy. I imagined her lips between my legs. We moved together, and we stopped together, breathing heavily.

"Good morning." Ann smiled.

"You made it really good indeed." I touched the screen. "I wish I was there with you."

I hated the distance.

"You will be."

She asked about my plans for the day. I opened my mouth to speak and halted.

"I can't talk calmly seeing your naked body," I growled.

"Should I get dressed?" Ann asked.

"Oh, God, no."

Ann laughed and moved the camera closer, stopped on her chest, and then touched and squeezed her breasts lightly with her free hand. She played with her nipple, and I noticed I was staring like a hungry teenager. She moved her phone lower and parted her legs.

"If I were there with you, I would lick and suck on you till you begged me to stop," I breathed.

Where did this kind of talk come from? I guess this was what the distance made me do.

Ann put her fingers to her flesh and started drawing slow circles.

"What else would you do?" she murmured.

I started talking, and it just poured out. I said that I would cover every inch of her body with my lips, the details I imagined I tried to express with words.

Ann's body rocked, and she begged, "More, please."

By the end, she was making animal noises, her body shaking so hard it was difficult for her to hold the camera.

The sweat was glinting on her skin, and when she came, she was repeating my name over and over.

"Oh, my." She moved the camera to her face.

My body pulsed with desire from what I saw and heard, and I was surprised by how I enjoyed talking. I was wet now. Very, very wet.

"I need to—" When my fingers connected with my hot flesh, I moaned; I was almost on the peak already. Ann started caressing her body, sucking on her finger, watching me, her finger leaving a wet trace on the areola of her breast. A strong power shook my body, making me feel every inch of myself. I came out loud.

"You are amazing," Ann exclaimed. "I could do this all night."

I smiled, feeling like melted sugar.

"We need to do it again," I told her eagerly.

"Yes," she murmured; the intensity of the last moments was taking hold.

"Sweet dreams," I said.

"They will be sweet now." She winked.

"Bye, Ann."

"Bye." She paused, looking at me, and switched off the call. I didn't know it was possible to feel this way, to reach this intensity being thousands of miles away.

I guessed she had wanted to do it earlier, but she waited for a Saturday, knowing I'd have more time for myself. I closed my eyes and laid there, during a morning in late March.

Before going to the hospital that day, I took a detour to a coffee shop and ordered a latte and a croissant, this time not to-go. I'd had enough of constant running and takeout food. I savored the freshest pastry, thinking about the dual life I had now. One where I was a good girlfriend helping an injured boyfriend, and another where I was crazy about a woman, our evening talks, constant presence and since today intense orgasms just seeing each other through the phone. Was it called cybersex? I smiled to myself.

During these past weeks, Mark grew close with Ivan. Numerous times I went to the hospital and saw them crack up with laughter about some private jokes, talking about football and the latest TV shows.

Mark was getting restless from lying down all the time. His family, friends, and I all kept him company during visiting hours. He started working one to two hours a day online. His boss was happy and had even come once to see Mark and asked if he needed a better laptop or any gadgets to get him back to work as soon as possible. Books, TV shows, and Ivan were his distraction when we couldn't visit.

On some days, Mark was cheerful, some days irritated. But with me, he was never acrid. He wanted to be home. For two to three more weeks, he wouldn't be able to put any weight on his legs, and he needed to lay still to make sure the bones were growing back together as they should.

Mark's insurance paid to have a full-time nurse at home, so he persuaded Ivan to take an unpaid vacation from the hospital to help him at home. Ivan agreed; the money was much better, and he enjoyed Mark's company.

"I am being paid for chatting with a pal," he joked.

"You also need to shower him and clean up after him," Mark said.

"Those are just details." Ivan smiled. "We get to work out together, so it's my dream job."

"You have to work out me," Mark said, but he wasn't bitter. Ivan's positivity was contagious.

The day before Mark got home, I spent time cleaning the flat. Ivan helped install a medical bed; thank heavens we had rented a huge apartment, so there was a place for this monster of a bed. Ivan noticed a frown on my face.

"Don't worry. It's only for two to three weeks and he'll be back in your bed," he promised.

I started to fix the pillow to hide my face, my cheeks burning red.

In the evening, Ann called me.

"I am glad Mark will be out of the hospital. This means he's getting better, but …" Her voice trailed off. "But it means we can't talk in the mornings anymore."

I knew what she meant; I had grown so comfortable with our evening talks. My evening, her morning. I rushed back from work to talk to her, and sometimes I sat in the cafe just to speak to her while having a cup of hot chocolate. Now it would change. I would need to squeeze our calls in when I was not at home. I could say that I was meeting Mom, but it would work only once or twice a week.

"I know, and I'm so sorry. I will call you anytime I can. And as soon as Mark can move by himself, I will tell him everything. Ivan said that it's too early to judge. So far, Mark's legs are healing well, but it all can change. The hospital is letting him go because he can get the care he needs at home because of insurance. If we didn't have this help, he would have stayed in the hospital. And the bright side is that patients at home seem to get better much faster."

"It's not only that." Ann rubbed her forehead and looked away from the camera.

"What is it?"

"You will be spending much more time with him." She was so vulnerable, my strong woman. "It's not jealousy, or it is jealousy, I don't know." She looked back at the camera. "I am afraid your feelings for him will rekindle."

My heart skipped a beat. So that's what she was thinking.

"Ann, I need you like I need to breathe. The feelings I have for you are so massive." I tried to show the size with my arm, and she laughed. "I feel them in my heart and my mind every minute. And my soul, it needs to be close to you. The life here is my old life, and my new life is by your side."

"But if you hadn't met me, you would have stayed with Mark."

"Maybe, but most probably no. I have met you, and you are a pillar of bright light showing me the way."

Ann was smiling, her eyes slightly red.

"I need you to remember that you need to put yourself first, not me, not Mark. You need to do what you think is best for you. I can't be the reason you leave him, if you don't really want it. Julie, think about yourself first."

"You are my person, and I am yours," I assured her. "And I need you to know that I am not like your parents. I am not leaving you. I choose you."

"I love you," Ann whispered, a tear sliding down her cheek. "Sorry."

It was the first time I had seen her so raw, so open, so easy to wound. She rarely exposed her feelings like that, and I wanted to shield her from the fears she had.

"Please wait for me," I pleaded.

"Of course," she laughed, wiping the tears from her cheeks.

"Do you know that I love you?" I couldn't touch her, but she had to know.

~

The next day, Mark was home. He was so happy to be in familiar surroundings.

"The smell, I can finally breathe in the smell of home. Do you know that hospital's stench of chlorine and disinfectant?" he asked.

I nodded.

"It makes you go crazy; it clings to everything, and you don't get used to it."

I took the day off from work to help Mark settle in and to show Ivan everything. All day, Mark was chatting happily and was throwing me intense glances. In the evening, I brought them both a beer to celebrate the homecoming.

By the time Ivan left, Mark was barely keeping himself awake. The long day and the move were taking their toll.

I wished him good night and he murmured a reply. I quietly switched off the light and closed the door. My plan was to have as many people as possible visit Mark so we wouldn't stay alone together for long. The time before bedtime would be tricky, though. With no one around, he might want to cuddle or kiss good night. I still had to figure out how to avoid it.

As it happened, mornings were easy. Ivan had a key to the apartment, and most days he was there before I woke up. We had breakfast, and I enjoyed their company. I still enjoyed Mark's company when there wasn't a hint of intimacy.

It was a bright spring morning, the sun lighting the kitchen in a balmy hue. The birds were chirping outside, and a savory smell of green tea tinkled my nose as the three of us were sitting at the table. Mark was in a wheelchair, his legs secured.

"So, your parents will visit today," I said after the last sip.

"Excellent." He nodded. "What time? Also I need to work today."

"They will get here at 3 p.m., and you need to rest."

"I have a busy schedule." Mark smiled and looked at Ivan, who rolled his eyes.

"Yes." I stood and pecked him on the cheek. "I should get to work."

I started clearing the table.

"Don't worry, I've got it," Ivan said, standing up from his chair.

I glanced at him. "Really?"

"It's in my contract." He grinned.

"That's handy." I winked at Mark. "Can we keep him?"

I pulled on my clothes and applied a smudge of makeup before rushing to the door. It was still early, which meant there was more time to speak to Ann.

This morning she sent me a photo of her in the bathroom mirror. She was wearing only shorts with her left hand she was covering herself, right holding the camera, a small, sexy smile on her lips. The text said: "I had a little wine." I loved when Ann was tipsy.

"You made my morning, you look so … inviting," I texted back.

I couldn't dwell on the photo during breakfast, so when I bought a coffee to go and was standing outside the coffee shop, I took my time looking at her curves. The spring was finally coming to Kyiv, and the sun started to warm the ground, swelling buds were ready to burst open. It was pleasant to stand away from the stream of people running to their offices. I called Ann, and when she picked up, her words were a bit slurry on the edges.

"I was at Jack and John's. Ian is away for a couple of days on a school trip, so they are having 'sex days', as they say. I left them to themselves as soon as I could and they went to the club to get more drinks," she giggled.

"I bet they are having a great time," I replied with a grin.

"Oh yes, when they are by themselves, they can't keep their hands off each other. I wish you were here," she breathed. "Sorry, I know you can't do anything about it. Sometimes I look at my couch and remember you there, your body, your eyes locking on mine, and I say to myself 'that wasn't real', that it was all a dream."

She was sad, I could hear it, and my heart sank.

"It was not a dream, but I see you a lot in *my* dreams," I tried to lighten the mood.

I heard her taking a sip.

"Please don't drink alone," I pleaded, my smile quickly turning to a frown.

She slurred, "Ah, who cares anyway?"

"Ann, I care, and you know it."

"Just leave him," she said harshly. "Now you are living together, and it makes me so crazy I feel like I am crawling up the walls. Does he touch you? Do you like when he is trapped between your legs? Does he make you feel as good as I do?" Her voice cracked at the end.

"You know nothing is happening between us," I assured her. "He isn't even healed enough to have sex." That was a wrong thing to say.

"But he still has working hands and a mouth! And I know you love when somebody sucks on you."

"When that somebody is you!" My body tensed as an angry heat burned in my throat.

"How do you want me to feel about you still living with your ex-boyfriend?" She paused. "He doesn't even know that he is your *ex*-boyfriend."

"Ann," I pleaded, I didn't know what to say. She was right, and if I was her, I would be jealous too.

"I am sorry. I need to hang up before I say more things I am going to regret. You do the things you need to do. They are the right things. I am just hurting. Julie, I love you so much." With that, she hung up.

I called her back immediately, but the call went straight to voicemail. I called again, and again. She switched off the phone. Tears pricked my eyes as I sat on the bench, hiding my face from the rushing crowd. No one looked my way.

I thought I was doing the right thing, staying with Mark so I wouldn't hurt him more when he was hurting so much already. But I hurt Ann in the process. I wanted to be with her so much, but I still couldn't run, not yet. Mark still couldn't walk, but he had a great support system of friends and parents. If I left, he could spiral into depression, which wouldn't help at all. Both of my decisions had hurt people I cared about.

I took a shaky breath and went to the metro station, my coffee cold in my hand and sun hiding behind the clouds.

That day, my boss asked me to help with a last-minute task, so the day was so busy I almost didn't have time to look away from the computer. It was a nice distraction from the dark thoughts coiling in my mind.

When I stepped into the crisp spring evening, my phone vibrated in my hand. Ann. I ducked into a quiet alley and took the call.

"Julie, I am so sorry," Ann said as soon as I picked up.

"It's okay," I sighed sadly.

"No, it's not. Please, listen to me. You asked me to wait, and I am waiting and will wait. What I said was unacceptable, about you leaving Mark. I know that you don't have sex with him, but since I saw his photo on Facebook, damn, he is smoking hot. I can't stop imagining you two entangled together. I know it's not true, but I have a good imagination. You are doing what is right, and please know that I support you and will always be here for you. Always."

"Ann." I started crying, the stress of the whole day of silence crashing in on me. "I don't know what the right thing is. Me staying here hurts you. Maybe Mark doesn't need me anymore?"

"Only you know the answer to that. Do you think he'll be okay if you break up with him now?"

I knew the answer.

"No, it will crush him."

I was sobbing the full force now.

"Oh my God, Julie, please don't cry. Can you hear me?"

"Yes," I whispered.

"Listen to me, I am sorry I rushed you before. It was the stupid wine. I shouldn't have gotten so drunk when I came home. But I miss you so much, and you asked me, and I …" She paused. "I am so sorry."

"I love you." These boilerplate words couldn't show the force inside me, the powerful feeling that squeezed my heart every time I heard her voice. "As soon as Mark is better, I am leaving."

"I do hope he gets better soon," Ann said. "How selfish of me."

"Please don't turn off the phone on me again," I begged.

"I won't, I was just *so* angry. I wanted to compare myself to him, I wanted you to know that he would be okay by himself, I wanted to persuade you to come to me. How stupid and drunk I was."

I laughed. "I like when you are tipsy, but with me, when I am near." I glanced around to check I was alone on the street. "I love how you arch your back, how you melt under my fingertips, how your gaze is unfocused, and you still try to catch my eye, the wine on your lips, the taste of you."

The images in my head warmed me deep to the core.

"When you say things like that, I will drink only with you." Her voice was light.

I heard her other phone ringing, her work phone.

"Damn," she cursed. "I need to go to the office. Julie, I am so sorry for what happened. I am here and I am waiting, and I love you."

"And I should be going now. Bye, Ann."

"Bye." She hung up.

I looked at the dark street around and felt calmer than I had in weeks.

Chapter 28

JULIE

$\mathcal{T}$ ime rushed by. Mark got stronger at home, and he was allowed to try to stand soon enough. During these weeks, I tried to speak to Ann as much as possible, but she was so busy at work, staying in the office long hours, and our schedules didn't match. I sent her long voice messages, and she wrote me emails. I missed our talks, but we both were falling back in our old lives. Ann worked and surfed, and I worked and cared for Mark.

He didn't insist on physical intimacy, but we started talking a lot after work. Long spring evenings, when it was still dark outside, we sought each other's company. He asked about my job, my parents, when I was cooking dinners. I was an awful cook, but he endured the burned and overcooked dishes with a smile.

I had the strangest feeling that Ann had withdrawn a little after that drunk encounter. I called her many times and she didn't pick up, later replying she was still in the office. They were opening a second office in Los Angeles, and she was managing the set up.

Once, she finally picked up.

"Hi, Julie," she said somewhat carefully.

"Ann, finally. How are you?"

"I am okay, and you?"

"No, no, no," I said. "Not that regular answer. How are you *really*?"

She paused, and I heard her taking a shaky breath.

"What do you want to hear?" she asked, almost whispering.

"The truth."

"I am miserable. I am here, I am waiting as I promised. Every moment I am alone I think about you, every moment I am not alone I try not to think about you. But I can't call you because by that time you are home with Mark. And I am sorry, but it hurts, and even though I said I would wait, I hate every moment of it, every moment you are there with him. I try to fill those alone moments with something, anything to distract myself. The office opening came in handy. I am so busy working with new teams, I come home dead tired. Meeting you was the best thing that happened in my life, but living without you is the hardest," she ended. "And how are you?"

I sniffed, tears rolling down my face.

"I miss you so much," I said.

"I am trying hard for it to be enough. I need you, Julie, by my side. How's Mark?"

"He is almost standing already, by himself. Can you imagine?"

There was silence.

"Hello?" I asked.

"I thought he was bed bound and practically couldn't move," she said, her voice strained, the words carefully measured.

"He was, but during the past few weeks with Ivan's

help, he is much better. I think he will try to walk in just a few days."

"Weeks? Walk? Why—" Ann stumbled, struggling to find the words. "Why are you still there?"

My heart skipped a beat. "He needs me."

Again, a long pause.

"I need to go. Julie, I love you. Bye."

"Wait—"

But she hung up.

I stared at my blank phone screen. I felt abandoned by her, even though she had a right to treat me like that.

Chapter 29

JULIE

*T*hat evening, I went straight to my mom's apartment from work. She hugged me and we sat in the kitchen, hot tea steaming from our mugs.

"How are you?" she asked tentatively.

I told her about Ann.

"I see what she is doing. She is giving you space."

"Space for what?" I asked.

"Put yourself in her place. Imagine she moved in with her ex-girlfriend."

I shuddered.

"How would you feel?"

I closed my eyes to imagine it. My Ann wrapped in unfamiliar hands, her head leaning on the girl's shoulder, their hands entwined, fingers touching. A cold wire squeezed my heart.

"I would think that girlfriend would try to win her back," I murmured.

"And it would be a real threat, right? You are not even in the same country, and that woman could take advantage of her at any time. I am not surprised Ann works hard on pushing thoughts of you in Mark's arms away," Mom said.

"But it's not true! There is nothing between us!"

"Isn't there? You warmed up to him, don't you see? Your past is pulling you back, and Ann feels it. So she is giving you time to decide."

"Decide what?" I felt stupid, but I couldn't follow where this conversation was going.

My Mom watched me, patience in her eyes. "To decide if you want to stay here with Mark."

I stood abruptly, my heart hammering. "No," I breathed, but it sounded weak even to me.

Mom raised an eyebrow.

"No," I repeated firmly this time.

"Are you sure?"

"Yes." I could see what she meant. "Of course it would be much easier to stay with Mark. But—" Ann's smiling face appeared in my mind. "I am in love with her."

I fell back in the chair, staring unblinking at the lacy tablecloth. Mom came closer and wrapped her hands around me. I took a few heaving breaths.

"Mom, what should I do?" My voice cracked.

She patted my hair lightly. "You know what to do, honey."

But did I really know?

When I left their apartment building, I called Ann but got her voicemail again. The evening was warm, and the summer heat would soon hit the city. I opened my email app and typed: "I am so sorry I made you feel this way."

Lots of other words swarmed in my head, but I wanted

to tell them to her, not type them in a stupid email. I called her again, but there was still no reply. I hit send and went home to Mark.

Chapter 30

*T*he cold drops hammered on my cheeks, slicing my skin. The dark clouds covered the horizon. It was the calm before the storm, and I was still sitting on my board looking in the depth of nothingness.

She was so far away, and she was with him. What was she doing right this minute? Was she in his arms?

My feet were freezing in the water. I put my hands down, the coldness gripping my fingers. Good. I missed her so much. I was tired of this feeling, and it numbed me. It numbed everything around me. She had to choose; me or him. I gave her time and it killed me, this waiting. She called me, she wrote to me, I waited. I opened her message every time with dread, fearing it would be the last one, saying she found her way back to her old life. My muscles tensed trying to fill the hole in my chest.

I jerked, pulling my right leg to the left, shifting the balance to fall, and I plunged into the cold water. The wetsuit saved me from the major impact, but I still skipped a breath when my head was pulled underwater. I wanted to feel something, anything, not this emptiness. I screamed, the water muffling the sound, bubbles of air rushing up my cheeks.

I wanted to peel off the wetsuit, I wanted that cold on my skin, because when she left, she took all the warmth with her. She wiped away all the colors of the world.

The cord that was attached to the board pulled on my leg, and I emerged from the water. Everything was grey still, the storm closer. I wanted to stay here, to get lost in it. But I heard *dangerous, dangerous, dangerous*, it was my muffled brain trying to scream, but the pain in my heart sliced back: *Who cares?*

I pressed my forehead to the board; it was time to get back. I took in a shuddered breath, a chill going down my core, and I swam back to the beach.

Chapter 31

JULIE

*M*ark was hopping on crutches in the apartment when I opened the door. His face was filled with concentration, and his brows were furrowed together. When he saw me, his face lit up, and he stopped in the middle of the room.

"Are you allowed to do that?" I laughed.

"Ivan said I need to train."

"And how is it?"

"Difficult, but I can do it, and I can finally get out of the bed by myself," he said. "I hope you don't mind, but I invited Alex and Christina over this Saturday."

"No, it's okay, I haven't seen them in a while anyway," I replied.

Christina had given birth to a baby boy, and I saw them only a handful of times. They were not yet sleep deprived and over the moon.

"Will they bring the baby?" I asked.

"No, Denis will stay with a nanny," Mark said, looking closely at me.

I turned away, retrieving my phone from the bag. No new notifications.

I went to the bathroom to change into my home clothes—comfy pants and Mark's old t-shirt. I looked at it and realized that it would hurt Ann if she knew. I didn't even try, right? I took off the shirt and fished my old one from the closet.

I checked the phone again, still seeing no reply. Tiredness was sweeping over me as I shuffled into the kitchen. Mark was sitting on the windowsill, and his crutches stood by the wall.

"Come here," he said.

I stiffened but stepped closer. He took my hand in his gently, his familiar rough skin wrapping around mine. Mark gestured for me to sit, and I perched on the pillow beside him, my heart beating faster.

"Julie," he said, peering into my eyes. "I wanted to say thank you for being with me during all these weeks. You were always here, always supportive of me."

At what cost? I thought bitterly.

"Sure, it's okay. You were in that accident partially because of me."

He was moving his finger, caressing the inside of my palm, and after these words his finger stopped midway.

"Why do you say that?" he asked.

"If I hadn't left, you wouldn't have been preparing a welcome party for me, and if you hadn't gone to that store to buy those ridiculous balloons, everything would be okay."

"Oh my God, Julie, it's not your fault! It could have happened anywhere and at any time. Look at me," he ordered. "It was just a stupid accident. Those first days in the hospital, I blamed myself over and over. There was a voice saying *what if,* and it thundered in my head. Then I realized where I was and that nothing in the past could be changed. I gradually stopped blaming myself." He squeezed my hand gently. "And now it appears you were thinking it was your fault all this time! I am almost fine now. Give me a few weeks and I'll be running," he chuckled.

"But what if—"

"No what ifs, Julie." He pressed a finger to my lips, silencing me. His finger stayed there, drawing the line of my lower lip. "There is nothing good about dwelling on the past. And it's neither my nor your fault."

I looked down, my eyes stinging. Mark put his hands around me, my head leaning on his broad chest.

He rocked me. "Thank you for always being here for me."

The word always echoed in me, in Ann's voice. I had abandoned her, and now those treacherous tears rolled down my cheeks. Mark's hands moved to hold me tighter.

Chapter 32

I closed my laptop for the day and looked around the office. It was almost empty. A guy a few desks from me was staring tentatively at the string of code on his monitor. My phone pinged, showing Ann's name on the lock screen. My heart started beating faster. Finally, she replied.

I unlocked the screen.

"Julie, my love. You remember it, right? I need you to know, to remember, to feel, that I love you. When I met you in that bar, I didn't know that one person could be my home, could accept me wholly, and could love me. You were my star, you lit up my life, I didn't feel alone anymore. Thank you for showing me that I am capable of feeling, to love a person till I can't breathe. You filled me to the brim and left. These quiet walls press in on me. I am so sorry, but I can't live like this anymore. I can't wait. During these past weeks, I hit rock bottom. I am alone again. You are somewhere there, in another part of the planet, and I am here, crumbling down to the emptiness inside. I can't do this anymore. Your absence is killing me. I love you, God, how I love you. And this waiting is destroying me now. I am cutting myself off from you. I am so sorry.

"These last days have been the hardest ones of my life. I finally understand that you are choosing him. I understand that you chose him when you boarded that plane and asked me to stay here. I am still here, and I will always be here. But I can't do it anymore. By the time you read this, there won't be any way for you to contact me. I love you, Julie. And I wish you were here. I wish you never left, but my wishes are not important. Forgive me for not waiting as you asked, but if I waited and hoped even for one more minute, there wouldn't be me anymore. I will always love you. You need to know that. Goodbye."

That *Goodbye* blurred. My tears were falling on the screen, silently. Sitting here, on this uncomfortable office chair, I could barely breathe. I had ruined us. There was no more *us*. Here I was, quietly crying, while the storm roared in my ears. I hurt her so much when I left to help Mark and saved him from the pain, but saving Mark killed the one I loved. She lost faith in us, and I made her wait too long.

But she was wrong. She thought I was like her parents, who just left her. No. I made the right decision to help Mark, but it took too long.

I picked up my jacket, my purse, and left the building. Outside, it was warm, almost summer. And deep down I knew that I should have left much earlier. I should have left when Mark got home. And now, he was almost walking, and I was still cradling his feelings, while Ann was left hurting. Was there still a chance to save us?

I called her. As she said, she had blocked me everywhere. All messengers, social media, and calls ended before the first ring. Even her email got returned.

Stepping one foot in front of the other, I reached my

front door, standing there with the keys in my hand. I had a plan, but not today. Coward. Soon, soon I would run back to the love of my life, pleading with her to take me back. I plastered a smile on my face and slid my key in the lock.

Chapter 33

ANN

My phone rang in the middle of the night. It sliced through the thick fog of my sleep. It was an unknown number.

"Hello?" I said, my voice croaked from non-use.

"Hello, my name is Ilana, I am calling from the Tel Aviv Medical Center. Your grandmother, Mary, had a stroke. Now she is in intensive care. We are doing everything we can. You were first on her list of contacts—"

"What do you mean?" My heart hammered in my chest, my heart which had silently broken the last few days, gave a final crack. I didn't understand what was happening.

"I am sorry, Ann. We will do everything possible, but given her age, you should be ready."

"No, not her," I whispered to myself more than to the nurse on the phone. "I could be there in twenty hours. I am in LA. Do you think …" My voice trailed off.

"If you can, please come."

"Do you think she'll make it?" I whimpered.

"I can't promise anything. Right now, everything depends on her body and will."

"Okay, I will be there as soon as I can." My voice sounded mechanical at this point.

"We'll be waiting for you, Ann." With that, she hung up.

This was not happening, not Mary. I hated Julie that moment. She had shown me what my life could be, how I could be loved and love back, how I was not a freak. And then she took it all with her and left me here alone. And now Mary, how could she? She knew I was lost now, and she was also leaving me.

And then it happened, my broken heart, the sharp shards sliced my skin from the inside. I took a quick breath, surprised by the pain, I pressed my palm to the middle of my ribcage. I tried to save it from crashing, but it was too late. My parents were gone, Julie was gone, Mary was almost gone, my heart was broken, and I was alone.

I dropped to my pillow and pressed my nose, my mouth down, stopping the flow of oxygen, and I wailed. Inhuman sounds filled my ears and my hollow body, muffled by the pillow. And I finally broke, this thread of light that had been inside me, was gone.

I decided not to call Julie. She was busy with her life now.

Chapter 34

JULIE

*C*hristina, still standing in the doorway declared, "No talk about babies, please. Denis is fine, but I am so tired of reading about babies, changing diapers, and everyone giving me advice on how it's right to do this and that. I love him to the moon, but I need a few minutes of not being a mom."

We knew that she couldn't breastfeed, and she had asked us to prepare a few bottles of wine.

When I came home last night, I rushed to the bathroom, calling to Mark that I was tired after a difficult day in the office. I cried my eyes out under that hot stream of water, hiding my sobs. Now I knew that I was afraid, afraid to break up with Mark, afraid to change my life. Why had I thought that Ann would wait for me forever?

I hid my feelings deep. Just one more day. I had to smile at Alex, at Christina, and at those trusting eyes of Mark. I would do it soon. I was just waiting for the right moment, or so I kept repeating to myself. In the morning, I spent a few minutes looking at her photo. Ann was strong, I was not. I shook my head trying to pull back into the moment, in that small corridor of our apartment.

"I wouldn't ask much anyway." I shrugged.

"Oh, I know Julie. It's not you who I am worried about." Christina gazed pointedly at Mark.

He blushed.

"You can ask me anything." Alex winked at Mark. Mark's face lit up.

"We ordered pizza. I hope you don't mind," I said as we all stepped into the living room.

"Thank God. Our nanny, Sophia, helped me lose a few pounds after my pregnancy and all she cooked was green rabbit food. It was healthy, but I missed grease."

We lounged on the sofa drinking wine and eating from the cheese platter I had managed to scrape together. They asked about Mark's legs, congratulating him on the speed of his recovery.

Mark and Alex moved to the balcony so Alex could smoke.

Christina looked at me.

"You look thinner. Is everything alright?" she asked.

I took a sip of wine, hiding my eyes. "Yes, sure, why?"

"I don't know, something is different about you. You have dark circles under your eyes. I am sorry if it's not my place to ask, but how are you?"

"I am fine, honestly. I need to sort something out, but I am okay, trust me."

I could still breathe, still function through life, but a huge chunk of my heart was ripped out. Other than that, I was totally great.

I heard bits and pieces of Alex's excited speech about Denis's little fingers. I smiled watching him, as he always wanted to be a father.

Christina followed my gaze. "He's a natural, you know.

I love Denis, but sometimes I think I am losing myself. I don't have a free minute. Sophia came ten days ago, so now it's a bit easier. You can't complain about being a parent, and when women find out that I can't breastfeed, they look down on me, making me feel like I am less of a mom, like I am missing the crucial bonding period."

Christina never questioned my decision of being childfree, and she had never once told me that I'd change my mind.

"I want to go back to the office. Staying at home all the time drives me crazy. But again, the pressure from other people, even my mom, that I am not spending enough time with my baby, and that work is more important." She dropped her head in her hands. "This is so confusing."

"People judge every decision if you dedicate your life into becoming a mother," I said.

Christina took a huge sip of wine.

"And you know,"—she looked at Alex—"secretly I am so happy that I don't breastfeed. I am free to do more things. I don't believe that if my body won't produce milk, I won't have a bond with Denis." She paused, looking at me. "Sorry, I am blabbering about motherhood, and I know how you feel about it."

"No problem. I admire the way you are handling it. You are not afraid to do what you need, not stopping your life, but weaving Denis in your old one. I am glad you are going back to work," I told her.

"They need me in the office." She shrugged.

I smiled. "It is wonderful to be needed."

"Oh yes, I am not only a mother, after all. And you know, Alex supports it."

That moment, the balcony door opened, and Alex stepped in.

"What do I support?"

"Me," Christina said simply.

"Of course." Alex sat near her and enveloped her in a hug. He kissed Christina, lingering there for a few seconds. She leaned into him.

"You know, we booked a hotel room in a center for the next weekend. Denis will stay with Sophia and my parents, and we'll have a day for ourselves." Christina blushed.

"And night." Alex winked at Mark.

As I watched them, my thoughts went to Ann, to my silent phone. I took three huge gulps of wine, trying to silence my mind.

When they left, I perched on the sofa with a glass of wine, numb from the alcohol and guilt.

Mark sat close to me, our hips touching. He was walking much better now but still winced when he sat.

I looked at him, seeing the few days' stubble I always loved, deep green eyes looking into mine, and the soft light made his hair gold. I could see myself doing it, staying with him, forgetting the ten days I had in LA, pretending it was just a fling, an experiment. I could see myself with Mark, but what I saw was our past. There was no future; both of us had ghosts of desire standing by our sides.

He touched my cheek lightly, slowly drawing my chin closer, and then he kissed me, tenderly at first, but quickly gaining more force. And I kissed him back. Familiar movements made me breathless, my mind shut down, and only my body responded to him.

Could I live as I lived before? Mark moved his hand down my neck, only touching me with his fingertips as though I was made of glass. Slowly, his hand moved under my shirt, taking a bra strap down. I felt the heat rising in the pit of my stomach as he cupped my breast, trapping my nipple between his fingers. Did I want this?

No. No!

What was I doing?

I bolted from the sofa, my heart hammering. I noticed my hand shot in front of me in protest.

"I …" I stammered. It was time. "I love someone else."

Surprise changed to hurt in a second on Mark's face.

"What? Who?" he demanded.

"It's Ann," I said. His eyes showed nothing; he took time to place the name. I didn't talk much about her with him.

"How?" he whispered.

I sat on the other side of the sofa and told him everything, his eyes growing darker with each second.

"So, if it wasn't for the accident, you would have left me months ago?"

"Yes, the same day probably," I said.

"Wow," he exhaled slowly, covered his face with both hands, and rubbed his eyes.

"I am sorry, Mark."

He removed his hands and looked up at me. "You know, the moment the car hit me, I was laying on the ground, the pain still was in the background when an image appeared. I saw myself holding a tiny baby, bundled in my arms. I had a feeling of pure love that moment, and then the pain and shock hit me. I was thinking that the vision I had might never come true as the asphalt pressed into my cheek."

I closed my eyes sadly. "Oh, Mark."

"And during these months of recovery, you were always close, and I thought, I *hoped*, you had changed your mind, and that the image I had seen would come to life one day."

I shuddered.

His voice turned bitter. "And now it appears you stayed with me for all the wrong reasons."

"Should have I left you there in a hospital?"

He paused and thought about it for a moment.

"Thank you for not doing that. It would have crushed me." He took my hand. "Thank you for staying and giving me hope to turn to, even if it was false hope. But still, it helped me put one broken leg in front of the other. All the while I saw that something was not right with you; your mind was always elsewhere."

I nodded.

"Can I ask you one question?" he asked.

"Sure."

"If you haven't met Ann, would we have stayed together? Would we have a family?"

I watched him closely.

"I guess you know the answer. We would have stayed together until you asked me to have a baby."

"So you would have left anyway?"

"I guess so."

Mark was looking at me with such sad eyes.

"But I love you, Julie."

"I know Mark, but think about it. Would you have chosen a childfree life with me?"

He was silent.

"You would have had second thoughts, you'd resent me, and kids everywhere around you would be a constant reminder of what you could have had. I guess our relationship was doomed from the start," I said.

"You weren't so sure in the beginning! You did not know that you hated kids so much." Mark swept his arm in an angry gesture.

"I don't hate them. I just don't want to have kids of my own. I was younger, and society demanded that women become mothers. But now I am sure and have been sure for years. You knew it."

"Really? You wouldn't change for me, for us?"

I shook my head. "No. Here is an easy question for you now: Would you have chosen me and stayed childfree or would you have rather been a father with somebody else?"

Mark was looking at me and then he looked away, out the window. We both knew the answer.

"You are right. Damn, now I feel as if I am breaking up with you."

I inhaled deeply. "We had our fun together, but it's time for us to both have what we truly want." I moved closer to Mark. "I wish with all my heart for you to have a happy family, with lots of babies." He smiled as I said it. "But I won't be a part of it."

Mark took my hand in his. "I guess deep in my heart I knew. Can I hug you?"

Instead, I hugged him. I felt his heart beating next to mine. This was goodbye.

"Can you show me her picture? You went to her in the US, and I never even saw her," he asked.

I unlocked the phone and showed him Ann's photo. She was standing on the beach, the wind playing in her hair, and the warm light of sunset lighting up her features.

Mark studied the photo, then me, and he winked.

"Wow."

I smiled.

"You know, it's true what they say. It doesn't hurt my pride as much since it's a woman. If you were leaving me for a guy, it would have been hell. But here,"—he pointed to the photo—"I know what you mean. How did you …" He tried to find the correct word. "Are you a lesbian?"

"I don't really know. I loved you. But with Ann, everything was different. It was more intense. Maybe I am bisexual? I don't want to label myself. One thing I know for sure is that I want to be with her. But …"

"But?" Mark asked.

"I made her wait for too long and she withdrew from me, from my life. She thought we were getting back together." I gestured to the space between Mark and me. "It was a blow for her, me staying here with you."

"I can imagine. It would have driven me crazy."

"Thank you, Mark." Everyone kept saying it.

He took my phone from the table and gave it to me. "Call her."

I looked at him.

"As you said, it's time for us to get what we want."

I took the phone. Mark kissed my cheek and stood with a grunt.

"I will take a shower, and meanwhile you get your woman back." He tilted his head. "So strange," he murmured and shuffled to the bathroom.

There was no way to reach Ann, as she had blocked my calls, but I tried anyway. I called again and again, with no luck. I opened my contact list and scrolled down to Jack. His caller ID made my heart beat faster. I pressed his name.

"Hello?" I greeted.

"Julie, hi." His voice brought so many pleasant memories. "How are you?"

"Jack, I need to talk to Ann, but I can't reach her."

"She is away."

"What? Where?"

"She's on a plane to Tel Aviv now. Her grandmother had a stroke, a big one. They don't know if she's going to make it." He was talking slow, being careful with me.

My heart sank. Ann's grandmother was the only

relative Ann had who supported her and talked to her. They were close.

I remembered Ann calling her grandmother when I was with her in LA, how happy she was to share her news.

"Why didn't she call me?" I asked, more to myself.

"Julie, she was not in a good place recently, and you probably know why." He tried to keep a reproach from his tone, but I felt it anyway.

"How long ago did she board the plane?" I asked.

"About three or four hours ago."

"Do you know the name of the hospital she's headed to?"

I fumbled to find a pen and a piece of paper, so the grocery store bill would do.

"It's Tel Aviv Medical Center," Jack said.

"And do you know her grandmother's name?"

"They have the same last name. She is Mary."

"Thank you so much." There was an awkward pause. "How was Ann?"

He stayed silent for a beat.

"She was withdrawn, quiet, and sad almost all the time." He cleared his throat. "But can I ask you a question?"

"Sure."

"Do you still want to be with her? I saw you two together, you are like two parts of one organism. I can't figure out how the distance is breaking it …"

This broke my heart.

"I will fix it, Jack. I am flying to Tel Aviv."

Jack repeated this to somebody, and I heard Ian replying, "I know."

I smiled, this little mystery boy.

"Julie, she needs you. Will Mark be okay without you for a couple of days?"

"I talked to Mark, and it's over."

"I told you," I heard Ian saying. Was the boy some kind of prodigy?

"Sorry, Jack. Say hi to John, but I need to run," I said.

"Bye, Julie. I hope it's not too late."

That blow hitched my breath. *No, it's not,* I thought.

Chapter 35

ANN

On the plane I looked around. The seat on my right was empty, the illuminated window on my left showing the busy life of airport workers. Only one thing made me put one foot in front of the other and crawl here was the hope of Mary being alright in the end. And one thing that chilled me to the bone was realizing that while I would be on the flight there wouldn't be any way to get in touch with me.

So, I sat there, waiting, trying to survive this thirteen-hour flight, then my connection, and then four hours more and I would be there. I prayed for her to hold on. All I did these days was pray to the gods who I hoped knew about me.

The plane rattled to the runway. An elderly couple sat in the middle row, her face pale as she clutched her husband's hand. I watched how he looked at her, soothed her fear, and cradled her head on his shoulder.

A sob escaped me. I watched this love and turned away to the window. I had this love, and I had lost it. Was I letting go of her too easily? Had she made a choice already?

Life without Julie … an awful thought crept under my skin. I could do it. I lived without her before. I could live without her again. One single tear rolled down my cheek, and I caught the gaze of that elderly woman. She was scared, but she looked at me, with worry in her eyes, and then she searched my face and smiled.

The warmth tried to penetrate my shell, but all it brought, a prayer, a prayer for Mary to be alive, so she could help me mend my life after this crash. My heart, though, it wouldn't be mended, ever.

I nodded to the woman and closed my eyes before leaning my head back on the headrest.

Chapter 36

JULIE

*A*fter I hung up, I opened a flights app. The earliest flight to Tel Aviv was at 6 a.m. I looked at the clock, seeing it was midnight. By the time I got to the hospital, after having been through security checks and customs if it went fast and easy, Ann would have been there for an hour. I booked the tickets immediately; it was a three-hour flight from Kyiv to Tel Aviv.

Mark found me shoving my necessities in my carryon bag. His eyes widened. He was tired, the corners of his lips tugging down.

"Are you leaving already?"

I told him about my call. Mark sat on the bed and watched me silently. Then he went to the kitchen and brought me some snacks.

"So you won't be hungry. You are always famished on planes."

The girl he loved was leaving. Only an hour ago he was sure we were on the way to a happy life together with a family, and now everything was different.

When I was ready and had double checked to make

sure I had packed everything, there were still two hours left before I would leave for the airport.

"Sit with me. Do you want some tea?" Mark asked.

"Yes, okay."

We moved to the kitchen, and I looked around. I didn't know when I would see it again. I loved this place; the spot on the windowsill was my favorite place in the apartment.

"Are you going to find a new place to live?" I asked.

"Not now. I need some time to get back on my feet, literally, and then we'll see. It's too much to think about now."

Two steaming cups sat between us, and I studied Mark.

"I am sorry," I said. "I am sorry that I couldn't give you what you wanted."

"I know, but it doesn't make it easier." He ran a hand through his hair. "And I didn't even fight for you."

I laughed. "It's real life, not some kind of movie."

He was silent.

"Thank you again, for staying with me. You put me above your relationship."

I nodded, doing one good thing had hurt another person badly.

We talked about our future, how uncertain everything was. I hoped so much that he would be in his happy place soon. But it was time for me to go.

I dressed and opened the Uber app. The car was seven minutes away. I hugged Mark.

"Good luck, Julie."

"Goodbye."

I had closed the door on my previous life.

Chapter 37

*T*he airport, security check, boarding my flight, it was all a blur. And after those long hours, I found myself in a taxi rushing to the hospital in Tel Aviv.

The building was massive, and I prayed that I'd find Ann fast. I was close.

A pleasant woman at the reception desk gave me directions to the waiting room and the room number where Mary was staying. I was sure Ann was not in the waiting room. All of the corridors looked the same. I became lost in the numbers, and I needed to ask directions twice. A panic rose in me as I rushed through the halls.

And then I saw her. Ann was sitting in a plastic chair, her shoulders slouched, her face hidden in her hands. She didn't hear me walking closer.

I touched her shoulder, and she looked up. Her red-rimmed eyes fixed on mine, the pain swirling there. I dropped to my knees at her chair. Putting my arms around her, I needed to feel her close, to protect her from the pain.

Her familiar perfume hit me.

"I am so sorry," I whispered. I was sorry for everything,

for Mark's accident, for my absence, for making her wait, and for her grandmother.

Ann was sobbing in my arms, and I held her tighter.

"I am here," I whispered as I touched her neck, her hair. God, how I missed her. "I love you," I kept saying over and over again.

Still, she didn't say a word.

I was afraid to ask about her grandmother, fearing the worst. Her breathing was ragged, but Ann calmed down as I held her. And then she looked at me, tears on her face. I moved closer, inches between our lips. I wasn't sure if she would move away. I wasn't sure what she felt about me. Would she take me back?

The world around stopped as I touched her cheek with my lips, kissed her tears, and tasted the salt on my tongue.

Ann wasn't moving.

"I was waiting for you," she said finally. "But I couldn't do it anymore. You stayed with him."

"I am here," I breathed as I moved closer to her mouth. Still, she wasn't moving.

"Julie, I …" Her eyes searched my face, but her hands were clenched on her lap; she didn't touch me. "I can't do it. You need to leave."

It hit me, like an invisible hand slapping my face. I scooted over.

"What?" My voice broke.

"I can't look at you and know that you didn't choose me. You left me! You rushed into my life, I fell in love with you, and poof, you were gone in the blink of an eye."

Ann stood and took a step back from me. My Ann, the person I loved the most, I had hurt the most.

"Please forgive me," I pleaded. "I messed up. I thought I was doing the right thing. But I kept hurting you by staying away, staying away with him. He needed me, and then I missed the moment when I should have left, and I stayed, and I didn't notice when my old life started to tug me back. And you still waited, even though I saw how difficult it was for you. You begged me to come, and I ignored it. You need to know that I never once thought I wouldn't be returning to you, it just took longer, and it's all my fault. My lingering didn't mean that I chose him. It was always you."

She still didn't move.

"I told myself that I was not like your parents, but I was. I woke up each morning in that place without you, but I kept telling myself soon, soon I would break up with him and go to you. And days turned into weeks, but you were still there, loving me, while I lived a double life. And when I was almost ready, you sent me that message, and I knew what I had done, I broke your heart with my stupid lingering. Because, Ann, you are the strong one, and I am a coward. I was afraid to move, everything was okay, Mark was getting better, and you waited. Your withdrawal was my trigger. I love you, Ann. Please take me back. Please let me make it right. Please let me love you. I am so sorry."

My eyes blurred, but in the midst of my tears, a bright ocean looked back at me. I was too late; she didn't need me anymore.

She still was silent.

"I love you, Ann," I murmured.

A small smile appeared on her lips.

"I started building a protective wall for myself again, and here you are. With just a few words, you became a bulldozer and demolished that wall into pebbles," she said. "Are you still with Mark?"

I shook my head.

Ann kneeled at my side.

"Promise me one thing," she said. I sniffed and nodded. "Please don't ask me to wait ever again."

I nodded again, and she smiled. Ann brushed a tear from my eyelashes. "I love you, Julie." And her lips touched mine.

A powerful wave of relief washed over me as I kissed her back. I moved my hand through her hair, pressing her closer. I needed her to feel my love, and our hearts hammered together.

This time, she held me as I crashed in her arms. "I am so happy to see you."

Chapter 38

JULIE

I looked around and remembered where we were. Ann's face fell as she glanced in the empty corridor.

"How is Mary?" I asked.

"She had a stroke when she was in the grocery store, and they rushed her here. She was stable, but when I arrived, her heart failed again." Her voice was shaking. "The doctors moved her into intensive care, and she was in this room."—Ann gestured to the door in front of us —"They asked me to wait."

"I am so sorry." I put my arm around her, and Ann's head nested on my shoulder.

"I need her. It's too early for her to leave. She wanted to meet you so much." Ann was crying again.

I was rocking her in my arms when a couple rushed around the corner. They were both in their late fifties, dressed immaculately. The couple stopped in their tracks and looked at us. Ann stiffened in my arms when she saw them. The man glanced at Ann, then at me, and bolted back the way he came. The woman stayed, and she looked at the man saying, "Oh, Jonathan."

She stepped closer to us. And then I saw it, her beauty, the face I loved but in an older version.

Ann stood, shielding me. Her mother had the same ocean blue eyes, but her nose was different. A web of wrinkles cut deep around her full lips. A light bob with flicked ends hugged her tired face and a linen cream-colored suit sat perfectly on the slender body. The woman stopped right in front of Ann; they were even the same height.

"How is she?" Ann's mother asked. Her voice was different but pleasant.

Ann replied, saying in a few words what she told me.

The woman's face fell, tears pooling at the corners of her eyes.

"She'll be alright," Ann's mother said, hope shimmering in her voice. She was still watching Ann, and then she slowly put a hand to Ann's cheek, gently stroking it.

"I missed you," Ann's mother said. "I missed you so much."

Ann's face didn't change its expression.

"I wanted to be back in your life, but I …" Her voice trailed off, and she took a deep breath. "I am so ashamed of what we did to you. I was afraid to reach out."

Tears were running down the woman's face, but she looked directly into Ann's eyes. "I am such a coward. I was afraid of your rejection. But we—I—deserved it. It was such a stupid thing. It doesn't matter who you love as long as the person treats you well. You being gay shattered our reality."

Ann sneered, "Shattered *your* reality? Suddenly I did

not have any family, and I was kicked out of my parents' home. How could you do that?"

"And I regret it ever since. You can't imagine how we hurt," the woman retorted sadly.

"Can you hear yourself? It's always about you, how you feel, how you hurt. Have you ever stopped to think about how I felt? The parents I loved never wanted to see me again because of who I was attracted to. I can't control it. But you,"—she pointed a finger at her mom—"you were always so focused on me being perfect. You had my life planned out, and when it appeared I was different, that I didn't match your perfect description, you threw me out! Mary was the one person who stood by my side."

Ann's mother was pale, but she listened, every word as a whiplash on her.

"You are right. There is no excuse for what we did," she finally replied, as her lips trembled. But suddenly, a fire lit in her eyes. "Ann, I will try for the rest of my life to fix what I have done wrong."

"Four years! You needed four years to realize it." Ann was shaking her head. "Not four days, but years! Dad," she corrected herself, "*Jonathan*, can't even be in the same room with me."

Jonathan appeared from the corner of the corridor. Apparently, he had not left; he was standing there all this time. While Ann's mother's face was pale as a sheet, Jonathan's was red, and huge, red-rimmed eyes bore into Ann.

His face was handsome, and he was extremely tall. He clutched the hem of his dark brown jacket that was the same color of his eyes. The thinning fair hair was cropped short, and a flush crept across his cheeks. It was heartbreaking to see so much pain woven into his face.

"I can." His voice was deep. "Ann, I want you back in

our life. I want to be close to you. I missed you so much, my little girl. But I was so afraid to reach out to you. We are two proud old souls, your mom and me. Mules would be a better description. We did an awful thing, and it took us weeks to realize it. And then for years we stayed silent." He shook his head, his shoulders sagging lower. "We lost you. We missed everything. By the time we wanted to reach out, you were climbing the career ladder with such force—"

"How do you even know that?" Ann exclaimed, her eyes going wide in shock.

"We scraped bits and pieces from the internet." Jonathan looked away. "Numerous times we picked up the phone to call you and froze. Many times I came back from work to find Eve sitting in her car, keys in the ignition, staring nowhere, crying."

"What were you so afraid of?" Ann demanded, her voice sharp.

"This." Eve gestured around them. "You throwing us out, not wanting anything to do with us."

"Like you did to me," Ann said quietly.

"Like we did," Jonathan echoed.

"Mom believed we would sort it out, but with each passing year she was disappointed in me. She didn't forgive me. Mary said that it was not her who needed to forgive us, it's you," Eve said.

"How could you have been so arrogant, so proud? You valued your precious friends' opinions about what they would say, and you worried they would call me a freak." Ann gestured to herself. By leaving her, they created so many false statements within Ann about who she was. "You needed their approval more than you needed me."

All this time I stood behind, watching this verbal sparring. But when I heard what she thought about herself,

I stepped closer and took her hand in mine. She squeezed it lightly.

Jonathan and Eve looked at me, to our entwined hands.

A small smile appeared on Eve's lips.

"I am so happy you are not alone," she said.

"It's none of your business," Ann replied, but there wasn't any venom in her words.

A nurse appeared around the corner, and she rushed to our group. When she reached Ann, she said, "Perfect, the family is together." We all looked at each other, and Jonathan smiled. "Mary's heart is steady now. We will watch her closely for a week. Right now, she's still unconscious."

"Will she be alright?" Ann and Eve asked simultaneously.

"We will monitor her. This was one stroke, not two. Given her age, it might happen again. She needs to take a bunch of pills now, every day; they will support her heart. So, yes, hopefully she'll be alright," nurse explained. "We will bring her back to this room in an hour and hook her up to the monitors. Meanwhile, you can go to the cafeteria."

We thanked her, and she went into the room to prepare it. "She'll be fine," Ann murmured, hope in her voice. I smiled. "Let's go to the cafeteria," she added, looking at me.

"Ann," Jonathan said, "can we try to win you back?" Her parents' expressions made me realize their lives depended on what they would hear next.

"Do as you wish," Ann said, but a small smile was tugging on her lips.

I had never seen two happier faces.

Chapter 39

*A*nn had walked silently to the cafeteria, as she processed what had happened. Her parents stayed behind. The cafeteria was a huge room with windows from floor to ceiling. An acerbic smell of a hand sanitizer mixed with coffee and mashed potatoes. The well-worn chairs were mostly occupied; a family tried to sound upbeat, while their faces were tired; a group of doctors in white scrubs discussed something hurriedly over the paper cups of coffee, dark stethoscopes hanging uselessly on their chests. A low murmur hung in the air, prickled with someone's exclaim from time to time. We bought coffee and settled in the far east corner. A white dented table was scrubbed clean, the chair uncomfortably cold.

"Wow," Ann said, sitting in front of me.

"Yes, *wow*." I smiled.

"Will you allow them back?" I asked.

"We'll see what they do. Maybe nothing will change."

"They looked pretty desperate out there," I remarked with a shrug.

"Yeah." Ann stirred her cappuccino, deep in thought. "And you know, the stupid thing is that I want them back, even after all they did."

She watched me, so close. How I had missed those eyes, her open face? I still couldn't believe I was here, by her side. I took her hand.

"It's not stupid. They are your parents. They have deep faults. They made a grave mistake they didn't know how to fix. I am not saying you need to forgive them now, but if you are willing to give them a chance, it might do you some good. We all make mistakes."

I was stroking her palm. She moved her hand and entwined her fingers with mine.

"Oh, we'll see. But it was nice when they said all those things." She shook her head, leaning in. "How did you find me anyway?"

"I called Jack," I said, and her eyes widened in surprise. "He thinks we are two parts of one organism."

She laughed. After the good news about Mary, Ann was relieved, like a huge weight had been lifted from her shoulders.

"I wanted to ask you one thing." My hand started trembling a little, and I squeezed Ann's fingers, but she saw. She nodded slowly.

"Can,"—I took a deep breath—"can we skip Barcelona for now and go straight to your home? If you still want to, that is, if you still need me." I dropped my gaze to her cup; my heart beat at the speed of light. "If you'd have me."

She was silent.

"Are you sure? Are you sure about Mark?" she asked after a few moments.

"Ann, I was always sure. Even though it took me longer to come and find you, I was always sure about one thing: My future is with you."

She nodded, her face unreadable. "Okay."

I raised a curious brow. "Okay means okay, I hear you, or okay you can come live with me and be my partner?"

"The latter," she said nonchalantly with a shrug, but a light was playing in her eyes, the lips in a soft curl.

I laughed, feeling weightless that she was taking me back. I pressed her hand to my lips and watched her.

"I'm happy you came back." She was glowing.

And we stayed like this, looking at each other in the bustling cafeteria of the Tel Aviv hospital.

"How did Mark take it?" Ann broke the silence after a while.

"Pretty good actually. He said it didn't hurt him as much since I was leaving him for a woman," I laughed. "Anyway, he agreed that we wanted different things, and deep down he knew I won't give him what he wanted."

"Kids," Ann said with a frown.

I nodded. "It took him by surprise, but we both knew deep down inside that we would go our different ways eventually. And I am so sorry I kept you waiting, but he needed me. I just wouldn't have forgiven myself if I left him there broken in the hospital."

"I thought you might want to stay with him."

"I know, you gave me space. But all I wanted all this time was to be with you. That dull pain that was with me all the time was the missing piece. And after getting that goodbye message from you, I woke up. I'm sorry you thought I had chosen him."

"That message was the hardest thing I ever did. But I couldn't breathe anymore. I couldn't breathe without you, so I had to cut myself off from you."

I understood the twisted feelings she had and faulted myself.

"Do you want to meet my family? Since we are pretty

close to Kyiv. On the way back to LA, we could swing by," I said.

"Do they all know about me?"

"My mom was on team Ann from the beginning, and my dad knew I was bisexual long before I knew. They will be so excited! My brother, it will be a surprise for him, but he's so busy with his son that he won't pay any attention to us, and his wife, Christina, will be thrilled."

"I would love to," Ann replied, a huge smile on her face.

After an hour in the cafeteria, we went back to Mary's room. Ann's parents were in the same spot where we had left them.

"They still didn't bring her back," Eve said, rubbing an eyebrow and pacing between a narrow hall.

Jonathan looked at me, cleared his throat and said, "Sorry, we didn't get a chance to introduce ourselves." He stepped closer to me and stretched out his hand. "Jonathan."

"Julie," I said, finding his hand was big and warm.

"I would hug you, but it's probably too early. I see how she looks at you," Ann's mother said, shaking my hand with a wink. "Eve."

They were nice, and they were trying. It would take them time to win Ann back, but I was sure they'd make every effort possible.

We heard noises from the adjoining corridor, and a hospital bed rolled into view. The nurse we had met before was leading the way with two nurses in tow.

On the bed lay an older woman. Her skin was pale, and her long, curly grey hair sprawled on the pillow. Blue eyes, Ann's eyes but darker, scanned the group, and a smile spread on her face. Her eyes lingered on me for a moment, and she nodded slightly.

The nurse rolled the bed into the room and started working with the machines near her, each press accompanied by a beep. Finally, she finished. After explaining a few things about them, she left.

Mary looked at the people surrounding her. "So, my heart needs to stop beating in order for you all to get back together."

Eve glanced at Ann, and Ann took my hand.

"How are you? Does it hurt?" Ann asked.

Mary waved slightly. "Ah, it's okay. I am not that young anymore. Introduce me to your girlfriend." She winked at me as I felt my cheeks burning. "I hoped you'd have good taste."

Ann put her hands around my waist and moved me closer to Mary.

"This is Julie," Ann said, beaming.

"Hello." I smiled nervously, my pulse fastening, a deep rolling feeling in my stomach. Mary's eyes searched my face, and I knew how important it was for Ann that she liked me. But all I could do was stand there, Ann's hand anchoring me.

"How's your boyfriend?" Mary asked me; of course she knew.

"We broke up," I explained, swallowing over the lump in my throat.

"Finally," she murmured, the slight crease of her elbow smoothing. "It was a difficult thing for you to do, but I guess it was the right thing."

I nodded. I knew it was the right thing, it just took too long.

Mary turned to Eve. "Did you talk to her?" she asked.

"We did."

"And I suppose it went well since you all are in the same room," Mary said, giving a satisfied sigh.

"We hope so," Jonathan chuckled and turned to his daughter. She shook her head but smiled.

"Perfect, so now I can go."

All heads turned to Mary with a gasp.

"What?" Ann whispered, her hands trembling.

"Oh, okay, not now, but the second stroke may come when I am in a less crowded place. I did what I wanted, and I am happy to see you all together. Now, I need to rest." She pressed a button to call a nurse as everyone looked incredulously at her.

A minute later, the nurse appeared. She said that Mary should stay at the hospital for a week. And when Ann asked about the possibility of a second stroke, she said it was possible, but if Mary took her pills, it might never happen.

Mary was already sleeping lightly in her bed when the nurse finished. Ann kissed her cheek and said we'd be back the next day. Eve did the same, and Jonathan squeezed Mary's hand.

"We are going to stay in the hotel," Eve said when we stepped out of the room.

"Julie and I will stay at Mary's," Ann told her.

"Sure."

Ann called a taxi, and we said an awkward goodbye. Outside the hospital, I noticed the heat. Summer was in full force here already.

Through the taxi window, I watched the city. The cafes were full of people as we crawled by, the savory smells of frying food wafted in the car. When we turned to the road that ran by the seashore I looked up, two seagulls were circling in a slow dance. It had all started here. Ann watched me closely.

"I still can't believe you're here," she murmured.

I reminded her happily, "With you."

We got out of the taxi near a white five-story building. Ann led the way to the entrance, punched the code, and we stopped before the elevator doors. You could feel the energy cracking between us; our eyes were locked.

When the elevator doors closed, I couldn't take it anymore. I needed to feel her skin on mine, and I rushed to kiss Ann, pressing her to the wall. Mercifully, the elevator slowly rumbled upwards, giving us a few minutes. Her full lips were on mine, my tongue was touching hers, and we were both stealing breaths in-between.

Out of the elevator, we were breathing hard. While Ann fumbled with her keys, I touched the bare skin of her arm, sending goosebumps all over it. And then finally we were inside.

Ann pressed me to the door, slipping my shirt over my head, unlatching my bra. Her arms caressed my body, trying to cover every inch of my skin, while our mouths crushed each other, fervently moving. I took off her shirt and threw it on the floor. Her breasts, peaked, held some kind of magic over me. I sucked her nipples while fumbling with her zipper and reached into her pants. She was so wet that I growled with pleasure.

Ann found her way into my jeans and cupped my chin to connect our lips. We touched each other, our bodies pressing together, feeling everything. I felt liquid spreading under my fingertips as Ann moaned my name. Her fingers sent waves of desire through my body, moving faster, till my knees almost buckled when I came. But I wanted more, I needed her taste in my mouth. Going down on my knees, I got what I wanted, making her scream and beg.

Our bodies were covered in sweat, and they radiated

heat. I kissed her thigh and whispered, "Welcome to Tel Aviv."

"Oh, I love your welcomes," she breathed with a laugh.

Chapter 40

JULIE

*T*he next week was full of love. We couldn't keep our hands from each other; we were always touching, feeling our presence. Mary's little apartment became our heaven, where we hid from the heat and learned our bodies all over again.

Mary was doing much better, and with each passing day, the color returned to her face.

"Did you two ruin my apartment already?" she asked.

My face turned crimson red, and Mary laughed.

"We'll get it ready for your arrival." Ann winked.

We spent mornings in the hospital, bringing fresh coffee to Mary. She asked me about Kyiv, about my parents, my life. Mary was particularly interested in why I had decided to be childfree.

"I guess I am a bit jealous of modern women. They have a choice to be who they want. When I was young, I didn't have that choice," she said.

During those days, Ann and I worked remotely. I called my manager as soon as I was in Tel Aviv explaining the emergency situation. It was a low season between two major projects, and I didn't have a lot of tasks, only maintenance and fix requests. I said I'd be back in Kyiv in two weeks and that I would like to meet with the team, and I asked if it was possible for me to work remotely from now on.

"I don't see any problem with that. You proved to be an excellent designer, so it doesn't matter where you work as long as you deliver your tasks," she said.

So, it was settled. I would take a few days off while moving from Kyiv to LA, and then the next big project that would require all my attention would begin.

In the evenings, we strolled by the sea, enjoying the sunsets. Once, we found ourselves in front of the hotel where everything had started.

"Would you like to have a drink with me?" I asked.

"Of course." Ann looked deep in my eyes, hers twinkling in the evening light.

We ended up drinking a few cocktails, remembering that first evening.

"Meet me in the restroom," Ann whispered, her hot breath on my neck. As she was moving away, I watched her back. I would not have believed anyone if they had told me that night I had seen her for the first time here that in more than half a year I would be leaving my old life behind to be with this woman.

I looked around as I stood up. There were no Benzon employees this time. It was quiet, with a few couples and a man with a laptop.

I left a bill on the counter and went after Ann. She closed the door behind us.

"I like your dress," she said slyly.

I nodded; it was a short white summer dress that hugged my body. Ann was wearing red lipstick, a white shirt, jeans shorts, and her boots. She skipped wearing a bra today, so my eyes kept falling to her breasts, her nipples outlined under her t-shirt. She looked like a badass rider, like she had just climbed off her motorcycle.

Ann stepped closer and kissed me. I knew I would be covered in her lipstick, with smudges of it on my neck and my lips. I was hungry for her. Ann's body pressed to mine; she held my hips and pulled down my panties. With a final bite on my lip, she slid to her knees, pulled my dress up, and kissed me between my legs. She sucked, licked, and bit gently while my back was pressed to a chill wall.

Chapter 41

JULIE

$\mathcal{W}$e left Tel Aviv a few days later after Mary returned home. She recovered so fast, her body pumped on the yoga she did daily. Ann asked her to promise to visit us in LA soon.

"Sure. Eve made me promise the same."

Eve and Jonathan would stay with Mary for a few more weeks. Ann called Eve asking to let her know if Mary's state worsened. But we all hoped she would be fine, as she was taking her pills diligently.

Back in Kyiv, we rented an Airbnb apartment. I texted Mark to let him know I needed to grab my things, and he replied with a time I should be there. "I will be out," the message said.

Ann stopped dead on the threshold of our apartment, boxes in her hands.

"It's so …" She stopped, looking around. "Homey."

"It was."

All my clothes and stuff I wanted to take to LA fit in two large suitcases. The rest of my things we packed into boxes, and my dad would pick them up later.

The doorbell rang. Ann turned, questioning me. I shrugged and went to open the door.

Mark stood in the doorway, and a crutch supported his weight.

"Sorry, but I wanted to see you one last time before you left," he said.

He was standing on his legs much better than the last time I saw him, but his face—it was sad. There were dark circles under his eyes, few days stubble.

"I missed you," he said so quietly I was sure Ann didn't hear it from the room she was in.

"Oh, Mark." I took his hand, but the truth was that in the last two weeks I didn't have a minute to think about him.

"I am not alone," I said.

Mark nodded.

"Do you want to meet her?" I asked.

He nodded again, his eyes never leaving my face.

Mark stepped in the hall of his apartment, then took off his shoes and jacket. I went in to call Ann; she was wearing black jeans that hugged her slim legs and a black top that showed a sliver of her fit belly. She ran a hand with red nails through her hair; she was nervous.

"Hi, Mark," she greeted hesitantly.

"Hello."

They both looked at each other, eyeing each other up.

"So, you are the girlfriend," he said, his hard eyes scanning Ann.

"Yes." She took a deep breath.

An awkward silence settled between us.

"We are almost finished packing. Fifteen minutes and we'll be out," I said, clearing my throat.

"I'll be in the kitchen," he retorted flatly. Mark was

moving much better now, but he limped severely on his left leg, the side that had been hit.

I asked Ann to finish packing. "I need to talk to him."

She frowned, glancing from me to where he'd disappeared to. "Sure, go."

Mark was making himself tea in the kitchen when I entered.

"Do you want a cup of tea?" he asked.

"I don't think that is a good idea," I said.

He shrugged. "She seems nice."

I perched on the chair near the kitchen table, the place on the windowsill was not mine anymore. Nothing here was.

"You know, sometimes I think to hell with all these future plans, this imaginary family. I want you back." There was calmness in his voice but such a regret in his eyes.

"You don't really think that."

He sighed, "Maybe, or maybe not."

"I am not sure your life can be fulfilled without a family."

"Are you happy, Julie?"

"Yes, I am."

He nodded and took a sip of his tea, his eyes far away. "Good."

I wanted to help him, to shield him from the pain, but I couldn't really help since I was the one who had caused this pain.

Ann stepped quietly into the kitchen.

"I'm ready," she announced. Ann noticed the quietness between us and took a deep breath. "Mark, I am sorry for what happened."

"Thanks," he shrugged, a wall of calmness still on his face. But his heart, his dear to me heart, was breaking.

We put on our jackets and shoes and started hauling the suitcases out into the hall.

"Bye," Ann murmured and was out the door.

I paused and hugged him.

"Bye, Mark," I whispered.

"I love you, Julie." His voice was raw as he murmured into my hair. This was his goodbye.

Tears stung my eyes. I went out into the hall, never meeting his gaze.

Ann saw my tears but was quiet all the way back in the taxi, my suitcases rumbling in the back.

"He still loves you." It was a statement. "He wants you back."

I took a deep breath. "He mistakes what he really wants."

"I am not sure he does."

"I hate hurting him," I said, a dull ache in my chest crushing me.

Ann nodded, her eyes sympathetic, and took my hand.

Back in the apartment, I changed and was quiet for a while, preparing the tea in the kitchen.

"I have an idea on how to make your bad thoughts go away," Ann told me. She was standing in her underwear at the threshold. "You can only watch," she added.

She perched on the stool in front of me, back pressed to the wall. She lowered her bra straps, eyes locked on mine. She touched her belly slowly, then the skin between her thighs. Next, she unhooked her bra, showing her full breasts. She caressed them.

"I see you are getting hungry." She smiled and moved her hand into her lace panties. Sucking in a breath, I moved closer but followed the rules of the game she was playing. Her hand moved in circles, and her hips rocked on that rickety chair.

"Oh, hell," I exclaimed, and I dropped to my knees, tugging on her panties, kissing her fingers and the flesh they were touching.

Chapter 42

*M*y parents loved Ann. Mom was beaming from the moment we entered their apartment. Their English wasn't flawless, but they tried. Ann was so nervous meeting them that her hands were shaking all the way. She had spent half an hour choosing flowers for them.

Within five minutes, she relaxed and talked about LA, slowly, trying to use simple words. I translated a bit.

Dad brought his special chocolate liquor he made, and we all laughed more, our cheeks rosy.

One thing I didn't know how to do was tell Alex that I was leaving.

"Speak to Christina first," my dad suggested. "He's a bit old-fashioned, but he'll be alright."

I groaned, "I don't have time. We're leaving the day after tomorrow."

"Let me call him and ask them to visit tomorrow. You will introduce Ann to them here," Mom told me.

Every time I mentioned Alex, Ann stiffened. She was

afraid he would react like her parents had. I laughed it off, but deep down I knew such a possibility existed.

The next day, we went to my parents' apartment. Mom opened the door and hugged us both. The baby was in the bedroom, and the adults gathered in the living room.

When we entered the room, Alex froze, Christina sized up Ann from head to toe.

"Hey," I said hesitantly with a nervous smile. "This is Ann. She's my girlfriend."

I had never brought friends to our family gathering, and there was a question in Alex's eyes.

"I mean like my lover, not a friend. We are together," I clarified.

Christina's eyes widened, and a smile spread on her lips. Alex's face was blank, his eyes darting between Ann and me.

"Are you a lesbian?" he asked eventually.

"She's bisexual," my dad stated calmly. "She had a boyfriend, don't you remember?"

Chrisitna waved at Alex, like *don't mind him*.

"That's so cool!" She was beaming. "I've never had a queer friend before, and now I have a family member! Tell me everything, how did you two meet? How did it all start?"

And we told them everything. Ann was blushing profoundly as I was telling our story, darting nervous glances to quiet Alex.

"This is so romantic," Christina exclaimed giddily. "When are you two leaving? I want to spend time with you. This is so exciting."

When we said tomorrow, her face fell.

"But you are welcome to visit my house in LA. Everyone is welcome." Ann looked around the room. "I would love to have you all." My heart melted, and I took

Ann's hand in mine. Alex followed this gesture with his eyes. Everyone fell quiet upon seeing Alex stiffen.

"What about Mark?" he asked.

"You know we always wanted different things," I said.

"But couldn't you have just given him what he had asked?" Alex demanded. Christina looked incredulously at her husband and shook her head.

"No, Alex, I couldn't," I said slowly. "Not to him, not to anyone else. You know about my decision on being childfree, but you kept ignoring it."

"But he is a great guy!"

"He is, and feel free to stay friends with him. But I love Ann, and you could at least be polite," I said. "You haven't said one word to her."

"It's okay," Ann murmured, looking down.

"No, it's not," Alex said, running a hand through his shortly cut hair and taking a deep breath. "I am sorry." He was looking at Ann. "My sister seems to really love you since she ran to another part of the world to be with you. And I must say, Julie, you have an excellent taste in women."

My mom snorted, and Ann's cheeks grew red.

"Now that we are all on the same page, tell me about your plans for your life in LA. How are you going to work?" Christina asked.

I said that for now I would continue working remotely with my Ukrainian team, and later we'd see how it goes.

"This is so liberating, the ability to work from anywhere," my dad chimed in. "I wish it had been so widespread back in my day."

"You are not that old." My mom punched him lightly in the ribs, rolling her eyes.

The rest of the day went by fast, but the atmosphere in the room was so warm that I never wanted to leave it. Alex melted to Ann and asked a million questions about surfing. He had always wanted to try it.

"I can teach you if you want. Julie is natural, and it might be in your blood too," Ann said. "Or we can hire an instructor."

"No, I'd prefer it to be you," he said. Alex winked at me when he saw me beaming.

The next day, my parents went with us to the airport. It was a sunny day, with not a cloud in the sky. The heat hadn't yet hit Kyiv, and the city was drowned in lush greenery, my favorite time of the year.

I checked my emotional state; it didn't hurt that I was leaving. I could visit or come back anytime. I didn't think Ann would mind moving here. These previous couple of days Kyiv had gotten under her skin, and she called it a magic city.

I looked at Ann. The whole morning she had watched me as if she was afraid I'd vanish or change my mind. Her warm presence beside me told me that we were up to something new and beautiful.

The new project at work would start in six days, giving me time to settle in.

I looked at the city from the taxi window. Would I miss it? I would. I looked at my dad sitting in the front passenger seat of the taxi. He noticed me watching and smiled reassuringly.

My mom was talking to Ann, asking about her travels. I studied them both, so at ease with each other.

Mom never really grew close to Mark. It seemed she didn't want to open up to him, that she had a feeling it would all end eventually. But with Ann, they clicked instantly, and it wouldn't have surprised me if they visited us soon. Not so much to see me, but to get to know Ann.

During the taxi ride, Ann was holding my hand, and she never dropped it. I looked at the tall pine trees that started after the city ended. It was still ten minutes to the airport, and I marveled about how my life had changed, how it had taken a one-hundred-eighty-degree turn.

Mark's hurt still haunted me; it was never easy to break up. I wished with all my heart that he'd meet somebody soon.

At the airport, my parents stayed till we left for a security check.

"We'll see you soon," my mom said, tears in her eyes. "Be happy." She touched my cheek.

I pressed her close to me in a hug, my light and support.

"I will miss you so much," I said. She just nodded, her chin quivering. The next moment, my dad embraced me.

"I know you'll be happy there. This country was always too small for you. And Ann, she'll take care of you," he assured me.

I nodded. "I love you, Dad."

"I love you too."

I felt my cheeks getting wet, tears sliding down. I started to sniffle lightly.

"Don't cry, honey. We'll visit you soon."

I loved them both so much. They hugged Ann, and we disappeared into the crowd as we made our way to the security check.

Ann put her hand on my shoulder. "I am so sorry," she said.

"Ah, they'll be alright."

"And you?"

"I am happy." I looked into her ocean blue eyes. "I am

with the person I love."

And we stepped closer to a new life.

Ann's huge truck revved under me as I looked out the window. It was my city now, my LA. I leaned in and kissed Ann's cheek. I'd now live in the city of sunshine, palms, and ocean. I took a deep breath, anticipation taking over.

"Welcome home," Ann said when we entered the house. It was exactly how I remembered it, warm and full of light. Ann's place, our place now.

I took a shower and put on my lace negligee that I remembered Ann loved. We were tired after the road, so we decided to go straight to sleep and start tomorrow. We would unpack, and I would settle my life here.

When I entered the bedroom, the view stopped me in my tracks. Ann was lying on her belly, flipping through her book, completely naked.

Water was glistening on her back, on the pale skin of her tights. She saw me looking and raised a brow.

"You are ethereal," I breathed.

She scanned my negligee, pausing on places that it didn't hide.

"Come here," she murmured.

I stepped closer and sat on the edge of the bed. Ann's eyes feasted on me, her hand on my neck pulling me to her. Our lips connected, and I leaned into her. Her naked body grazed mine. I was hers, and she was mine. Our tongues met, and my finger slowly traced her collarbone, wet from the shower. I moved between her breasts and felt her heart hammer under my palm.

"I love you," I whispered.

"Always," she replied, and we melted into each other.

Chapter 43

a year had gone by since I moved to LA. The transition was smooth, and not really having close friends back home, I started to find them here. Ann, Jack, John, and Ian were my LA family now, and my parents had visited twice already. My dad and John had so many similarities that they loved spending time together. Fishing was a hobby they both loved dearly, and they could spend whole days out fishing, leaving Mom and Jack to lounge with us.

Mary appeared to be the wisest and funniest person I had ever met. She came to Los Angeles three times, saying that being around younger people made her realize that her heart needed to work for a little while longer, as she still had so many things to do. We were trying to persuade her to move here, to rent a small apartment close to us. She was still thinking about it.

When I first moved here, I spent a lot of time working on the project designing a new product from scratch. It took almost all my time during those first months. From my laptop, I just dropped into Ann's arms. It was a time of change in my life that inspired me to create.

The app I was working on got released one month later, and it hit the top of the AppStore in a week, bringing attention to the main office. Once they found out the person who created the visuals lived in LA, they invited me for an interview. So, now I was in the process of officially relocating to the LA office.

I loved their policy of remote work. I could go to the office or stay at home as long as I wanted to. The most important thing for them was that I got the job done, and with their system, it was easy to track my progress.

Ann and I usually didn't see each other in the office on the days we went in. She worked with different people and left me with my new team that was so diverse and interesting I could actually find friends there.

Jack and I started running in the mornings trying to start a good habit but mostly failing spectacularly.

Instead I surfed, oh my, I surfed. Ann and I spent countless hours on the water, the power of the ocean beating in my veins. I always felt that I needed to live close to the water.

Alex and Christina still hadn't visited. Alex didn't want to leave the baby with a nanny for a long time and did not want to fly with him so far away. But now, it seemed they actually were ready, and they had been discussing dates.

After I broke up with Mark, Alex tried to stay friends with him, but he told me that Mark withdrew. Seeing Alex reminded him of me, Mark had told Alex. So, after a few nights out, Mark said that it was better for him to stop meeting with Alex. Mark confessed it was difficult for him not to ask questions about me.

I never saw Mark after the day I left. We didn't stay in touch. He sent me a feeble happy birthday greeting, and I politely replied. That was all. Alex said that he bumped into Mark in the restaurant a few weeks ago, and he was with a pretty young girl, too young as Alex pointed out, but he looked happy, and she had warm eyes that never left Mark. I hoped he'd found his happiness.

Because I had found mine, Ann. As the year went by, I realized she was my everything. She was my light, my support, my day, and my night. She worked fiercely to make me feel at home here, and here the puzzle clicked, two souls finding each other.

Living with a woman was so different than living with a man. We talked a lot. We explained our thoughts, fears, and emotions. I memorized every inch of her body and holding her in my arms still made me the happiest person on earth.

Chapter 44

ANN

$\mathcal{I}$t was this day exactly a year ago when Julie moved into my house. We needed to celebrate, so I prepared a picnic and drove us both to the beach. We nestled in the shade, the heat already making the early summer hot. We were wearing bikinis, and Julie's body was tanned already, the sun clinging easily to her skin.

She laughed when she found my gaze sliding down her navel, going up and pausing on her breasts, barely covered by the thin fabric. She always made me hungry for her touch.

I looked into her eyes. "I was thinking," I said and took a deep breath, moving closer to her. The anticipation, fear, excitement, all mixed in my heart.

She grazed my chin with her fingers. "What?" she whispered.

"Would you like …" I stuttered. My heart was so loud in my chest. "Would you be interested in spending your life with me as my wife?"

She prepped on her elbow. "Are you proposing?" She smiled.

"Actually, I am," I laughed and opened my palm. A delicate ring was lying there. It was white gold with a stone that shone brightly under the sun. My heart skipped a beat as I looked at Julie's face.

"Will you marry me?" I asked.

There wasn't a moment of hesitation. Julie instantly threw her hands around me.

"Yes. Yes! I want to spend every moment of my life with you."

A wave of relief and happiness washed over me. I found her lips with mine and kissed the woman I loved. Then, I took her hand, sand clinging to my palm, and slid the ring on her finger. It fit perfectly.

"You know, I love you." I smiled.

"Oh, I know." She kissed me again, sweetness on her tongue.

I was going to marry the woman of my dreams. Sun warmed our bodies, and the ocean waves whispered just a few feet away. My lips pressed against Julie's, and I realized that my life was a miracle.

Acknowledgments

I want to thank the team of Creative James Media who believed in this book. When you are at the very beginning, the first *yes* means a world to you. Especially when you are not a native speaker and writing in another language is something like a charade.

I am immensely grateful to Abby Orlandi, who read my book and saw the potential. The constant support of Jean Lowd, who was always just a message away, always guiding and encouraging, thank you. Ashley Oliver, who made me see the plotholes, those simple sentences, lack of descriptions, I needed it and I'm so grateful for your work on my book.

To my beta readers who read the first versions of the book and actually made me believe that the pile of handwritten pages in two and a half notebooks can be turned into something real.

A special gratitude award goes to my parents. To my Grandmother who always asked me about the process, and always nudged me to continue. To my Mom who accepted that I decided to write as there was no pause between that book I started to write when I was eight, and when I picked another story many years later.

To my friends who listened to the story and made the right comments in the right places. To the constant interest and support.

And thank *you*.

About the Author

Laura May is a pseudonym of a Ukrainian-American author. Laura lived in Kyiv till her mid-twenties. Now she can be found traveling around the world.

The One Woman is her debut novel published by Creative James Media.

Check latest updates on LauraMayAuthor.com and Instagram.com/LauraMayAuthor/